The Summer Playbook

JAQUELINE SNOWE

PUBLISHED 2024

Published by: Jaqueline Snowe

Cover Design: Star Child Designs

Editing: Katherine McIntyre

Formatting: Jennifer Laslie

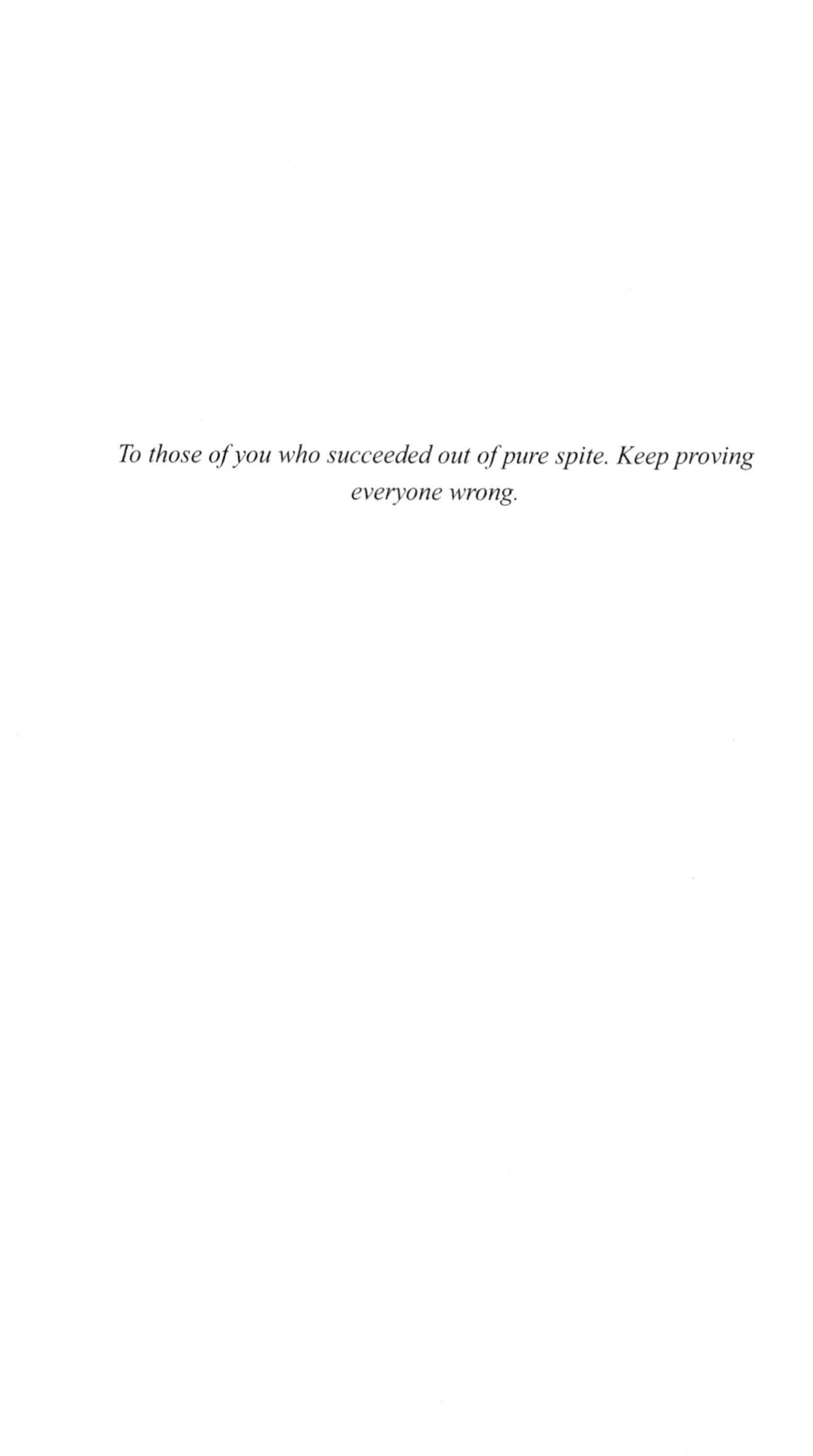

To those of you who succeeded out of pure spite. Keep proving everyone wrong.

THE SUMMER PLAYBOOK

Mackenzie Mallinson is an expert at two things—playing soccer and talking about soccer. Wait, there's a third too. Crushing on her best friend's twin brother, the star quarterback for the football team, but *no one* knows about that. Her senior year is her last shot at fun before entering the pros, and she refuses to let soccer be the only thing that defines her. She wants to live life to the fullest, and that requires a summer bucket list.

Dean Romano might have a line of people wanting his signature, but he's been off his game since someone he trusted hurt him last year. Once the life of the party, he misses the old version of himself. Not the guy who slept around version, but the fun, carefree, let's enjoy my time on earth version. With his senior year on the team starting, he wants to get back to having a good time, and the perfect opportunity arises: *The Summer Playbook.*

Mack needs to let loose but wants to do it with someone she trusts. Dean wants to find his mojo again with someone who doesn't care about his potential NFL career. The two pair up to complete a bucket list of fun while ensuring there are no feelings involved. Some items are easy, like dance on a bar or go to a concert, but skinny dipping? Body shots? Things heat up, but they both agreed their deal ends once they check off every item on the list. The question remains: is love something you cross off a list or a game you can win?

CHAPTER **ONE**

Mack

You ever feel guilty for having a slightly, tiny negative thought when so much around you is going well? It's a horrible feeling to be thankful and happy yet have discontent growing roots in your veins.

I had *so damn much* going well for me. I'd excelled at school and had finished my junior soccer season with some of the best stats. My window for playing for the NSWL hadn't closed yet, and if I continued my workouts, I could be invited to play.

My social media following had quadrupled since my stats went up. Young girls looked up to me at games. They wore my jersey and wanted my signature. Me. Mackenzie Violet Mallinson. The school stores sold posters with my face. They had giveaways with my uniform. My best friend Lorelei and I were on billboards promoting girls' soccer all over town. People recognized me, and every single time, my heart sped up, and my soul said *you're living your dream.*

That was awesome.

My teammates were more like family. My own parents were the most supportive in the world. I spun my tanzanite ring on my thumb, staring at the vibrant color. The deep blue-violet hue matched my hair. When my parents gifted it to me, they told me the story of how it formed was similar to me: strong and capable of surviving lots of pressure and changes.

Like a bully of a coach who always told me I'd be nothing on the field. That'd I'd never achieve my dream of playing in the pros.

"You'll never get that far, Mackenzie, but it's cute you think so."

Yeah, my high school coach effed me up. She was the reason I put my life and soul into soccer, missing out on so many other parts of growing up. Despite getting a D1 scholarship and living out my dream at Central State, she remained in my head—and in my life as my parents' best friend.

I carried some trauma from that wonderful asshole of a woman.

The latest root of my insecurity? My life outside of soccer. The lack of experiences I had because of *ensuring I would make it to spite Coach Emily.*

Seriously, Emily was too sweet of a name to be a horrible human being.

I eyed the vodka sprite in front of me, swallowing down the feeling that I was annoying. I couldn't share my worry with my friends that I wanted to *live more*. They had their own shit going on, real issues that weren't pathetic like mine. Lorelei's internship was kicking her ass, but it was her chance to prove herself. Alejandra's parents were going through a divorce with her fourteen-year-old sister still at home. Mally's girlfriend cheated on her, broke her heart and soul. Those issues were legit. Mine were not.

We were at our summer roundtable. Every Tuesday at six, we met at one of the hole-in-the-wall bars to talk about our lives. Vee—who had to take summer courses, or she wouldn't graduate—created an agenda of topics that we'd approved the night before.

Was this extra? My god, yes. But we trained together, worked out together, partied together, and spent hours on a bus together. We could talk all the time, but carving out a place without soccer made it more special.

Again, I had the best life in the world. Just no experience with love.

My skin heated at my blip of insecurity.

"Vee better have put Xavier Reed as a topic agenda today." Ale slid into the booth next to me, her beer sloshing over her hand and onto the table. She dabbed a napkin on it before whistling toward the bar. "You see him? Do you see his ass? Do you? Because I am a healthy, alive human, and my eyes work. He is the finest person I have ever observed in my existence."

I snorted. "He's gorgeous."

"His dark skin? The way those jeans fit his thighs? I want to climb him."

"Climb who?" Lorelei slid across from me, her face flushed and her smile lines ingrained into her forehead. Her joy was my favorite thing about her. She was smart, led with her heart, and was my ride or die.

"New football player." I jutted my chin toward the bar. A few of the guys were there, mainly juniors and seniors who lived on campus over the summer. I scanned them for the familiar head of dark locks, the broad shoulders that led to lean hips and thick thighs. They weren't Xavier-size, but Dean Romano had swagger and talent that very few could match, and I couldn't stop myself from seeking him out everywhere we went.

My crush had started as something silly. He was objectively gorgeous and the star quarterback for our school. Everyone had some form of infatuation with him. Minus my best friend, who happened to be his twin sister.

The ever-present twist in my gut tightened, and I took another sip. We weren't huge partiers—couldn't afford to—but the thought of numbing my mind for a few hours was inviting. *Stop thinking about all you missed out on. Stop thinking about Dean.*

"Ah. Xavier Reed." Lorelei nodded before swirling her straw in her drink. She'd opted for a mule tonight. "Luca told me a bit about him. Great player, a lot of strength, and I think Luca even mentioned he has a good personality?"

"Luca said that?" I teased, earning a fake glare from my best friend.

"Maybe not that exactly, you dick, but it was context." She stuck her tongue out at me, and I did it right back.

I wish I knew the word or feeling for how I felt about Lorelei and Luca. Watching my best friend find the love of her life and getting the support and swoon she needed made me inexplicably happy. He brought out the best in her, and she deserved every single second of it. But humans were complicated, and somewhere, deep down and hidden, rooted in insecurity, was jealousy.

I didn't want Luca. I just dreamed of finding someone like that.

"Girlies, I have an aggressive agenda today, so please hold gossip for after our meeting." Vee smirked as she reached into her jean jacket and pulled out a folded sheet of paper. "Creating this list is what's holding me together."

"Going hard on the drama tonight, I see," Lo fired, her smile growing. "Holding you *together?* Is this because I asked to create the itinerary today?"

"No. Maybe. I don't… look, y'all, can I get real for a second?" Vee's eyes widened, and she bit the inside of her cheek. "I fucked around and found out, all right."

I sat up straighter. Vee was always the wild child, the party animal who defined the term life of the party. She feared nothing and no one. Frowning, I leaned closer to her. "Vee, what happened?"

"Coach talked to me last week, and my grades suck. Studying is hard for me. I don't… I don't learn by reading a book, you know? I failed two classes last semester, along with barely getting by." Vee sniffed and ran a hand through her hair, her gaze searching the bar in the distance. "My summer classes and creating these lists are what's keeping me from a breakdown."

"Well shit, Vee, you can make every list for everything." Lo grabbed Vee's hand and squeezed. "What can we do to help? You need us to quiz you?"

"I don't know." Vee sighed, met our gaze. "This is my chance to clean up my act. If I lose my starting spot because of partying and grades, my brother will kill me."

"Whatever you need, we'll do," I said, making my voice louder. I had a loud voice that carried across a field, bar, countryside. I could whistle with my fingers, and it was a talent I rarely used. "Lo is pretty much the dad of the group, with her confrontations and loyalty. Plus, she can use her stern dad tone on you. It works on me."

"I do not—" Lo paused, tilted her head and laughed. "Damn. I am the dad of the group."

"We know." I rolled my eyes.

"You're blunt but the best shoulder to cry on. Plus, you would absolutely be my call if I were in jail. You answer your phone on the first ring. No one does that anymore." Vee held up her glass and cheered Lo's.

"Do I carry Dad Energy?"

"BDE, but instead of dick, it's dad." I met Mally's eyes, and she giggled. "We need to get you shirt that says BDE. Luca will *hate* it."

"If she's the dad, Mally is the mom. She wants everyone to be happy and succeed in life. Even if her world is crumbling, she holds her head high and gives us the tough love pep talk. She cleans us up when we need it and holds our hair back when we puke. She has the Big Mom Energy we all strive to have," Ale said, reaching over and squeezing Mally's forearm.

Mally's eyes watered, and she gave a small smile. "Thank you. I needed that today. Being cheated on has destroyed me, and I'm struggling to handle it. These weekly hangs are what I look forward to the most."

"It knocked you down, not destroyed," Lo said, hitting the table with her hand. "Cheating is reflection of her, not you. Now, these gatherings are perfect for us. We all have our reasons for this, so let's lay them on the table. Whip 'em out."

"You have a way with words, Lo." Ale rolled her eyes. "But in an effort to open up and expose how we're all messes, I'll share mine too." She adjusted her long black braids and stared at the center of the table. "My parents are going through a divorce, and I don't want to talk about it. I might cry."

"Have you ever been here on a Friday night? Literally everyone cries," I teased.

We all laughed, and Ale visibly relaxed. That soothed me. I studied people's body language on the field to anticipate their next move. Watching for habits or tension, stress or panic helped me plan my attack. But to know my girls were struggling hurt me. How could I share my little insecurities when they were dealing with real shit?

Sensing the change in topic, Vee cleared her throat. "Oi, is everyone present for our Girl Gang Gathering?"

Ale rolled her eyes, but her smile was back. "Clearly. Now get to the juicy stuff. I need something easy to talk about after all these damn feelings."

I met Lo's eyes, and she narrowed them in agreement. She and I hadn't dished our stuff tonight, and I was fine with that. Mine seemed trivial and silly, where hers was about balancing the internship and fun. Our topics weren't as heavy. Our friends needed our focus more.

Damn, I adored these girls so much. They were my family, and when we were going through something, we helped each other out. I put my arm around Ale, and she nuzzled closer. Personal space didn't exist if you were an athlete. The concept just wasn't allowed.

"Now, first order of business. Hairstyles. Lorelei and Ale indicated they wanted to get new cuts." Vee started a timer on her phone. "You each have two minutes to state your goals."

"I'll go first." Ale leaned onto her elbows, her face serious. "I want bangs."

"No!"

"No way!"

"Ah," I mumbled. "Are you… sure?"

"I know. I prepared for this moment, but look how cute these photos are?" She set her phone in the middle with a picture of Camillo Cabello, who rocked bangs. "I like this."

"She probably doesn't have to run as much as we do," I said. "You know how annoying it'll be sweating all season with them on your face? It'll drive you crazy."

"And you'll break out." Vee winced. "Will we support you? Yes. But it would be a disservice to our friendship if we didn't try to talk you out of it."

Ale groaned and focused on Lorelei. "You're quiet, Daddy."

"Gah, do not use that on me." Lo shook her head before shrugging. "But my argument is that hair grows back."

"We don't have your superhuman power to grow hair overnight, Lo," I said. "It took me five years to get this length." I held the end of my long blonde hair, admiring the split ends already. "Even with all the vitamins, my hair is fragile."

"I could pluck my brows, and they'd be back in the night." Lo laughed at herself, her innate self-confidence oozing out. "Ale, I say do it. As the father of the group, my opinion has more weight."

"It's decided." Ale hit the table as the buzzer went off. "Now, Lo, your hair?"

"Oh. Mine isn't as controversial as yours. I want to add some caramel lowlights to it."

The group all agreed they'd look amazing. Easy topic.

"Next item: sports gambling. What are our thoughts as athletes?" Vee tapped her finger, and Mally *jumped* in.

"I love the idea, even though there are some weird gray areas with being athletes ourselves. Maybe it's an ego thing or a lifegoal unlocked, but I love seeing my name on the apps." She spoke with her hands and seemed so much like her old self that it made me smile. "See, Mack gets it. She agrees."

"Oh, no. I was just enjoying your manic hand energy."

"I say we switch topics to how we can get Mally back to doing pottery again." Vee picked up the pen and crossed out the next item on the list. "As leader of the list, I'm regrouping. Let's focus on how we can each do something this summer to be better."

Lo nodded a few times. "I need to create a schedule to balance training and my internship, friends and Luca. I can report out on my scheduling next week because I feel like I'm spiraling when it comes to priorities. My brother and I—" she paused, and my stomach dropped.

Her and Dean *what?*

"I need to focus on my relationship with him too. He's been acting weird. Anyway, that's my thing. Ale, what's yours?"

"Fuck. Drinking?" She pinched her nose and let out the longest, grumpiest sigh I had ever heard from her. "I don't… know."

"Can I suggest something?" I said, my voice softer. "What if you focused on spending quality time with your mom, dad, and sister separately?"

"Oh, I like that idea." Vee nodded. "Your sister is obsessed the lake and movies. Plan a day with her."

"And your mom loves getting her nails done and books." Lo nudged her. "Mack is right. You can put your energy into your separate relationships until you know the new family vibes."

"I can do that, yeah." Ale ran her hands together, determination forming in her eyes. "I'll report out next week what I've done."

"Even if it's a FaceTime or a phone call, that counts. Your family is changing, and it might be for the best. You don't know, but you gotta put all your badass, best person in the world energy into them," I said. "I understand you're struggling but they need you, Ale. You're the emotional support person for the team, and it's hard, but your family can't do this without you."

"Fuckkkk, I love you girls. Enough for me. Move on. Mally, what is your plan?"

"Cry. Eat ice cream. Get a tattoo I'll regret for the rest of my life." She shrugged. "Just kidding. Don't… guys, don't look at me like that."

I snorted. "How are you going to get back into pottery? You and your ex both met there, but it's a huge part of you. She doesn't get to take that from you."

"I can sign us up for a class?" Vee said, raising her voice. "I absolutely suck though."

"And you should be focusing on summer school," Lo said, her delivery kind. "You should find a class, Mally. I'll go with you some night. Maybe it'll help me relieve stress."

Mally chewed her lip. "Okay, next week, I'll have a class signed up."

Vee jotted notes down on her notebook before glancing up. She had a thoughtful, targeted look on her eyes as she tapped her purple pen on the table. She often got *that look* when she had an idea. Usually, they were terrible ones like getting cheese fries at midnight or ordering a thousand little plastic babies the size of a quarter so we could hide them all over campus. Her attention was focused on me, and I swallowed.

Everyone else had shared *something.* I couldn't just… exist and cheer them on, could I? I'd be the ultimate wingwoman, hype-man, captain, coach, whatever else worked. I didn't want to share my worries because, hello! They had real issues! I had a weird case of envy because they all did exciting things and had love lives and felt all the feelings.

I've done soccer and soccer and soccer some more. Thanks to Emily the Evil, I refused all fun things, and regret clawed at my throat. I hated that I missed the senior ditch day, the camping drink everyone did, the concerts and dancing in the rain and hooking up with people from other schools.

It was my final year before going to a women's soccer team, playing professionally, and forgoing anything fun. I'd played by the rules my whole twenty-one years. The most scandalous thing I'd ever done was accidentally shoplift a WWJD bracelet when I was eight. My mom found out and made me return it, tears running down my face.

"Mallinson," Vee said, her voice firm. "We've all whipped it out."

"And by it, you mean feelings?" I clarified, buying myself more time.

"Obviously. Our Girl Gang is about trust and making a plan to report updates every week. Yours can't just be more viral videos on social or working out."

Viral videos on soccer and working out... for soccer. It was always about proving Emily wrong and demanding a place for myself. Which I did, didn't I? I could... let go a bit?

"Is that... is that what you all think I do?" I asked, hating how my stomach clenched.

"Um... yes? That is...I mean, girl," Lo said, her brows furrowed as she stared at me with too much awareness in her large brown eyes. *Eyes just like her brother's.* "You're Mack fucking Mallinson. You kick ass on the field and have a legion of followers."

"Yeah, but I don't do anything *fun.* I haven't had my heart broken because I don't invest myself in dates, not really. I've never had a wild night of sex that blew my mind."

"Shit," Ale hissed.

"Yeah." I fanned my face, my skin already reddening. Curse of being pale. I could be mad, sad, or horny, and my cheeks would flush like I ran up four flights of stairs. "Soccer is my past, present, and future, but before senior year takes off... I want to experience *all the shit I missed out on,*" I yelled, then immediately clasped a hand over my mouth.

People stared at us.

"You need a bucket list!" Vee's eyes lit up. "A Summer Playbook of dares."

"Wait, *what*?" I sniffed.

"Vee's right." Lorelei grinned and released my hand. "You've said for years you have no regrets in life, which is amazing because I have like four that I'll never get over. But anyway. You need to channel that same energy into this! You love a challenge to the point it's scary."

"Oh shit, remember the running challenge last year?" Ale laughed. "She almost shattered an ankle just to beat us."

"I didn't break anything except all your hopes because I won," I said, puffing my chest. "But okay, talk to me about this idea."

"You're competitive. It's sexy. If we make a list that you have to do or you'll lose, it'll fire you up." Lorelei grabbed a pen from her purse and used a bar napkin. "I hereby declare this is The Summer Playbook of dares to get you to live wildly before senior year starts. And if you don't complete this by December, you lose."

"Whoa, December?" The competitive part of me roared, needing to know the parameters and easiest way to win. "What's on the list?"

"See, you're already interested." Lo's eyes danced with amusement. "This is gonna be so much fun. As long as you're game. This is about you."

They all watched me, their eyes wide and joyful. My heart banged against my ribcage, a continuous *thud-thud, thud-thud* that felt like worry. But…there was a speck of excitement. A blip of hope. Would this silly checklist help get me out of this funk?

Vee's eyes were wide with excitement, and even Mally had stopped frowning as she waited for my response. My friends were going through real shit, and if this list could help them, I'd do it in a heartbeat. Without overthinking, I slammed my hand on the table, saying, "I'm in."

Whoops and hollers went around the table, and I laughed with them. This felt right. This felt good. Like a big *fuck you, Coach Emily.*

A shadow approached the table. Three of them, actually, and my breath caught in my throat at our visitors. Luca Monroe,

Callum O'Toole, and Dean Romano. Callum leaned against the table, scanning us with his playful eyes.

"I have aggressive FOMO, ladies. Why are we cheering? I want in, whatever it is." His face lit up in mischief as he moved his gaze to each of us, slow and cocky.

Callum was gorgeous and a total without-a-doubt playboy. He was loud and crass and flirted with anything and was proud of it. I admired his swagger and confidence, but I didn't like the challenge in his eyes.

He didn't capture my attention though. Dean Romano, Lo's twin brother and our Central State quarterback, demanded it. He wore a simple black shirt and jeans, but the backwards hat and dark brown eyes drew me to him in aggressive kind of way. He stood next to Luca and Callum, but his gaze was elsewhere.

"We're coming up with The Summer Playbook for Mackenzie." Lo jutted her chin toward the napkin. "Any ideas, Callum?"

"Is this naughty?" he asked, smirking as he winked at me. "Mack needs naughtier in her life."

"Not this again." I shoved my hair out of my face as my skin heated. Like I'd done a million times before, I peeked up to expect Dean to be long gone, but he remained and studied me with his intense gaze. That look always made my skin tingle.

Callum yanked the napkin out of Lo's hands and read the title. He sucked in a breath and stared at me, hard. "The list is blank."

"You interrupted us as we were getting started," Lo fired back.

Dean ran a hand over his face, his jaw set in a hard line. His gaze bored into mine, his unreadable as always. With a quick shake of his head, he left the table. Luca shrugged and followed him, but Callum waved a hand in the air. "Don't worry about Romano. He's having a moment. Now, let's make this shit. I've been bored for a minute, and this sounds exhilarating. Public sex has to be on there, at least twice."

"Never thought I'd say this, Callum, but I'm glad you're here." Vee cheered her drink with his, and he clinked it back.

"I'm the king of trouble, so Mack, how much fun are we going to have?"

CHAPTER **TWO**

Dean

I couldn't believe Callum dragged me out for this. A list of fun? Of getting into trouble? I had enough trouble to last a lifetime, and it was *trouble* that had put me in this damn funk. Gripping the back of my neck, I found my way to the bar. If I was being peer-pressured into acting social, then I deserved a drink. Maybe two of them. Summer hours were the best because no one was here. It was hot as an armpit outside, humid, and only upperclassmen with jobs or summer classes remained on Central State campus.

Previous me would've hated how slow it was because I craved attention. Without the crowds, how could I hook up with the hottest girl here? How could I pose and high five and get free drinks? God, I wasn't the biggest fan of myself, looking back the last few years. My mom referred to my underclassmen years as my first and second season of life, where the writers were still brainstorming the show before the main character—me—figured their shit out. She, along with my dad and sister, had no idea about why I'd changed from my party-animal, attention-seeking self to this more reserved, quiet version. I'd never tell them. It hurt too much, and the guilt… I was so fucking sick of it. My entire body tightened with anger, even months after. I lifted my fingers once I reached the copper bar top, and the pretty bartender met my eyes.

Old me would've enjoyed the way her outfit fit her body. Current me didn't. Current me liked the slow pace of summer. There were fewer people to bother me, to recognize me, and to ask for a photo. Even now, after Callum demanded I come out for a drink, eight girls who wanted a selfie lingered at the entrance. A simple interaction shouldn't piss me off. Maybe they were real fans, or maybe they wanted clout to say they met some of the team, but *just a photo* was how it had started with *her.* The reason my soul had a chip in it where I couldn't trust anyone again.

When the first girl I fell for pretended to be pregnant, lied about it, then cheated on me and became pregnant with *someone else's baby,* I got fucked up. Couldn't trust anyone. Was terrified to even look at a girl.

"Romanooo, wait up." Callum caught up to me. The bastard said my name like it was ten syllables long. If he wasn't the kindest fucker in the world, I'd probably hate him. He befriended everyone alive, never got flustered, and made everyone around him happier.

He was also convincing as hell and always got what he wanted—which was me coming out with him and Luca. The two overbearing dudes refused to let me live in my head. Did Callum have any idea about the truth? No. But he was empathetic as hell and had more emotional intelligence than anyone I knew.

"O'Toole." I sighed as he joined me against the bar. Our arms touched, and I shoved him away. I believed in personal space. He didn't.

"I promised you I'd buy you a round for coming out tonight." He pushed up onto his elbows and looked over the bar. "Oh, they have cherries. I've been craving an Old Fashioned, but this place doesn't have the nice ice cubes. Isn't it weird how an ice cube can make or break a drink? Like those slushies with the small cube ice at the drive-in?"

The bartender returned with my beer.

"Oh, hello there, you are gorgeous. Could I get an Old Fashioned with Maker's? I'm feeling myself tonight. And three shots of whatever you have that won't kill us. My dude here needs a pick-me-up."

"Does he?" The bartender winked at me, her tongue dancing on her lower lip. Her dark hair hung down to her waist, and she had all the things that used to entice me about women: curves, sultry lips, eyes that shouted mischief, and an ass to hold onto. But instead of even a blip of interest, my libido was dead. Gone. Out of the country.

"My beer is fine."

"False." Callum put his arm around me, squeezing my shoulder. "Jabroni, it's so nice having you here."

"I see you every day, O'Toole. What are you doing?"

"Cheering you up. I can tell you're down, bro, and not sure why. I'm not asking, that's your business, but I'd be a shit teammate if I didn't pull you out of your ass."

My jaw tightened, and a million different feelings flew through my chest. Gratitude, pain, guilt, and happiness. How lucky was I that my teammates were trying to help me? I sipped the beer and met Callum's puppy-face. He always looked like Christmas was the next day. "I've been in a weird headspace."

"I get it. We all have moments like that. It's life."

"I doubt you've ever had a down moment, Cal. You're annoyingly happy all the fucking time."

"Mm, I wouldn't say that."

Luca joined my other side, his serious face scanning the crowd. "I hate people."

I snorted. "Wow, you're a ray of sunshine."

"I need new roommates. Jesus, you two are like clouds in the night. It's hard being the ray of sunlight all the time with you two grumping around. You've always been this way, Luca. It's part of your charm. Lo is all smiles, and you're frowns. It's fitting." Callum grinned as the bartender handed three shots to us. "Ah, beautiful, thank you, gorgeous."

"I'm not doing this," Luca growled. "I don't do shots."

"Ah, but what about the summer playbook our girls are doing?"

"*Our* girls?" Luca said, his tone going dark. "Not *your* girls, Callum."

"I beg to differ. I'm invited to girls' night *and* will help Mack with her naughty and wild list. Pretty sure that makes me one of them." Callum smirked and tossed the shot back with ease. "Ah, tequila. Yes. Makes me feel spicier."

Mack and a naughty and wild list…a warm, unfamiliar tension weaved its way in my gut thinking about her and those adjectives together.

"God, you're annoying," Luca said. He downed the shot, didn't show a single emotion, and hit his fist on the bar. "Lo doesn't invite me to girls' nights."

"Yeah, because you're with her. It's different. I can't make up the rules, but it's cute how your jealousy is showing. You should tuck it back in, Monroe."

"*Callum, come here!*"

He craned his neck. "Ah, your woman needs me. I shouldn't keep Lo waiting, hm?"

Callum hit my shoulder before returning to the table with the girls. I could almost feel Luca's irritation in the air, swirling around us in a cloud of gray. He was my best friend and closest teammate, and he was the definition of grumpy. Was I really turning into that because of what happened? *Because of Jessica.*

"Some days I hate him." Luca pinched his nose. "Others, he's great."

"I know the feeling." I chewed the inside of my cheek, watching Callum slide into the booth so that he was next to Mack and Lo. Mackenzie Mallinson—my sister's teammate and best friend—rested her head on his shoulder like he was some sort of comfort. A weird, unfamiliar pang formed in my chest, but I blamed it on the damn tequila shot. "I think this list is a dumb idea. Who needs a checklist to have fun?"

"You're asking the wrong person here, but Lo looks happy, more than happy, so we are gonna support this notion even if it's the worst thing to ever exist."

"Worse than bacon-scented candles?" I teased. I bought Luca one for our Christmas gift exchange two years ago, and holy shit, the dude hated it. Every time I lit it, he walked into the kitchen excited for bacon only to be fooled. It was honestly an excellent prank.

"Fuck your dumbass candle." Luca's lips twitched. "It feels good to see you joke.

"I *can* be funny when I want to."

"On that note, when the fuck are you gonna tell your sister the truth about what happened? You're testing my patience on hiding this from her. I will not let you cause a strain in our relationship, and she keeps asking what the hell is going on."

"You've made it clear," I grumbled. Luca was a good dude, the best teammate, and honestly great for my twin sister. The problem was, I selfishly missed him being mine first. He was still a great ass friend, but his allegiance shifted when Lo was involved. He knew what happened to me last fall and pushed me to talk about it, when I would rather lick the floor of this bar than mention feelings.

Or *her.*

Or me.

I chugged the rest of the beer, ignoring his glare. Sometimes —like now—I was glad he was on my team on the field because he could be scary as shit.

"Dean, it fucked you up. You haven't spoken about with anyone but me, and I honor that, but you're changed."

"Of course I'm different." I gripped the back of my neck, the same dark thoughts circling like they had since last fall. It had been eight months since *it happened,* and everything still hurt. I'd pushed myself physically to distract and in the process, accidentally alienated those closest to me.

My family was big on feelings and hashing things out, but it was like all those experiences didn't mean shit now. "I… need more time."

"I physically am repelled by what I'm about to say to you, so know this is how desperate I am." He cleared his throat and stared at the ceiling. "Christ, help me. Okay. Here it goes. You should have your own list to get your head out of your ass."

GYHOOYA.

"The GYHOOYA list?" I made an acronym. It was a useless, unbearable character trait of mine that showed up in the worst moments. Like the time Lo had her girls' days to relax and have fun, so it was the AGDTRAHF, pronounced *ahg-dtra-huff.*

Useless. But amusing to me, so that meant something.

"You're a fucking idiot." Luca closed his eyes. "I'm heading to the bathroom then joining Lo. She made me promise to have her head home early since she works tomorrow."

"She's loving her internship, right?"

"Talk. To. Her." Luca spared me no glance as he pushed off the bar, leaving me alone with my fucked-up acronym humor and sad thoughts.

AHST—pronounced *ah-st.*

Rolling my shoulders, I leaned against the bar and took in the scene. Focusing on the five senses helped me settle whenever my insides got weird. It smelled like beer and cleaner, an awful combination. That and the sweat from everyone around me. June was hot in central Illinois. The bar top was sticky and a little humid. My skin prickled with sweat, and I dug my toes into my shoes. My mouth tasted like tequila and lime, and I breathed in the tangy scent.

Luca's words resonated with me. I needed to speak to my sister. I'd been avoiding her whenever shit felt too heavy or real, which she of course assumed had something to do with her and Luca being together.

It didn't. It was my own shit holding me back.

A familiar pleasant scent of flowers and sunscreen hit me as Mack Mallinson leaned against the bar, her arm an inch from mine. She wore her long blonde hair down in waves, and the tips were purple. My lips curved up. "I didn't notice your hair earlier. I like it."

"Oh." She held up the ends and flicked them over her shoulder. "Thanks. I need to get them redone soon."

"You keeping purple? It suits you."

She bit her lip and glanced down, like she was nervous. I frowned, hating that I could've possibly made her uncomfortable. We'd been around each other on and off for years, and she was cute as hell, but she was my sister's best friend, so that was an automatic no in every sense of the word. I blamed my protective brother instincts on the urge to warn her about this list. Nothing else.

"So, about this playbook thing—"

"Can I practice something on you real quick?" she asked, her eyes wide.

Her skin was flushed, her cheeks redder than before. Her

large blue eyes almost matched her hair, and I noted she barely wore any makeup. Her freckles stood out, and they were cute. Her lashes were also super long and dark. She was pretty, no doubt about it.

"Practice what?"

She huffed and glanced back at the table. I followed her gaze and found all of the girls and my teammate staring at us. I stood straighter. What was going on? Why was Callum winking at her?

"Uh, the plan is… was…look, I have to ask some guy if they want to do a shot with me. It's the first item in the playbook."

I scanned the bar, weighing at her options. They all seemed like horrible choices. Beefcakes would stare at her chest, and Mustache seemed a little creepy. *This is a dumb idea.* "If you don't want to, don't do it. They mean well, but friends are the worst sometimes."

"No, that's the thing. I do. I need to push myself out of my comfort zone and *live*." She gripped the edge so hard her knuckles were white.

The urge to comfort her had me leaning closer. She sucked in a breath as I bent my head, which made me feel even worse. Her friends would hear it from me if they pressured her into something she didn't want to do. "Mack, you're nervous. If you're not wanting—"

"Can I practice with you? Just for a second?"

Her large eyes pleaded with me, and *fuck,* I was a sucker for blue eyes. As someone who grew up with dark brown, blue eyes on a woman usually were my kryptonite. I expected the usual blahness to hit me, the nothingness I felt around the opposite sex, but instead, my stomach tightened with… something. Mack was always cute in the sporty, adorable way.

Lo's best friend. Back off.

Sighing, I nodded. "If you think it'll help, sure."

"Thanks, Dean." She swallowed, hard. Her throat bobbed, and she pushed her hair behind her ears. She had a birthmark on her left cheek, right below her eye, and I'd never noticed how her lashes fanned over her cheeks when she blinked.

"Hit on me," I said, amused.

She sighed, blinking a million times before she clasped her hands in front of her. "Can I buy you a shot, please?"

I fought a smile—second time in the span of five minutes. I was a new person. "Can I offer feedback?"

"Please. Yes. All of it. I don't… I never do this." She groaned, and one of her tank top straps slid off, showcasing a very bright pink bra.

My finger twitched with the urge to touch it. *Interesting.* I let my gaze drop for a second to the tight black tank that hugged her toned body. Her cutoff jean shorts went high, and she had a shoestring as a belt. Seeing the loop there made my fingers ache to yank it. She didn't want my opinion on how cute she was though. She'd asked for feedback on hitting on a dude.

"First off, you're clenching your hands together. This isn't a job interview. You're asking a man, who is generally an idiot. He's gonna be happy you're talking to him."

"No hand clenching. Got it." She released her fingers but then held them in the air at an awkward angle. "What do I do then?

I couldn't stop the laugh that came out. She was goofy. "Lean on the bar. Put your arms there, lean forward a little bit, and tilt your head."

"Oh. That's much better. Yes. Like this?" She did what I said, the movement causing her tank top to drop in the front. Mack had nice tits. I usually saw her in sports bras or working out, and that hid the curves spilling out right now.

She stared at me, her brows furrowed. *Shit.* She'd asked a question. "Yes, much better."

She ran a finger over her lip as she said, "Can I buy you a shot, buddy?"

"Don't say buddy." I laughed again. Three laughs in one night. 3L1N. "No dude wants to be called buddy."

She groaned and rested her forehead on the wooden top. Her tank top dipped low in the back, so the movement showcased all her back muscles, and a wave of appreciation washed over me. Mack was talented as hell, strong, and a kickass athlete.

"My summer playbook is dumb," she mumbled. "I can't believe I agreed to this."

I couldn't either, but I learned early on with Lo that sometimes my opinion wasn't needed. "Chin up, Mack. You can do this. Do the lean on the bar, hold my gaze, and ask if you can buy me a shot."

She ran her hand over her hair, a blue ring on her thumb catching my eye. I wanted to ask about it, but she did as I said. "Hey, can I buy you a drink? I couldn't stop staring at your eyes and figured a drink was an easy way to see them up close."

Her normal chipper voice turned husky. Her cheeks pinkened at the tops, and she wet her bottom lip as her gaze dropped to my mouth. My stomach tightened as a bolt of interest pulled me toward her. This was *Mack.* My sister's best friend, the tomboy, the soccer star, the girl who could probably outrun me. Her cloudy blue eyes widened the longer I stared, and I coughed to ground myself.

"Killed it." I exhaled, worry churning in my gut. It had been so damn long since I felt anything like attraction that a simple, dorky pickup line worked. It wasn't Mack. It was my long-lost libido coming back.

"Really?" She beamed. "That was okay?"

I nodded. The tequila shot hit me, the nice buzz easing the tension in my shoulders. "Mack, if you aren't comfortable, you really don't have to do this."

"That's the thing, Romano." She chewed the inside of her cheek, her attention moving from my face to the TV in the bar. "I've played it safe for so long. I've only done things that make me comfortable. It's time I pushed myself off the field. This is my final summer before professional soccer becomes my life. I'm doing the list they come up with. Plus, we're all working through stuff, and you should've seen how happy the girls were to get on board with this. You should have one too, you know. Before you have your senior season here and get drafted. Life will be different. Now, wish me luck. I think I want the guy in the orange backwards hat. I'm a sucker for that look."

She pushed off without sparing me a glance. The muscles in her back rippled as she moved about twenty feet toward some dude in a hat. I watched her. How could I not? If the guy said anything to make her upset, I'd intervene. Someone had to keep her safe. She was a pretty blonde with a heart of gold, who was too dang trusting.

Trust.

Betrayal.

And there went my mood.

Talking with Mack had distracted me more than I realized, but now my mind returned to the fall, and my twisted feelings of anger and sadness warped my personality once more. I ordered another shot, my max absolutely two because I never wanted to lose control again, and saw the guy laugh at Mack.

Was he laughing *at* her or with her?

Her familiar cackle carried across the bar, and a sinking, annoyed feeling weighed me down. I liked her practicing with me, and I wanted her to succeed, so what the fuck was this?

"Dean Romano." A woman slid up next to me, her voice sweet and sultry.

An aggressive wave of perfume had me coughing as I faced my new friend. She had bright red hair, large brown eyes, and a figure that would've made my mouth water. She was gorgeous, case closed, no notes. I scanned her head to toe, waiting for the flicker of desire to hit me. It had five minutes ago with Mack, so I knew my libido was trying to get back to normal, but not a thing occurred.

So why had it happened with Mack?

"What are you drinking tonight, handsome?" She scooted closer so our arms touched.

The bartender slid me my shot, and I downed it. "That. Last one for me."

"Aw, are you sure?"

"Sweetheart, you are beautiful. It's not you, it's me, okay?" I tapped the bar, scanning to see Mack and her guy taking a shot together. I swallowed down the strange, unrecognizable feeling and forced a smile. "If you're wanting some company, find Xavier. He's new to town and needs to be shown around. I heard he has a thing for redheads too."

She didn't spare me a second glance, on to find her next mission. My jaw tightened, the need to warn Xavier gripping me in the throat. He had to be careful about who to trust, who to sleep with. People were vicious. They were cruel.

I'd learned that the hard way.

Jessica *had* turned me into this distrusting, angry dude who couldn't enjoy the summer before my senior year, and it wasn't fucking fair. I needed to avoid this feeling, burn some energy to settle down before I tried to sleep. Sleeping or working out were the two things that helped me not think, well, those and then the little bit of helping Mack.

Speaking of…

She grinned maniacally as she came back to where I was, her eyes lit up and her hands waving in front of her chest. "Oh my god, oh my god. I did it. I did it, Dean."

"Yeah?" I almost smiled. She was so damn happy it was hard not to mirror that. "Seemed like you did alright then, Mallinson."

"My heart is racing. Wow, that was more nerve-wracking than a soccer game. How sad is that?" She cackled. "I'd rather face down our rivals than approach a guy at a bar."

"The field is where you feel the most at home, the safest. I'm the same."

"Yeah, I imagine you are." She smiled, this time smaller, like we had a shared secret. "Thanks for letting me practice. There was no way I could've done that cold turkey. Nope. No way."

"Happy to help."

"I get to hold my head high as I return to the table. Thanks to you. Oh hey, wait." She scrunched her nose, leaned onto the bar, and repeated the question she'd practiced earlier. "Can I buy you a drink, as a thank you?"

"You're a dork." I laughed. "I'm good though."

"I tried. Look at me though, throwing around pickup lines like it's no big deal. I'm growing!" She raised her hands, the movement causing her shirt to ride up and show off her very toned stomach.

Lust hit me again. The second time that night.

"Well, if you don't want a drink, come join us."

"I have an early day tomorrow, so I'm heading out. But Mack," I paused, unsure what I wanted to say. I couldn't exactly thank her for helping me laugh or distracting me from myself. She stared at me, lips parted and a half smile on her face. So open. So trusting. "Be careful with these challenges."

"Sure." She frowned and studied me for a beat before waving. "Have a good night, Dean. See you around."

She walked away, leaving me alone and feeling like I upset her. I paid my tab, eyed my group of friends and sister all laughing and hanging out, and hated how alone I felt. It was time I got my shit together, but I didn't know where to start.

Tomorrow. I'd figure it out tomorrow.

CHAPTER **THREE**

Mack

There were very few times I agreed with Vee when it came to finances. The girl was wild and came from wealth, so spending money was easy for her. A hobby, almost. So for her to suggest we meet up at the football house instead of a bar to come up with list ideas a few days later, I almost didn't believe it.

I nervously chewed my lip, thinking about who else lived at the football house. *Dean.* I hadn't seen him since the bar, not that I would've. We circumvented each other whenever we were in the same room, and while he'd been kind to me at the bar, he wasn't… he didn't do that. It was small chatter usually, where I tried not to tell him he was sexy, and I'd talk about the weather.

Making this list at the house, where he could hear? My nerves were in overdrive. I felt embarrassed. He had to think I was lame to have a checklist of adventure. He didn't have a list. He always lived his life to the fullest in every sense of the word. But I didn't want to spend money at a bar, *and* Callum was there.

Mack: Okay, heading out soon.

Soccer camp finished an hour ago, so I showered off the sweat and sunscreen. My farmer's tan was out of control. When I removed my socks, they looked like they were still freaking on. It'd been that way forever, and I eyed my foot, wincing. Super not sexy to have feet that were so pale and white they could guide a plane to land at night.

I usually didn't get dressed up for anything, but I planned to wear something nicer than my workout gear. *Is that trying too hard?*

Did I secretly want Dean to see me and look me up and down? Did I hope I saw a flash of interest in his eyes? It was foolish. Ugh. He was Lo's twin brother, a total womanizer, and never committed to anything besides football. *But a fling with him would be fun...*

"Shut up, brain." I rubbed my temples, annoyed at myself, and opted to wear a simple black sundress sans bra because it had a built-in one and it was summer. I threw on my High-top Chucks and tied the laces around my ankles. Mascara was my armor, and after two sprays of my perfume, I walked toward the football house. It wasn't too far since Lo wanted to be close to Luca.

Maybe it would be a good thing to be there. Xavier would be home, taking up Lo's old room, and Oliver. They'd be great to try things with, plus, they were easy to look at. The one rule that wasn't established with the playbook was *who* I did the challenges on or with. It would be too restrictive. As long as I kept that caveat in there, I could use the guys I was sorta comfortable with to knock some challenges out.

There was a light summer breeze, and I closed my eyes, smelling the fresh cut grass and rain in the air. I smiled, absolutely loving this combination. I was a summer girl, through and through. No pumpkin-spiced, fall loving for me. I was all summer showers, barbecues, swimming parties, and days at the lake. Fourth of July was my favorite holiday, and the smell of mosquito repellent and sunscreen brought me joy.

"Do you often stare up at the sky with a smile like that?"

That voice.

"Hi, Dean." I blinked my eyes open, a blip of panic rooting deep in my stomach. Shit. He wore a cutoff shirt, showcasing his ripped arms, and black running shorts. His damn backwards hat and Ray Bans perfected his look of utter sexiness. He was like an ice cream cone of *my type.* I wanted to lick him.

"What's with the grin?" His lips quirked up, and he took off the sunglasses and put them on his hat.

"The scent." I inhaled again, my skin prickling as his gaze moved from my face toward my legs. "I love it."

"Is someone having a bonfire or something?"

"No. It's the scent of summer," I said, really homing in on my crazy. "It's like sunscreen and grass and swimming pool and *heat* combined into this perfect concoction. It makes me happy. That's all. I'm sure you have a favorite scent of something."

"Uh, I don't think I do. I mean, I love the smell after they take care of the field. Or that immediate change of air walking out of the locker room." Dean ran a hand over his jaw. "I've never thought about scents like that."

"It's my strongest sense. I know people by their smells." My face flushed, and I winced. "Not in a creepy way. In a… I recognize Lo's perfume and Mally's lotion or Callum's laundry detergent. It's just a thing I have."

Stop talking about smells. Talk about the weather.

"Man, is it gonna rain?" I squeaked.

"How do I smell then? Do I have one?" He stepped closer, his lips parted with interest.

"Everyone does." I gulped. He was close. Near enough I could see the lines of sweat dripping down his bicep. Did he just work out? Probably. He smelled of sweat and leather, woodsy too. He reminded me of a summer camping trip, only no fire yet. Could I tell him that? Absolutely the hell not. "But you smell fine."

"Fine."

"Yes. Totally fine. Good, some might say." I gripped the fabric of my dress, desperate to stop this. "Anyway, I'm off. Great seeing you, Romano." I quickened my pace toward the house, but not a second later, he was next to me. I eyed him. "What are you doing?"

"I'm walking to where I live. What are *you* doing?"

"Also walking to where you live."

He snorted. "Yeah, I figured. Luca texted us that the girls were coming over for some dumb chat about a dumb list and that if Callum added anything about Lo on the list, he would punch his *dumb* face."

"That sounds all on par."

We walked side by side, our fingers brushing for a second. A jolt of electricity burst through me from the small touch. An awkward, squawk-like sound escaped my throat, which I had to turn it into a cough and pray Dean assumed I swallowed a bug. This was where my life was at, that I *wanted* my crush to think I'd inhaled an insect rather than freaking out about our pinky fingers touching.

No wonder I need this list.

I sent another *fuck you* to Coach Emily to have me spiraling about a pinky touch. Was this her fault? Probably not this specifically, but I was mad at her all the same.

The house was in sight! I only needed to act chill and cool and sexy for twenty more seconds. Less, if I ran. But that would draw attention.

"You do any more dares since Tuesday?" Dean asked, his voice holding a twinge of amusement. "Ask to buy shots for more men?"

"Why the laughter, Romano? Is the idea of me doing that funny?"

"I've seen you try and wink, Mack, so yes." He nudged his arm with mine. "You were cute though. That helps."

"Wow, a compliment from you." I rolled my eyes, but holy shit, he said I was cute. Me! Dean Romano! My insides did back handsprings while my face was as hot as a damn fireball.

He never responded because Callum sat on their porch, nursing a beer and wearing a smirk made for mischief. "Damn, Mallinson, you look good. It's gonna have to come off though."

"What?" Dean asked, his voice lower. "Why…what did you say?"

"Why am I taking my clothes off?" I hopped up the stairs, thankful for the distraction from being near Dean. It was weird, how we'd been alone more this week than we had in years. My heart raced per usual, but there was a comfort with him that was hard to explain. He seemed… focused when he spoke to me, like he was really listening when before I was just a blob of a person who he spoke to when needed.

"Because part one of the playbook is this: wear an uncomfortable shirt out with friends. It's the first challenge, and you're going to want to thank me, I already know," he said, winking as he paused for a dramatic reveal. "I took care of it for all of us."

He tossed me a T-shirt, but it was rolled up and tied off with a rubber band.

"Is this mine?"

"Sure is. No returns. No take backs. We're going to pregame here, make the rest of the list, and then everyone is wearing one of these shirts to go out. If you refuse, then you're cut off. It's in the playbook, so its law."

"Obviously." I grinned, a blip of excitement weaving its way down my stomach. This sounded fun. "Where is everyone?"

"Porch." Callum eyed Dean, his expression changing from playful to curious. "You want to join us, Romano? I bought two extra shirts just in case you and Luca come along. He is obviously the Grumpy Cat one. But yours… join us in the back if you're down."

Callum held out his arm and wiggled his brows. "Ready, Mack Attack?"

"Do I have a choice?" I looped my arm through his and glanced at Dean over my shoulder. He watched us with a strange, distant expression. It seemed like he was sad, almost, but that made no sense. Maybe it was the longing in his eyes or the way the light hit his face, but I nodded. "Are you coming?"

He gripped the back of his neck, his jaw working before he shrugged. "Sure."

"Dude, yes, let's go!" Callum almost tossed me to the side. "I've been waiting for this, bro. I've missed you. Can we hug?"

"No."

"You need to stop hanging out with Luca. He's rubbing off on you."

"I don't know… I've seen Luca give more hugs since he's been with Lolo." I grinned, my heart swelling as Callum pulled Dean into a hug. Dean shoved him off immediately.

"Head to the back, Mack. I'll grab some beers and join you in a second. I want to get my man here his shirt."

A bubble of anticipation formed in my gut, not quite nerves or excitement. I asked Dean to hang, and he did. That felt cool, big even. With a smile still on my face, I walked outside to see Lo, Vee, and Ale sitting in lawn chairs with beers around their feet and packages lying in the middle in a perfect circle. "Well, this seems culty."

"Mallinson!" Ale stood and pulled me in for a hug. "This is going to be amazing. Did Callum tell you where he found this idea?"

"The shirts? No." I sat next to Lo, hitting her thigh as a greeting. She grinned back. "Why do you look suspicious?"

"Because I know what's in there, and I can't wait to watch everyone's faces." She covered her mouth with her hand, but her eyes lit up.

"I hate that you got a sneak preview." Vee rolled her eyes. "Freaking Callum."

"He's the one who saw the video on social media and shared it with me. So, it made sense to collaborate on this." Lo's gaze moved over my shoulder, toward the house. Surprise covered her face, but then she seemed pleased. "Oh my god."

I whipped around, and sure enough, Dean wore a shirt that was the body of Shrek. Green chest, a brown vest. It fit him like a glove, so at first glance, it seemed like *him.*

He pressed his lips together for a beat before turning around. "Okay, check me out. Get your comments over with now."

We all burst out laughing. He looked so ridiculous, but he somehow could still pull it off.

"I'll be your Fiona, Romano," Vee said, winking at him as he joined us. Callum practically beamed at the group, his face lighting up like a proud parent. "I'll peel back your layers."

Dean laughed. "O'Toole, there better be weird-as-fuck shirts in there. I can't do this alone."

"Don't worry, party people." Callum unbuttoned his flannel, revealing a bright blue T-shirt of a cat sitting on top of a tiger's head while swimming in the ocean. It was… ridiculous.

"How the hell did you find these? Like… what?" Lo laughed so hard her eyes watered.

"I have my ways. Now, there are four shirts in there for you. I bought Luca the Grumpy Cat shirt, but of course, he's not hanging with us tonight."

"He's reached his people limit for the week," Lo added.

"Each of you grab one of the packages. It doesn't matter who has what because they're all the same level of ridiculous. Once we have them on them, we go out and show them off."

"After we make the list though for Mack," Vee said, holding up a sheet of paper with the words THE SUMMER PLAYBOOK on the top. "This is top priority."

"Wearing a shirt that looks anything like the two of you," I said, pointing at Dean and Callum. "Is enough of going out of my comfort zone."

"Nice try. You're living it up this summer, girly. Now, let's pick our shirts."

My heart raced as Callum tossed the packages to each the girls. I held the purple package in my hand, spinning it. It matched my hair, and that had to be a good sign.

I tore the paper apart, anxious to see what Callum did to us. It wouldn't be good, I knew that. The man had no boundaries. I unrolled the shirt and gasped.

"Oh, oh, oh my god." I stared, my face heating. "This is… no."

"Let's see it." At some point, Dean sat next to me, and he leaned over so his face was a foot from mine as he stared at my shirt. "Jesus Christ. No way."

"I can't…. is this obscene?" I gulped. He was so close I could smell his cologne and see the curve of his jaw. If I wore *this shirt* in front of him, it would kill any secret chance I had at getting him to fall in love with me.

Dean shook his head before he cackled hard. It was a loud slap of laugh thunder, where it was almost contagious.

"Stop it. This will kill me," I said.

"Put it on now, please. Please, Mack." He laughed hard again, his eyes watering. "Callum is either evil or a genius or both."

"This is the least sexy thing I've ever seen. How will… people will gawk. At my *man chest.* "

"Yup. I can't stop staring at it either." He slapped his knee before moving his attention toward the other girls.

I held up the shirt, which was a very hairy, very bare man chest. Nipples and all. I believed in free the nipple, because hello, it's your body, so do what ya want, but this seemed… damn. Wow. I could… I could do this. I could be silly and bold.

My pulse spiked, but I put the shirt on over my outfit. It fit perfectly, almost like a dress. The others all giggled and freaked out about their shirts, but Dean watching distracted me. He started at my legs, moving up toward my chest, before he bit his lip. It almost seemed like interest, but I dismissed the thought immediately.

"SHUT THE FUCK UP!" Ale screamed, holding up her shirt of Shaquille O'Neal's face. "I love him. I love this man, and look at this shirt!"

It was enlarged, so his eyes were the size of her boobs. My lips curled up. "Whoa."

"Whoa yourself, nips," she quipped.

With Ale and I standing, Lo put on her shirt, Vee following after. Lo's shirt was a gorilla face, printed over and over, covering every single inch of the shirt and sleeves. Vee wore the same type only with Nic Cage's face.

I wasn't sure who won or lost with the worst shirt, but I was in the top two, either way.

Callum giggled the entire time, taking photos and filming us. "You all are so beautiful. Mack, especially."

"Did you make sure I got this one specifically?"

"Yes. But I regret it. It's very confusing. Your legs look sexy but then with the man chest… I have weird feelings."

I laughed, caught Dean's eyes, and quickly averted my attention. Callum flirted with anything and everyone, so I knew the compliment wasn't meant to express interest. However, hearing my legs called sexy did make me stand a little taller.

"Group photo, come on." Callum forced us all to stand together, really close, and Dean's arm came around me as we huddled.

My stomach swooped from his stupid Shrek-covered arm touching me, and I didn't want to admit it to Callum, but this silly shirt idea already had me doing things I normally wouldn't.

Adrenaline surged through, the urge to really live it up hitting me. After this year, there wouldn't be nights in the backyard of the football house or goofy shirt bar crawls with my girls. I'd be living in a host's house, working my ass off to make a name for myself professionally. This truly was my last summer of fun before proving Emily wrong and making it to the pros. "Okay, let's create this fucking playbook. Everything is fair game."

"You for real, for real?" Lo asked, her face thoughtful. "We can go *hard* or medium for you."

"Hard. I want it hard."

"That's what she said," Callum added, winking at me. "Vee, the first item on the summer playbook should be to sleep with five men."

Dean coughed.

"What? No. Not… medium. I want medium." My face

burned cherry red as I stumbled over my words. "I'm not a one-night stand person. I wish I was, but I'm not, and that's too far."

"Making out then," Vee said. "Or a tit squeeze."

"We're not putting a *tit squeeze* on this list," I said, grabbing Lo's beer and taking a long swing. "Someone needs to be rational here."

"I disagree." Ale grinned sheepishly at me. "We know you, Mack, and despite Callum's terrible start, we understand your limits. Now, you and your man chest pipe down. You trust us, and we love you. We got this."

I stared at my friends, my teammates, and sighed. "Okay, I need a goddamn drink though."

CHAPTER **FOUR**

Dean

"I'll come with you."

I joined Mack on her walk to the house to get a drink. I wanted one too, but I'd need about ten if I was in her position. She was handling the challenge well too. It impressed me. Seeing her gain courage at the bar the other night, then tonight, wearing that stupid fucking shirt, showed her innate pride and bravery.

I'd always found Mack cute, but her legs in her outfit right now were delectable. After not being attracted to anyone the last half a year, lust hit me hard and fast. Her calves were defined from years of training, and I wanted to feel them, run my tongue over them to see if her skin was as smooth as it looked.

"Are you joining in on the list to embarrass me?"

"Wait." I paused, clearing my inappropriate thoughts about my sister's best friend. "Why would I do that?"

"You're the king of one-night stands, and I can't even do them. I put on this strong face that I'm looking forward to these challenges when really I'm terrified." She pushed her hair behind her ears, her eyes wide and full of emotions.

Feelings weren't really my thing off the field. It might've been why I was still struggling to deal with the aftermath of what happened in the fall. Seeing her fear, excitement, and embarrassment in her expression stopped me though. She thought I'd embarrass her? I didn't like that. "There's nothing to be ashamed about not wanting to do one-night stands."

"Well, you're a player, and that's great. Good for you. But what if my friends, or former friends, put that shit on my list? I'm so competitive it's unhealthy. I'll have to complete the list, or I won't live with myself."

"You shouldn't do anything that you're not a fan of, Mack."

"The whole point of the list is to have me live it up, which is something I don't normally do." She groaned and stomped into our kitchen. "Where is the alcohol?"

"Beer or hard stuff?" I asked, trying not to stare at the bare man chest or her legs. Callum said it perfectly earlier: it was confusing. Her legs were sexy as hell, but the hairy man chest wasn't my preference.

SBC. Sexy but confusing.

"All of it." She rubbed her temples and took a deep breath. "Beer. I'd love a beer or two before heading back out there. I thought I'd be in here alone to have my freakout, but you're witnessing it, so I'm trying to be more chill."

I went to the fridge and pulled out a couple of bottles. "Don't be chill on my part. Let it all out, I can handle it."

"You're being nice to me. Why?"

"Why wouldn't I be?" I fired back, a little bothered by two negative comments from her. "Do you think I don't like you? I would never embarrass you on purpose, like you asked earlier, nor would I be cruel. I'm a little confused here."

"Fuck, you're right. I'm sorry, Dean." She walked closer

to me, her eyes filled with sympathy as she squeezed my forearm. "I feel like we've circled each other the past three years, never really hanging out or talking, but now we've been around each other more the last week. You're Dean Romano, the campus legend. The dude who can blink and have girls lined up. You're kind of untouchable in my mind, so I'm projecting my own BS on you. You're not mean and never have been to me. I shouldn't have made you question that."

I chewed my lip, taking in her words. She apologized so easily, so genuinely, and I envied her ability to do that. "I'm not really the campus legend anymore."

She snorted. "And what has changed from last season to now? Of course, you still are. Your damn face is everywhere, and you have fan accounts."

She has no idea what I went through. She never would. Instead of letting my mind go down that route, I changed direction. "I like how honest you are. It's refreshing."

"Oh. I can't help it. It's a personality flaw."

"Nah." I opened both our beers and tossed the caps in the trash. "If you're going to play professionally, you know you're gonna get catered to and used in some ways. That's how it is for me, so honesty is refreshing."

"That doesn't happen to women, Dean. The sports world is vastly different for you and me. I don't mean that to be combative to you, but it's the truth."

I handed her the beer, and our fingers brushed. The contact sent a jolt through my forearm, which was fucking weird. Clearing my throat, I pointed toward the door. "You're right. Lo and I have had a lot of talks about that and how utter bullshit it is. I've seen Lo and you work harder than some men I know, and the system is built to support us, not women."

"Exactly. Hey, maybe you're not so bad." She grinned and

let her eyes drop to my chest. "I'm kinda into Shrek. This look suits you."

"Mallinson," I barked out, laughing. I was not expecting that. "Are you *flirting* with me?"

"You? No. Shrek? Yes." Her eyes sparkled, and she walked out the back door, her hairy back sending the same conflicting thoughts through me. She was hot waist down.

I followed, more intrigued in this journey than I would've assumed. Since she'd practiced on me at the bar, I'd thought about her more and more. She wanted this summer to live it up, where I wanted this summer to return to normal.

Was my standard hooking up with random girls? Was it partying? I didn't know what *normal* meant to me now, but I liked how I felt hanging out with Lo and her friends. I enjoyed how they had fun. My teammates were great, but Callum was still in the partying phase. So were Oliver and Xavier. Luca never was, but now that I was changing, it was hard to find the new balance.

Mack held her head up high, her blonde and blue hair clashing with the black back hair on the T-shirt, and I grinned. Callum did a great job with these stupid shirts.

"What have you done to me?" Mack asked her crew, sitting in the lawn chair and crossing one leg over the other.

That meant her calf was facing me, inches from my own leg. It was tempting to touch it.

"We have the playbook. Now, most playbooks have a few standard plays that are basic. We have those. But then we have some special plays in there too for you," Callum said, his face almost manic with joy.

He loved this shit.

"Okay. Okay." Mack nodded to herself. "You know I'm competitive, so I'm going to do it all, but Callum, if there is anything… too much for me in there, I'm going to do it with you."

"Gladly." He beamed.

My stomach hardened. Do *what* with Callum? One-night stands? For whatever reason, the thought of that made me uncomfortable. Callum was a total playboy. He was never serious, ever. He lived life by the seat of his pants, and his personality was great to have as a teammate and friend because he was always a good time, but for Mack? No. She deserved more even if I couldn't explain it. Callum was a great dude but wasn't right for Mack.

I frowned and gripped the side of the chair tighter. "What did you put on the list for her to need you, O'Toole?"

"Oh, this and that." He winked at me. "Now, are you ready for the big reveal?"

Mack showed all her teeth in a grimace, her gaze darting from person to person before she took a huge breath, her chest rising and falling twice before she nodded. "Let's do this shit."

"Gah, I am so excited!" her friend Vee said, rocking back and forth even in her chair. She seemed to be the leader of this particular thing. "They are in no order, except we put the first one because it's already done. Now, here are the rules—"

"Fuck the rules, give me my playbook," Mack said, her eyes lighting up with fire. "I want to see it."

FTR—I liked that one. Fuck the Rules.

Vee tossed her the notebook, and Mack stared at the white page covered with blank ink. She gave nothing away as she studied it. The only indication she was still awake was her teeth gently nibbling the side of her lip. My own stomach lurched as Callum and the other girls grinned, watching her.

"Hm," Mack said, pursing her lips.

"Hm, what?" I asked, leaning closer to her. "Can I read over your shoulder? I'm dying."

"Oh, yeah, of course. You weren't here with these assholes." Mack scooted her chair closer to me, her flowery, summer scent calming my unnecessary nerves.

I read through the list, my mind going to inappropriate places.

- Buy a guy a shot
- Mixologist challenge – ask bartender to let you make a drink
- Skinny dipping
- Get a makeover
- Tattoo
- Take a body shot off someone
- Someone takes one off you
- Grind with a stranger
- Make out with two people in one night
- Hook up past first base with a stranger/someone
- Be naughty in public
- Ask three guys out
- Dance on a bar
- Streaking
- Dance in the rain
- Concert
- Join a game already going on with strangers
- Bonfire (talk to five strangers)
- Wear an outfit you normally wouldn't wear
- Dye your hair a new color
- Crash an event (or wedding for bonus points)
- Lose the cell phone for a whole day
- Strip poker

What the fuck did be naughty in public mean? And

streaking? Strip poker? Why were these people obsessed with getting Mack naked? Tattoo? Grinding? First base?

"What are you going to do first?" Lo asked, her voice filled with amusement. "I vote being naughty in public."

"Happy to help with that." Callum reached across *my lap* to squeeze Mack's leg.

He was so touchy. It made me want to kick him.

"The second one." Mack scrunched her nose and scratched across her hairy shirt chest. "Let's finish these drinks and head to a bar for the second one."

"Let's go!" Callum shouted, and everyone held up their beer, cheering Mack on about her playbook. "I should make my own list of crazy shit to do."

"You live a wild life; you don't need a list." Lo laughed, standing and folding up her chair. "A list would just convince you to do even dumber things. Honestly, I don't know how you haven't been arrested."

"Mm, technically I have no mug shot, but I've been in the back of a cop car before. So, your statement is kind of not true."

Everyone picked up their chairs and bottles, and I found myself gravitating toward Mack. I wanted to ask how she was feeling about all this. Was she excited? Nervous? Scared?

"Want help with the mixologist challenge?" I asked her as the group walked through the house toward the front door. "I can do it with you if you're anxious."

"Oh, I'm very nervous, but I think that's the point. I've played by the rules for so long, and this summer is me going outside the lines, you know?" She glanced up, her lashes fanning her eyes, and smirked. "You've lived life outside the lines for a while. Any tips?"

I swallowed. That was *old* me. She clearly still thought of me as a major playboy, a role I used to be fucking good at.

"Tips, huh? I guess… have fun and don't do anything you'll regret the next morning."

"The post-morning sads are the worst. I've had those, that's for sure." She leaned closer, her lips parting, and another bolt of desire went through me.

My libido had been broken after Jessica destroyed me, yet Mack woke it back up. It was terrible timing. Maybe I needed to wild out tonight too, to have it return with anyone but her.

"Do you have an opening line you use, or do you just exist and puff out your large chest?"

I laughed. "Wow, large chest?"

"Yes. You're stacked. And not just from Shrek either." She winked, and fuck, that charmed me.

"You know this, Romano. If you need a compliment, post a selfie online. You'll get comments asking to ride your face within minutes."

"Are you talking about *my brother* and face riding? Because that's a party foul. Dean, you're out if I hear that shit again." Lo came up, walking right in between Mack and me.

I wanted to shove her for that. The urge to ask Mack if she wanted to ride my face had been there, but Lo showed up before it could slip out. It would be terrible to say it aloud, but it didn't take away the desire to. "It was all Mallinson. She mentioned social media. It wasn't me; I swear."

"Liar. I know you're lying."

"He's not. It was me," Mack said, raising her brows at me in an adorable, flirty way.

"Okay then." Lo ignored me and looped her arm through Mack's. "Are you sure you're alright with this? I know you're tough, and I love you, but I need you to speak up if this is too much."

"Nah, I'm kind of excited. Plus, Vee needs this to focus on, and I want to have the summer of a lifetime."

"I actually bought you something, if you're up for it. I found a cheap polaroid camera and a little moleskin journal for you to document everything. If you want, of course."

"Wait. A camera? That prints pictures? Hell yes, Lolo. This is… I love it."

My lips curved up at her enthusiasm. Seeing her so damn happy eased the unwarranted tension that formed thinking about her and Callum together.

"Let's take a photo with our shirts. You can put it in the first page now, if you want?"

"You are the best friend ever, oh my god." Mack jumped in a circle. "Everyone, get in close!"

I scooted next to my sister and put my arm around her as everyone squished together. Mack stood right in front of me, and I pulled her close. I tried to ignore her curves or how she smelled or how she wiggled against me and let out a cute little sigh. She was happy, and I was selfish because I wanted to be a part of her joy.

"Gah! Look at this, it's so fucking cute!" Mack hopped up and down and shook the photo. Her smile stretched across her face; her radiant joy almost visible around her. "Let's go knock off an item on that list!"

"If you get naughty with the bartender, then you can check off two of them!" Callum shouted, causing the girls to giggle.

It should've had me feeling weird, hanging with the girls' soccer team. I'd never really done it before, never was interested, but now I couldn't imagine a more fun random night. We wore our dumb shirts, looking like a dorky gang, yet I smiled more than I had in months. Even if I wasn't a huge fan of this damn playbook…I kinda wanted to see it play out.

CHAPTER **FIVE**

Mack

"Okay, you little gremlins! We're running laps to warm up our muscles. Down and back three times, focus on good jogging form. You're going to hear me talk about fundamentals a lot this summer. Anyone know what that means?" I yelled.

"The basics?"

"Very close. They are using your body in the right way. When you practice a certain way, it becomes permanent in your mind. Now, three down and backs." I clapped my hands and blew my whistle. It rang across the thick air the next morning. Everything seemed a little brighter today. Maybe it was the air of badass I had now, knowing I made a motherfucking drink on my own. I'd asked the bartender, and he'd agreed, letting me create one and serve my friends. It was the best ten minutes of my college life, and I still had a little high from it.

And it has nothing to do with the fact Dean couldn't stop staring at you. It had to be the shirt. It was… eye-catching. That was the truth. I was used to people recognizing me if they were soccer fans, but last night was unparalleled. It was fun and wild and exactly what I wanted this summer.

To be more than just a soccer star. To have an experience that wasn't related to being on the field.

The seven-year-olds took off down the field in a chorus of giggles and cheers, pulling me from the memories. Some parents sat in the stands, clapping and shouting their daughters' names, encouraging them to hustle. The June sun burned bright without a cloud in the sky, and I grinned hard. The grass was freshly cut, and it smelled like sunscreen and summer. My skin prickled with sweat from the early morning humidity, and damn, I was lucky.

Between my challenge last night and day four of the camp, I was feeling good. Excited, even. I loved being in this coaching role because I knew everything I didn't want to be for these girls. I'd push them but remain positive. I'd never say anything that would have them doubt themselves, that was for damn sure.

Maybe this would be the summer I'd remember for the rest of my life. Instead of being the secondary character, I was taking over as the protagonist. Watch out, world!

The girls completed lap one and jogged toward the second. We practiced on the football field since ours was getting reseeded and redone the next two weeks. While I hated the truth, more participants signed up if we used the football field. It drew more people in, and even if I played with my heart and soul, sports were still a business. Just because I understood it didn't mean I liked it.

I wore my neon pink spandex and matching tank today and styled my hair in long French braids. They were my go-to look when I wanted to feel in charge.

"Coach Mack! Coach Mack!" A little girl with brown pigtails ran toward me from the entrance to the field. A tall figure walked behind her with familiar broad shoulders. She panted as she stopped in front of me, gasping for air. "I'm sorry! I'm late! I got lost!"

"Hey, it's okay. Take some deep breaths. Here, stand tall. Your lungs need air." I put my hands behind my head, opening up my chest for her to model. "Do this and do slow breaths."

Her cheeks were red as she gasped for air.

And the familiar shoulders turned into a very familiar face with that familiar tug low in my gut toward him.

Dean Romano approached us, his dark brown eyes scanning me up and down. A zing went through me at the gesture, but it didn't mean anything. Dean was a natural flirt. Not like Callum —he was what you'd call a massive ho. But Dean oozed sexual prowess and confidence, and he liked women. A year ago, I would've thought about that look for hours and weighed the consequences of acting on it.

That was over. The possible flirtation wouldn't go anywhere, and I was sick of getting my hopes up for something that wouldn't happen. He didn't see me like that even if his stare lingered on my legs. I had great legs.

"Hey, Dean, what brings you to our soccer camp today?"

"Gabby ended up wandering the concourse, freaking out about Coach Mack and being late." He smiled. "I told her you'd understand."

"Did ya now?" I narrowed my eyes at him. He had been a fun surprise last night, helping me with the drink challenge and encouraging me. Even though I gave up on anything happening between us, I'd always carry a minor, tiny crush on him.

"She told me she had to walk here from her house. By herself."

What?

I frowned. "Gabby, is that true? Did you walk here by yourself?"

She nodded. "My mom couldn't take me, and my dad is always at work. I can't miss this. Soccer is my dream. We watch your games, and I have your jersey!"

"You shouldn't come by yourself. Do you remember where you live? Can I take you back after?"

"Mack Mallinson will walk me back to my house? My friends will die!" Gabby cheered the way little girls did. It was endearing.

Dean met my gaze, his eyes warming as he smiled at me. It did feel cool as hell to have him witness this. I crouched and put a hand on Gabby's shoulder. "Yes, but I'll need to talk to your mom about letting you come alone. Now, you ran a lot, but being late is not tolerated if you want to be known as a serious athlete. Can you do two laps real quick while the team cheers you on?"

"Yes, Coach!"

She took off, going faster than everyone else despite her gasping for air five minutes ago. She was a hustler.

"Thanks for bringing her to me."

"Anything for Mack Mallinson." He lowered his voice.

"Hey, you." I glared at him. "You get fangirled over all the time, but I have my moments. Don't rain on my parade."

"That's not what I'm doing at all, I swear." His tone went saccharine.

"Little liar. You're teasing me."

"No, I like seeing you like this. In charge, admired." He smiled for real this time.

I felt that grin all the way to my toes.

My face heated, and I fanned it with my hand. *Dang summer temps.*

"Is one of your list items to sign autographs? Can you write your name on my ass?"

"I think it's time for you to go do football stuff. Bye, Dean."

He chuckled but walked closer to me. He smelled like leather and musk, like he'd just showered and put on cologne. His cutoff shirt showcased his biceps and *damn.* He was so hot. His messy brown hair and lips that were almost too full, along with his perfect eyebrows and long lashes. He could leave the field and pursue a modeling career with ease.

"I actually wanted to ask you what the next item on your playbook is."

"Mm. Well, I don't know yet." *Did he want to get naughty in public with me?*

Ha.

Definitely not saying it was *hooking up with a stranger* or *getting a tattoo* or *grinding with a stranger.* I gulped, unsure if he could read my mind or not. Dean had weird powers on the field. I wouldn't put it past him to have hidden talents.

"Do you have the list?"

"Of course, I do." I clapped, telling the girls to stretch after their run. "Gabby, you lead everyone in warm-up stretches today since you were late."

"Yes, Coach!"

"When do you have to do the next one?" asked Dean.

"You know about our Tuesday meetings."

"Yes, since Callum and Lorelei decided to become besties, I hear about them more than I care to."

I snorted. "Luca loves their friendship," I teased.

"Callum is a harmless goofball." He pursed his lips and stared at me, a thoughtful, serious expression overtaking his face as he waited.

"I have to show progress every Tuesday." My skin flushed. Talking about the list at the bar, with the music and a few drinks was easier. In the daylight, being so open about it was harder. More embarrassing. "Are you here to make fun of me?"

"No!" He held out his hands, waving them around. "The opposite, actually."

"What is the opposite of making fun of me?" I asked, amused. Was Dean…flustered? He blinked a lot, and his hands were in the air like little surrender flags.

He shifted his weight back and forth. "I had fun with you yesterday and the night at the bar."

"Fun with *me*?" I repeated, like a dummy. My stomach fluttered. Dean had fun with *me*? Alert the media!

"Yes. I've been in the same boat, working hard and grinding all the time. Your comment about senior year and life outside of soccer struck a chord, and I haven't stopped thinking about it. Could I join you on some of the items?"

"You want to join me on my Summer Playbook challenges?"

He nodded. He pressed his lips together as he stared at me. Dean and I had talked, obviously sharing Lo as a big part of our lives, but he had never looked at me like this. Intense, like he was *actually* seeing me. After all these years, I had his attention, and it was over this silly playbook. My mouth dried up, and that was rule number one—always stay hydrated. I broke eye contact and picked up a bottle of water, chugging half of it before glancing at him again.

Worry lines framed his eyes, and he seemed so…vulnerable. Dean Romano never looked anything less than badass, and my stomach twisted.

"Sure thing!" I smiled, forcing myself to be chill about this. He seemed sad, and that was just weird.

Think of Lo! She'd want me to make her twin not sad. Yes. She'd approve.

It had nothing to do with the fact I squealed inside every time he smiled and his dimple came out. None at all.

"Yeah?"

"I mean, Callum called dibs on some of them. But the others, well, not all of them. Most you can do. Yeah, some."

Not going past first base in public.

Not skinny dipping.

Not streaking.

The more I thought about it, my friends were the worst. This was a horny list.

"You're blushing hard." He grinned, and just like that, he was back. The sexy, unflappable Dean Romano. The handsome quarterback who got whatever he wanted, whenever he wanted.

"It's the sun. I burn easily. I'll be a tomato after this week," I said, my words coming out too fast.

"Right." He smirked, his gaze dropping to my legs again. "Which ones does Callum have dibs on?"

"Dancing on a bar, body shots, and getting a makeover."

Dean's jaw tightened, his gaze burning. "You don't need a makeover, and Callum shouldn't be doing body shots with you."

"Pretty sure Callum and I can do what we want, Dean," I fired back. "Can't imagine a better person to push myself with. I trust him. Now, I need to help these minions. If you choose to stay and help run drills with me, that could be fun. But no pressure. Head out if you want."

He tilted his head. "You're inviting me to stay?"

"Yeah." I shrugged, embarrassment taking over that I asked him. "Never mind. You probably have plans. Football plans. Quarterback plans."

"I don't." He pocketed his hands, rocking back on his heels. Now he looked cool and casual. "Need help? I'm a great drill sergeant."

"Okay then. Let's show these girls how to push themselves." I whistled for them to end their drill, and introduced Dean. "Now, he plays football, but he's really talented and can show us some insight on how to be a good player."

"My dad says soccer is real football," one of the girls said.

"Yeah, soccer is harder than football and has more action."

"And running."

"I hate football."

I fought a grin and gave up. Watching Dean's expression as these seven-year-olds tore his sport apart was priceless. There was no way he was used to this behavior. He usually sneezed, and people were there holding a tissue for him. I couldn't stop myself. "The girls speak the truth, Coach Romano."

"Wow, you all seem so tough." He crouched so he was at eye-level with them. A spark entered his eyes, like he enjoyed this. "Soccer is more popular worldwide for sure, but football is a testament to American sports."

"There are less games," the tallest girl said, nodding hard. "What position do you play?"

"Quarterback. I'm the one who throws the football to score touchdowns."

"Can you even kick?"

I snorted. "Okay, that's enough ladies."

"No, she has a great question. What's your name?" Dean asked, his voice gentle.

"Maria Cabrera."

"Okay, Maria Cabrera. How about we make a deal? We do some of Coach Mallinson's drills, and if you focus and work hard, you can show me how much better of a kicker you are than me."

"You got yourself a deal."

"That I do." He held out his hand. "A real deal requires a shake."

She shook his hand, hard, and puffed out her chest in a beautiful display of confidence. I loved that. I loved any time I could help a young athlete learn their value, learn what made them tough, and I held out a fist for her to bump. I would be their beacon of hope, always.

"Don't let this guy intimidate you. Your fear is the only enemy you have. Now, let's get to work!"

Dean stayed the entire three-hour clinic. To say that was unexpected was an understatement. I predicted me and twenty girls, not me and Dean Romano. I studied him as he picked up the cones and stacked them, sweat dripping down his face and arms. It was noon, the sun beating on us without a cloud in the sky.

I took a long swig of water and double-checked everything was picked up. The clinic was two weeks long with this age group, then I'd have a week off and repeat it with older girls. I got paid part-time wages for it, which was nice, but really, giving back to the younger athletes was part of the job. Not that I would tell my coach, but I would've done this for free. I wanted to be the person who I never had growing up—the cheerleader, the one who pushed you but built you up. There was a way to be encouraging and tough to help grow athletes instead of fucking them up.

"Hey, Romano, thanks for hanging around. This was unexpected." I held out the net bag, and he placed the last cones in it. Our fingers brushed, and a silly little thrill zinged up my arm. I smelled like sweat and sunscreen had a love child. This was no time to acknowledge my attraction to him.

"No problem. This was fun. Gabby and Lilah are tough as shit."

"Right? I love seeing their attitudes and determination. I knew what I wanted to do at this age, and I hated when adults told me it was stupid or unrealistic or not a real job. If I can help instill a sense of purpose for them, sign me the hell up."

"Adults mean well, but they have their own ideas of what the future is, and they try to force it on us. I see it all the time." He shrugged, a thoughtful, pained look crossing his face. "What's your plan now?

"Uh, gonna shower all this sweat off after I take Gabby back." I nodded toward the stands where Gabby waited.

"I'll walk with you."

"Oh, um, okay."

Be cool. Be chill.

Just a normal Friday morning, walking out of the stadium next to Dean. Despite how hot it was, he smelled so good. Sweat and soap and the cologne that I wanted to inhale. I had no idea why he wanted to walk me back, or why he'd volunteered to help me. We didn't *hang out* just the two of us.

Except he helped at the bar, and we hung out at the house… okay, so we never used to hang out.

My heart fluttered, and a tornado of butterflies swarmed my gut, slowing my brain down to try and find the right words. Did I say *what's up,* or was that too late? We'd been together for three hours, but the girls were the focus.

Focus on Gabby.

"Are you sure? I don't mind."

"We don't know what's waiting at home, and I'd prefer to make sure Gabby and you are safe. No big deal." He spoke with an air of authority, like there was no way I could defy him.

"Okie dokie, artichokie."

Oh my god.

This was not good. This was the ultimate dork status, and I closed my eyes, groaning. Maybe if I pretended it didn't happen, he would too. Avoiding his gaze, I jogged to Gabby. "Ready to head home?"

"Yes, Coach."

We exited the stadium, me still not acknowledging Dean's presence, as Gabby gabbed a lot. She talked about her three younger brothers, her mom, and her sister but never her dad. She wanted to be a pro soccer player and help her mom out, but it was hard when she never had a ride to practices or money for cleats.

She took us down four blocks before turning to an alley. It wasn't creepy, but I didn't like how secluded it was. "Gabs?"

"Yes, Coach?"

"If you can be ready early tomorrow, I'll walk here to get you first. Okay?"

"Okay."

"We can talk strategy." I shared a look with Dean, who frowned at the surroundings. I noted the garbage and evidence of people drinking. Crates and cigarette butts covered the ground as she turned right.

"That would be fun. I don't mind walking myself though. It's an easy walk."

She led us to a small house with toys in the yard. TV noise carried through the window, a woman's angry voice coming too. "I told you to get off the damn table!"

"That's Mom." Gabby sighed. "See you guys tomorrow!"

"See you soon, raccoon!" Dean said, a coy little smile on his face as he watched me. His smirk grew. "Okie dokie, artichokie. Are you a child?"

"What are you referring to? I have no recollection," I said, my tone accidentally taking on a British accent. Another thing I didn't mean to do when I was a liar.

"Once in a while, crocodile." He snickered at himself as he held out his arm, gesturing to me to go first. "You're a dork."

"I'm well aware of that, thank you." I held my head high. I figured most people were dorks, but society determined that *football* was just always cool. It was honestly bullshit. There were diehard Star War fans and Lord of the Rings stans who played sports. It was cool to be passionate about something, and my passions were just smells, soccer, and social media.

"Hey." He nudged his shoulder against mine, the contact of our bare skin sending alarm bells in my body at red alert.

Boy! Boy! Boy! Touching! Touching!

"Hm?" I cleared my throat, eyeing my empty water bottle. Worthless.

"You can have some of mine." He held out his, our fingers doing some weird flirty tango again.

I took a swig, definitely not thinking about our weird transitive property of kissing. Technically, his mouth touched the end, then mine did, so our mouths… *get ahold of yourself!*

"I was teasing, you know, about you being a dork. I like how you talk to the girls. It's refreshing. At their age, I had coaches ripping into me. It should be about fun and focus, sure, but seeing them get excited about soccer? That was some real shit."

"It makes me so happy. I love how so many of the soccer players now are talking about the league and being role models. The shut up and dribble thing makes me so angry because as humans, we look up to our athletes as who we want to be. If I'm going to enter that world, I want to do my best to be someone they are proud of." My eyes prickled again, this time from passion. "I realize I sound–"

"Incredible." He laughed and nudged my arm again. "You're sneakily wise, Mallinson. I know your secret now."

"Don't tell anyone." I fought the urge to smile, very content with Dean learning everything about me. The lilt of his voice, the way he leaned into me… yeah, big fan of Dean knowing my secrets.

We continued down the road, sharing his water, until we arrived at the apartment I shared with Lo. He'd been over numerous times, with and without Luca or Callum. Did I invite him in? Did I not?

Why was this awkward?

Chewing my lip, I unlocked the door and found him staring at me with his large, intense eyes. If this was how he looked at girls all the time, no wonder they threw themselves at him. He was a like a puppy dog with those big browns. "Care if I come in?"

"Lo's not home."

"That's fine. I figured we could hang, or if you're busy, I'll just take off."

We could hang? Him and me?

What the hell was happening?

CHAPTER **SIX**

Dean

The Summer Playbook

- ~~Buy a guy a shot~~
- ~~Mixologist challenge – ask bartender to let you make a drink~~
- Skinny dipping
- Get a makeover
- Tattoo
- Take a body shot off someone
- Someone takes one off you
- Grind with a stranger someone
- Make out with two people in one night
- Hook up past first base with a stranger/someone
- Be naughty in public
- Ask three guys out
- Dance on a bar
- Streaking
- Dance in the rain

- Concert
- Join a game already going on with strangers
- Bonfire (talk to five strangers)
- Wear an outfit you normally wouldn't wear
- Dye your hair a new color
- Crash an event (or wedding for bonus points)
- Lose the cell phone for a whole day
- Strip Poker

"This is a lot of shit," I said, whistling as I read the list again. A strange, grossly weird feeling grew in my chest thinking about Mack doing these things with some people who weren't me. *Skinny dipping. Streaking. Naughty in public. Make out. Hook up.* I ran a hand over my jaw, working it left to right as tension grew. "You could get into trouble with these."

"Don't start with me." She carried two large glasses of ice water, the condensation dripping down her hand.

My mouth watered. It was hot outside.

She handed it to me before yanking the paper out of my reach. "You weren't supposed to acknowledge *all* of them."

I fought a grin. "Absolutely not. I need to know how you're going to do every single one of them."

"Haven't figured that out yet, but I have to complete each one to win." She set her glass down on a coaster and undid one of her braids. With her focus on her hair, I let myself truly check Mack Mallinson out.

After a good night's sleep, it still wasn't clear why she of all people got the spark back for me. I spent most of the morning with her, and the pull was even stronger. I wanted to ask her a million questions, but my gaze wandered over her high cheekbones and her beautiful blue eyes, down her neck, and over her chest. Her tits pressed against the tight fabric, sweat still visible in her cleavage. Call me crazy, but I wanted to lick it up.

Her toned stomach and thick strong thighs had me questioning everything. I shouldn't be attracted to my sister's best friend. Not fucking now. I shook my head and caught her gaze. Her lips were pursed, like she was studying me.

I kinda liked her attention on me. It felt different. She wasn't staring in a way where she plotted to use me or needed something from me. It was refreshing.

She chewed her lip before asking, "Were you honest about joining me for *some* of them?"

I nodded.

"How would that work? For example, the wear an outfit you normally wouldn't. Does that mean you join me when I wear something strange, or—"

I shook my head. "I also wear something strange."

"So, if I have to make out with a rando, you make out with someone too?" The tips of her cheeks turned bright pink, almost matching her shirt.

I ignored her question because that wasn't something current me would do unless she asked me to. "I have a more important question. Are you comfortable just making out with someone random?" My heart thudded against my ribs, my muscles tense as shit waiting for her answer.

Why?

I wasn't sure. The thought of watching her hook up with someone felt gross, and the weighted pressure returned behind my chest. But I also didn't want to make out with a rando, not after what happened.

Whoa. You haven't thought about Jessica all day.

That was what Mack did to me. She brought me out of my headspace, and I craved being around her. In less than twenty-four hours, she'd distracted me so much from my life that I would move mountains to keep being near her. That was why the disgusting feeling was there. Nothing else.

She sighed and moved her attention toward the front window. She wet her bottom lip with her tongue as she spun the purple ring on her thumb. "I don't know. If I have a drink or two, I'll loosen up and maybe not freak out about it. But I need to do this. I have to put myself out there before I become that role model and live and breathe my job. I've been so focused and perfect all my life, and I wanna be a little unperfect."

"I understand, Mack, I really do. But you also need to know your limits." If she couldn't handle making out with someone, she sure as shit couldn't do more than that. Or skinny dip. Grinding my teeth, I forced my voice to come out calm. "I'll do whatever you want me to if you think you might need support."

"What is this, Dean?" She leaned onto her knees, her face set in serious lines. "We've gotten along, sure, but we don't hang out. What is this?"

"Uh," I opened my mouth, but nothing came out. Her question was legit. Valid. She opened up to me… I could do a varied version. "I'm not the most trusting person, and I've been…burned a few times. The bar, and last night...." I shook my head, laughing as I held her gaze. "I had fun with you. It's been a while since I enjoyed a night out. I've been stuck in my head, and you're easy to be around, so it let me just be free and myself. I'm selfish, okay? I'm begging you to let me come on your hot girl summer tour like a weird third wheel. I know it's pathetic."

HGST—Hot Girl Summer Tour. I was a third wheel on an event that sounded like HGTV.

"It's not." She smiled and set her hand on my knee, squeezing. "I'm probably crossing some boundary here, but Lo has been worried about you. I'm not getting in your business, but whatever it is you're going through, people care. They want to help."

My throat tightened, and I cleared it, pushing back into the couch and away from whatever spell Mack put on me. "I know she is. I'll talk to her. But joining you would help distract me. So, if you'll have me—"

"Saturday," she blurted out.

"What about it?"

"Come out with me Saturday." She swallowed, hard. "Callum and I were going to head to one of the bars on the west side. Join us."

"For the body shots?"

"Yes. There is a lot on the list, so I need to strategically do these, or I'll never complete them all. If I do the body shots, dance on the bar, maybe streak after, I could—"

I arched a brow, fighting the slap of annoyance swirling underneath my skin. I scratched at my forearm. "You're gonna streak with *Callum*?"

"Dean Romano. That man has seen more tits and ass than a locker room. I get naked all the time. That is the least of my worries." She laughed. "You're a bit of a… hm, well, you've had your fair share of hookups. How do you do it?"

"Clarify your question, Mack."

Her blush intensified. "How do you just flirt and know to kiss someone? How do you know its gonna lead to more? I think that's my problem. I've gone on dates, and at the end, it's obvious there's a kiss. Date two is more. Date three is sex. At a bar though?"

"You have rules about dates?" I teased. "Date three is sex?"

"Shut up. Yes. No." She groaned into her hands. "I regret this conversation."

"I sure as hell don't. This is great." I cackled, absolutely charmed by her. "You feel them out, see if you have chemistry.

Touch their chest, their arms. If they suck in a breath, you can kiss them. Men are simple and idiots."

Clearly, since someone almost conned me out of my future.

"That I agree with. Minus Luca. He's dreamy." She stood up, her ass right in front of my face in her tight-ass shorts.

I loved tits as much as the next guy, but asses were my thing. And Mack's was a ten out of ten. It was juicy and strong and thick and *what the hell!* Think of plays. Think of the guys on the team. Oliver's disgusting habit of not washing socks when he played well. Anything to stifle this spark for my sister's best friend.

Once I settled down the uncomfortable fact I was into Mack's ass, I rolled my eyes. "Luca is not *dreamy.*"

"Lies." She laughed as she set her empty glass on the counter and put her hands on her trim hips. "He treats Lo so damn well. She's a light, and he's a sexy goober moth just following her."

"Is that what girls want? A goober moth following them?"

"Sometimes, yes. We don't tolerate Luca slander in this apartment, Dean Romano. But for your information, girls like being the center of someone's attention. No distractions, full intensity. If that's a goober moth… then I want a goober moth once my career settles into place." She frowned, a cute line forming between her brows before she rubbed the spot with her finger. "Wow, that's a breakthrough."

"Happy to help, I think?"

She met my gaze, her eyes warming. "This might sound silly to you, the guy who's never had a real relationship, but I've always felt like I had to date or have a partner. I even felt pressure to find *the one* senior year because my cousins tell me dating after college sucks ass. But damn, after this chat, I think I'm happy being single and having fun until my life is figured out. Wow."

Have I had a legit relationship before?

Jessica didn't count, that was for sure.

She didn't mean the words like an insult, but they provided a little jab. "That doesn't sound silly to me. There's a comfort in knowing yourself."

"Thank you." She beamed before reaching for a box of peanut butter pretzels. "Want some? These are my favorite thing in the entire universe. They might seem simple, but the combination of flavors with the salt? Chef's kiss."

How could I say no to the invite? Not when she was so easy to be around. Plus, it was totally normal to befriend your twin's best friend…right?

The next week flew by, and Mack let me help at the camp each morning. My days were spent as an assistant coach for young athletes, my afternoons were all workouts, and my nights a weird combination of bored-to-death and trying to distract myself from spinning out.

Saturday arrived, and a burst of adrenaline went through me, the same way it did for game night. It was Mack's night to knock an item off her Playbook, and somehow, much to my annoyance, everyone was fucking tagging along. Not just Callum and I. Luca and Lo. Oliver. Callum. Me. Mack. Alejandra and Mally and Vee. Nine of us.

Too many damn people to go *out* and watch Mack make dumb choices. Yet, she smiled so damn big when we all arrived at their place, and her eyes sparkled when she saw me. I liked that feeling. I liked it a whole lot.

"Body shots! Body shots! Body shots!" Callum chanted, making everyone laugh. He went up to Mack and slung his arm around her as everyone filed outside. "You ready for this? I showered and used my nice cologne."

"You always smell good, and you know it." She leaned her head on his shoulder.

My left eye twitched in annoyance. I put on cologne tonight for the first time in months, and did she notice? No.

"I never said the body shots *had* to be you, you know. What if I find a sexy stranger I want to lick tequila off of?" Mack said, her mouth way too close to Callum's face.

He had such a punchable face, honestly. I'd never noticed before.

"My abs are better." Callum patted his stomach.

"Debatable," Lo said. She pretended to eye Callum up and down. "I've seen what we're dealing with. I lived next to you, remember?"

"Can we not do this?" Luca asked, sighing as he pulled Lo against his chest. "I understand you and Callum are close now, but I'd like it on record I despise it."

"You hate everything except Lo and your grandma," Callum fired back.

"Hey, he likes me!" Mack said.

"You're fine."

"Lo, you hear that? We're bonding. That was the nicest thing he has ever said to me!"

Everyone laughed, and I just kept my hands in my pockets, my nerves bubbling. I felt awkward. Me. I had always been the popular guy, the life of the party, the one people wanted to talk to or flirt with. That was *before.* It came with the quarterback role, but I didn't know this new version of myself.

"We need to leave before these shots wear off. I'm feeling groovy, people. Groovy!"

"And tipsy Mack is my favorite." Alejandra clapped her hands. "We're leaving. Let's go."

The group of us walked down the sidewalk toward the main party street on campus. There were six bars that all competed with each other with different specials, music nights, and tonight we were going to the raunchiest one. *Peter Jays.* The lights were darker, the music louder, and the girls wilder. No other way around it.

I fell behind the group, watching how my teammates laughed and teased the soccer girls. I liked it. I loved how Lo and I always had a great relationship, which spread to our teammates and friends. I never thought that us going to the same college would have our lives so intertwined, but Lo and I were friends for life.

Speaking of…

My sister slowed until she walked right next to me, her gaze blasting with curiosity. I tensed. I hadn't opened up to her. It felt too real, too uncomfortable. She'd support me and try to help, so I'd lied and avoided her the past few months. Something I never did.

"Is this because of Luca?"

"Is what?"

"The gap between us now. Our teammates are hanging out, having a good time, and I can feel the heavy cloud over you. I thought we were okay when Luca and I got together, but we have the twin thing, Dean. Something isn't right, and if I'm at fault, I need you to tell me."

"Lo, it's not you." My stomach twisted. I hated that she felt guilty. "You and Luca are great together."

"You say the words, but they seem empty."

She grabbed my forearm, stopping me from walking. Her wild hair was up in a ponytail, and the wind made it go in every direction. The summer humidity washed over me, making me sweat, and I braced myself for whatever she planned to say.

"I need you to tell me what's going on. It's eating at me, and

I can't help, and it's putting a strain on Luca and me. He won't tell me, and he constantly feels like he has to pick you over me, and that's a trigger for me. Do you think I'll judge? Or be mad? I won't, Dean. We did a blood oath. I'm there for you if you need to hide a body or if you're the father of ten babies."

I sucked in a breath. *It's a joke. She's joking.*

"Can we set a time to talk, please?"

My jaw ached from all the tension, and I nodded.

"Unless we just… aren't… close anymore? I know siblings grow apart. If that's the case and I'm clinging to what used to be, you can tell me that too. I'll adjust. But I can't do a goddamn thing until you talk to me."

She let go of my arm, gave me one more look, then returned to the group and grabbed Luca's hand.

Her words gutted me. She had been my best friend all my life, and here she was, thinking I didn't want to be close with her anymore. That she was *too clingy* as a sibling. Fuck. I wiped a hand over my face, irritated at myself. I never wanted to hurt my twin or have her doubt our friendship. But sharing what happened would be embarrassing and hard. I'd worked hard as hell to not think or talk about what went down last fall, but maybe that hadn't been the best plan of attack. Not when Luca was pissed and Lo felt mistreated.

I scrubbed a hand over my face. The excitement I had to spend the night with Mack disappeared as everyone stole her attention. Her melodic cackle—because that's what it was, a snorting honk sound that was ridiculous but charming—carried over to me, and it caused my lips to quirk up. She was having a good night, and that made me happy.

Lo's comments brought me down a bit, but being around this group gave me a sense of peace. I'd just get a beer and see what happened. Maybe I'd find some time to assist Mack, maybe not. At least being near people I trusted was a safety net in itself. Maybe the first legit step in getting over what happened was speaking to Lo. She'd know what to do.

Suddenly, it was like a weight lifted off me. *Of course* my sister would know what to do. She'd help me!

With that, a real smile broke out as we entered the bar. It wasn't too busy since it was early summer, but the bouncer shook my hand, talking about the season. A group of girls who sat at a high-top table all assessed me head to toe, the familiar tells of interest coming from them. Twirling the hair, sitting up straighter, touching their necks. I could…if I wanted, go over there and flirt?

Maybe I could try? See if my mojo came back?

I ran a hand down my chest, pumping myself up when a familiar scent of summer flowers hit me. Mack stood next to me, her wide eyes pleading with me as she gripped my hand.

"Okay, I'm nervous. Can you help me?"

CHAPTER **SEVEN**

Mack

Dean frowned, glanced around my shoulders, and pulled me close to him with a protective arm. "What's wrong?"

"Nothing... well, I'm fine. It's these challenges." I tried *not* to think about how good he smelled and how nice it was to have his arm around me. He had a good six inches on me, and his broad shoulders, strong arms, and overall height made me feel cute. And I wasn't a cute, petite woman.

My heart raced at how close we were. His mouth was right there, his full lips pulling down at the sides as he studied me. For one hot second, I was the center of his attention, and it made my skin burn with want and my thighs tremble. No wonder I had a huge crush on him all three years. Dean was so hot and protective.

"The body shots with Callum?"

Was it me, or did he say Callum's name with a strange lilt to his voice? I couldn't be sure. I'd had a couple of shots at the apartment before we left to help me loosen up, but now I was creating fake scenarios where I thought Dean wanted to do a body shot with me. If only. That was a dream. Having his tongue on me.

Shit.

"It's hot. Are you hot?" I fanned myself with my tied shirt. It didn't quite check off the list because I already owned it, but it was a bright red bandana shirt that tied in the back and meant no room for a bra. It showed a ton of skin, yet I was super toasty right now.

"It's humid but not bad outside. Mack, what's wrong? You know you don't have to do a thing if you're uncomfortable." His dark brows came together as he sighed. He kept his arm around my shoulders, squeezing. "You asked if I would help you. Of course. Name it."

"They want me to dance on the bar." My stomach bottomed out, the thought of actually doing it making me want to puke. I'd rather face down our biggest rivals on the field while battling a hangover than get on the bar.

"Hey, Mack, listen to me, please." He set his large hands on each of my shoulders, holding me in place. His gaze moved over my neck and bare arms before meeting my eyes. "This isn't about *them.* This is your list. You decide. Don't do the bar tonight."

"They came here to see that."

"Fuck that. They came to support you on your list."

I took a shaky breath before nodding. I liked his hands on my bare skin. They were rough and strong and *ugh.* My crush on Dean would probably never go away. He was too perfect. "You're being nice, Dean Romano."

"Yeah?" He smiled briefly. "We can mark that off on my own playbook, yeah? *Is nice.* Check."

I snorted. "You're ridiculous."

He shrugged and kept his hands on me. This was the longest

we had ever touched, and I was heating up. Was he not thinking about my skin like I was? I almost gasped when his gaze dropped to my chest, then down to my feet. Was he… checking me out?

"I'm assuming this outfit marks off that item?"

"Nope. I tried, but I already owned this, so it doesn't count, according to them."

He ran his teeth over his bottom lip as his eyes heated for one second, and my core burst on fire. *He's checking me out. Ohmygod. Be cool. Be chill.*

He released my arm and spun me around. I couldn't breathe. He twirled me as his brown eyes darkened. I had never felt so exposed. I was dying. What did he think? Why was he silent?

When I faced him again, his nostrils flared as he said, "You look good. I like the outfit."

"Uh, thanks, yeah, I'm a fan of it." *Ohmygod.* I cleared my throat, embarrassed and hot and *Dean checked me out.* "Anyway, thanks for the help. I'm gonna go do things. Stuff. And things!"

"Mack, whoa." He grabbed my forearm, preventing me from walking away.

I needed to escape! I was such a dork!

"Hm?" I refused to glance at him. My face had to be as red as the tied shirt, and with one look, he'd know.

"I didn't help you at all. Why are you—am I making you nervous?"

"Mmmmmm, maybe?"

"Wait. Why?" He frowned, hard, like he really didn't like my answer.

"Because I'm pretty sure you checked me out, and I think you're super hot. It's ridiculous, and you definitely looked me up and down, but I'm a dork, and I tried hiding it even though you definitely already know, and I am like so not your type even a little bit, which is fine, we all have our types, but now I'm talking so much and cannot stop—oh my god, kill me."

Dean stared at me for one beat then tilted his head back and *howled* with laughter. There was nothing sexy about this laugh. It was unhinged, loud, and was so goofy it made me laugh too.

"To clarify, I definitely checked you out." He grinned, his eyes sparkling at me. "And you think I'm hot?"

"Shut up. Shut up! That can't be the takeaway. Damn you, Dean Romano."

"You're cute when you're flustered."

"Grr."

"Did you just *grr* at me?"

"Yes. Because this is torture. Can we pretend the last five minutes never happened? 'Kay, thanks."

"Absolutely not." His grin grew. "Now, I recall one of your items on the list is joining a game. You can dance on a bar or do a body shot or get naughty in public, or… you could ask to join that darts match over there?"

Oh shit. "Dean, you beautiful genius. I could just kiss you!" I clapped. "Thank you. This is way more my speed."

"You're welcome. Want company, or you want to do it alone?"

"It doesn't *specify* that I can't bring a buddy, does it?"

"Nope."

"Then come on, buddy. Let's go play some darts and make new friends!"

"Cross that baby off!" I jumped in the air, swinging my hands around my head and cheering. I joined a dart game. Did I win?

No. Did I suck? Yes. But I met Jeremy, Greg, and Christina, who were juniors majoring in art, and it was exhilarating.

Dean didn't play, but he sat at the table nursing a beer the entire game, and having him there as support was incredible. I didn't need the crutch, but it felt nice to have someone. My friends were the best and meant well, but I liked having Dean join me on this too.

"Wait!" I gripped the back of his shirt as he walked toward our friends, pulling him toward me. I tried, and failed, to not notice how warm the shirt was and how good he smelled. Even in a bar that smelled like pee and stale beer, his scent was magical.

"Hm?" He faced me, his eyes dropping to my chest for a second.

"*You* said you were doing things too. That means *you* have to join a game!"

He pursed his lips, and I didn't give him a chance to make an excuse. "You're either in or out, Dean. If you can't do it, then—"

"I'll do it." He scanned the bar, his dark brown eyes narrowing like he was sizing up an opponent. "There." He jutted his chin toward a group of girls playing a drinking game in a booth. "Let's go."

"Wait, *I'm* not going. Those girls won't want me to hang with me, just you. You're Dean Romano! I'm just a—"

"Careful how you finish that sentence. *I'm just a* is not a good sentence starter when I know you're a badass woman with a lot of confidence." Dean's eyes flared. "You're coming with me. Now."

His tone had a bite to it. Not a mean one but a commanding, *don't fuck with me* vibe that had my legs moving for me, following him to the table of beautiful girls all giggling and throwing cards into a pile. He thought I was a badass woman with confidence, and god, that made my insides turn to goo. I wasn't, at all, but it felt nice for a hot second. It didn't last long. My age-old insecurities crept up my throat, making an uncomfortable ball of emotion form back there. *These girls were so pretty. Cool. Confident.* They'd take one look at me and judge.

Just like high school, when I was so focused on proving to *Emily* that I could be a pro athlete, I gave up on being cool, on making friends, on *living.* I'd been judged for always wearing practice gear to school or always being covered in sweat. One time, the cool girls covered my locker with perfume samples because they said I smelled.

Fuck.

"Ladies, how we doing tonight?" Dean asked, leaning on the edge of the booth.

"Hey," the girl with beautiful black hair said. Her lips were bright pink and her skin flawless. She eyed Dean up and down, smirking. "You coming to hit on us?"

"Actually, I'm not. You are all stunning, obviously, but my friend and I have a hot girl summer list to complete, and I was hoping you could help me. Mack, come on. See if we can join."

Shit. Just, be cool.

My shirt felt too tight, too small. Like I tried too hard. My hair was in a pony because that's all I really did, and my jeans were longer than normal. I only wore mascara, and I wish I knew makeup more. I squeezed my hands together as the women looked at me, and I focused on a spot on the table. "Hey, sorry to bother you."

"Mack Mallinson?" the pretty girl with red hair said. She leaned forward onto her elbows, her smile manic. "No fucking way. I love watching you play on the field. My siblings are huge women soccer stans."

I blushed, hard. "Oh, wow. Thank you!"

"Girl, sit. Right here. Oh my god, can I take a picture with you?"

Dean met my gaze, his eyes warming with pride and humor. He gently nudged my lower back so I could slide into the booth next to the girl. She leaned into me as she snapped a photo, and my mind couldn't catch up. They were excited to see me! Not Dean?

"So, what is this hot girl summer list you speak of?"

"Tell them, Mack." Dean positioned himself next to me, instead of sitting on the other side. It was tight, and our thighs pressed together. Not a single room for a hair between us. He moved his arm to the back ledge, so it rested right behind my neck, and his finger grazed my ear so quick I thought I imagined it.

That little motion sent a flurry of butterflies from my neck to my toes, taking a detour on the way straight to my nipples. They tightened with an aggressive need and wowzers.

"Well, I've been focused on soccer and practicing. I know my life is gonna get even stricter this year. My friends and I came up with a list to make sure I experience all the things I need to before senior year starts."

"And one item on the list is joining a game with strangers," Dean said, nudging me. "Which she did by joining the darts game."

We looked over, and the trio nodded at us.

"I'm obsessed with this idea," the red-haired girl said. "I'm Hattie. The blonde is Heidi and black-haired beauty is Bea. Seriously obsessed. How do we fit in?"

"I wanted to join her hot girl summer challenge, but that means I have to do everything too." He shrugged. "Your game looked fun."

"Oh my god, this is amazing. What else is on there?"

I pulled out the list, my face tingling from Dean's stare. He didn't try to hide the fact he watched me with a little smirk on his face. I loved and hated it. I had no idea what was happening, but this list had introduced me to six people I never would've met otherwise, and I was enjoying it so, so much.

Look at me, Emily, living it up!! God, I needed to get over that, but it was hard when her words haunted me all the time.

"I've done a few at this point." Pride had me sitting up straighter.

"Damn. This is sick." Heidi pointed at the body shots. "I mean, I'm happy to help with this one if you need it."

"Oh. Thank you." I blushed. "I think that one is taken care of already."

"Fair. If Dean Romano was going to put his tongue on me, I'd choose that too."

I snorted to cover up the sheer embarrassment of how much that comment made my skin tingle with electricity. Dean's mouth on me? I'd die. I'd combust like a phoenix, right in front of everyone. "Yeah, well, no, it's…two is good for one night."

"I want to create a list. Why don't we have a list?" Heidi asked.

"Because we aren't strict athletes?"

"Let's do one."

"Well, we need to help Mack Mallinson and Dean Romano first, then we can make you a list of whatever you want."

"My Horny Hattie list. It sounds great."

Dean laughed and nudged his shoulder into mine, the lines around his eyes softer than normal. He seemed relaxed and friendly. I liked this version of Dean. I also enjoyed his swagger and dominance on the field, but he'd lost a little of the playboy, flirt with everyone personality, and this calmer one was nice. "Hey," I said, leaning closer to him. "This is awesome."

He bent down, his mouth almost touching my forehead before he said, "I agree."

For a moment, it was just the two of us in the bar. The thuds of the music and laughter from the crowd faded, and it was Dean and me. His breath hit my face. His eyes moved along my jaw, stopping on my mouth. His thigh tensed next to mine. My lips parted as breathing became a challenge. Sucking in oxygen was asking too much. The moment captivated me, and I gasped, choking on my own breath.

"You okay, Mack Mallinson?" Bea asked.

I waved a hand in the air, my face turning fifty shades of red for the millionth time. "Wow, yes, breathing is hard."

"It really is." She laughed. "Okay, we're playing Kings Corner. You in?"

Ignoring the magnetic pull to Dean, I focused on the instructions as she dealt the cards. The game was easy enough, and honestly, it was more fun just chatting with them. They had a million questions for me about playing soccer, the team, what team I wanted to play for after college. Hattie's family had hosted for a team one year, and that was what made them become such huge fans.

Thirty minutes went by when the game ended. Dean won, annoyingly, but the time was so worth it. I thought they were mean girls and would make me feel like crap, but instead, I'd put myself out there, and it felt… fucking amazing.

Pretty girls like that don't care about tomboys like you. You think you can play soccer? Then prove it.

Coach Em was simply *wrong.*

"Seriously, we should hang again," I said as Dean scooted away from the booth and held out a hand for me. I didn't need help standing, but I wanted any reason to touch him.

"Wait. What?" Hattie stilled. "Did you ask us to hang out *again*?"

"Um, maybe?" Suddenly, I felt silly.

"Shut the fuck up, yes, please. Whatever you want to do, Mack Mallinson."

"First off, stop with both names. Pick one." I giggled, relief coursing through me. "Here, give me your number. We can grab a drink sometime."

"*Be cool, be cool. Mack Mallinson has your number,*" Heidi mumbled to herself, making the table laugh.

It was the perfect tension relief, and we waved before walking away. Dean put his hand on my lower back, his *bare* hand on my skin as he stilled me. "You have fangirls."

"I sure do!" I pursed my lips, shimmying a little. "I love this list. That was incredible, truly. I assumed they'd be all over you and mean girl it up, but I adored them. I *love* this."

Dean smirked. "Still feel like you could just kiss me?"

Swoop.

My stomach twirled.

"Romano, you are not flirting with me." I brushed past him, holding my breath to not breathe in his cologne. His only response was a deep chuckle, which I also ignored as I marched toward my friends. I barely took two steps before Lo and Callum grabbed my arms. "What is this? What's going on?"

Callum hummed. "It's body shot time. You're not backing out. We cleared it with the bartender. Lay on the bar, girlie. I chose rum."

CHAPTER **EIGHT**

Dean

"This is a terrible fucking idea." Luca stood next to me, arms crossed over his large chest as he stared at my sister, Mack, and Callum as they drew a crowd around them at the bar. A nervous, almost palpable worry bubbled in my veins at seeing her up there. Was she nervous? Excited? Did I want her to *need* me? A little, if I was being honest.

"Which part?"

"All of it. This damn list. Mack is uncomfortable but gives in to her dumbass friends."

"Those dumbasses are your friends and girlfriend."

"I stand by what I said." He grunted as Lo clapped her hands and chanted. People swarmed them. Both the sports dudes and fangirls all circled them, enticed by the excitement. "I can't keep this secret for you any longer, man. Lo is getting pissed, and I hate lying to her. I'll never betray you, but its time."

I ground my teeth together. "Lo approached me. We'll chat soon."

"I mean it. She's worried and has to hide her concern from me, because if she brings it up, she'll get pissed at you and me. Don't shut her out, okay? She'd cut off her own leg if it helped you."

"I fucking know." The weighted stress returned just like that. The entire time I was with Mack, it disappeared. Even now, I watched her laugh and nervously cover her face as the bartender—some attractive dude with tattoos—held a bottle of rum in the air. People clapped and hollered as Callum leaned over and bit her stomach.

Fuck.

That bastard was too goddamn much. *Is he licking her?*

"What the fuck is he doing?"

"Annoying me," Luca said.

I almost laughed. Luca was notoriously grumpy, but I couldn't say I blamed him. Callum irritated me too, specifically right now as he waved his arms in the air, wanting the crowd to be louder. He did the same on the field, which was great because the stands ate it up. Here though? Everyone was wilding out watching him touch Mack.

My feet rooted to the ground as Mack squealed. The bartender poured rum on her stomach, and Callum's mouth was on her. I fisted my hands, absolutely unclear why I hated him. Years of being teammates flew out the faded red bar door as he kept a hand on her thigh, holding her down. Everyone yelled louder, and how the fuck were there this many people here tonight? It was summer.

"Idiot." Luca scoffed. "Wait, what is happening? Is… *Lo, get the fuck down.*"

My best friend pushed through the crowd as my sister lay on the bar. This oughta be good. Luca was possessive, and my sister was wild. Faithful, loyal, all that shit for sure. But if Callum or Mack dared her to do something, she'd do it. She had to. It was in her blood. We used to get each other in trouble because neither of us could back down from a dare. Win or die trying was our unhealthy motto growing up. WODT. Not a great acronym.

I followed.

"Lo, no." Luca was already at the bar. There was a reason he was the best tight end in the game. Large and fast and quiet. He gripped her hip and covered her stomach with his other hand. "Not happening."

"I guess you better do it then, huh?"

He growled. "Only if its whiskey. Then I'm taking your ass home."

"God, he's such a simp for her," a girl next to me said, a dreamy look on her face. "I want a Luca Monroe."

I rolled my eyes.

Luca took a shot off my sister while I focused on anything but the scene. Mainly, I tried not to punch Callum in the face as he ripped his shirt off before laying on the bar. This couldn't be clean. Why was this allowed? I should talk to the manager.

"Mack, where do you want the shot? My stomach? Mouth?" Callum pushed up onto his elbows, eyeing her with a dumb smirk. He met my gaze, winking, before focusing on her.

I wanted to shove that wink up his ass.

"Do the tequila one! Lime in the mouth, salt on the stomach, shot in the belly button!" Heidi had somehow joined and stood right next to Mack. "Do it, do it, do it!"

Mack's hands shook, but she nodded. "That's what I want."

"You got this girl. It's harmless. Lick the salt. Do the shot. Then take this lime out of my mouth like a good girl," Callum goaded.

I needed a new roommate. Plain and simple.

Mack laughed and flicked his nipple. “You’re the worst. I’m not one of your playthings, remember that.”

I hate this. I fucking hate this. I should’ve volunteered.

“I’ll never forget, Mallinson. Now stop stalling. This will knock off another item!”

It happened slowly, each second of time punching my eyelids. Mack ran her tongue along Callum’s too-tanned stomach. Then she sucked up the tequila. Then she grabbed the lime from his mouth, their lips almost touching.

You would think the football team won a playoff game with how deafening the cheers were. Screams and high fives and hollers surrounded me, but all I thought about was the fact Mack had licked Callum’s stomach, and he’d licked hers.

I want to be the one to do that.

Unreasonable. Unlikely. Unfair to think it.

But willing something out of my mind had never worked before, and this was no different. I ground my teeth together, my heart pounding against my ribcage as the urge to punch something grew. Did I think I could be the one to do that, and Lo and everyone would think it was normal? No. Callum and Mack were closer friends than me and her. He was also a flirt and did this all the time.

Plus, Lo would murder me if I touched her best friend. Maybe not death, but a few stabs, and those would definitely hurt. She was one to kill by a million small cuts rather than a fatal blow. That was why she was terrifying. I ran a hand over my hair, digging my fingers into my scalp to ground myself. Luca and Lo waved a quick goodbye to everyone, stealing my move. I wanted to sneak out of here, but they left first. *Annoying.*

Mack’s cheeks glowed, and her eyes were wide and filled with joy. She hugged her teammates, then Callum, gave high fives to everyone before her gaze sought mine. It was a strange, unfamiliar feeling to watch the moment she saw me. Her already large eyes grew bigger, and her already curved lips smiled even more. She weaved through the few people between us, ignoring most of them before she arrived in front of me.

Curiosity got the best of me. What was she going to say? What did I *want* her to say?

"Dean Romano," she said, a little tipsy. She grabbed the collar of my shirt, her gaze on my mouth. My core tightened as her breath hit my face. She smelled like tequila.

If she kissed me, I'd lose my mind.

"Yes, Mallinson?" I said, my voice scratchy as hell. If it was any other girl, I'd say she'd know exactly how she affected me. But Mack had no idea.

"I did my body shots." She ran her palm over my pecs, the darks of her eyes blackening. "Know what that means?"

"You should drink water? Brush your teeth because Callum is filthy?"

"No." She giggled. "It's your turn."

"My turn to do a body shot *off of you*?"

She pursed her lips and shrugged. "I meant it's your turn to complete that challenge since we're in this together, Romano. If you want to do it off me, be my guest."

I can lick her. My blood heated. My cock stiffened just at the thought. She kept her hand on my chest as she stared at me with those large doe eyes. She had cute freckles on her face I hadn't really noticed before. The lighting in the bar was just right, and I wanted to trace the line of her nose, the curve of her jaw, yet my hand remained fisted at my side.

"Uh, you can also do it off someone else. Literally anyone in this place would do it off you or for you." She snorted and stepped back. "Of course, you'd rather do it with anyone else. How silly. Not me. No. No. No."

What? A wrinkle formed between her brows as she glanced down, backing away.

"Mackenzie." I gripped her wrist, preventing her from walking away. "I'm not putting my mouth on someone else."

"You can't back down. I did it. I've seen you make out with numerous random girls in the same night." She pointed at my chest and shoved. "Don't act like you're shy, cause you're not."

Shit. I was an idiot freshman and sophomore year. I made dumb choices and yeah, partied and hooked up a little too much. *Hence why I'm a hot mess now.*

"I'm not backing down. I'm saying I don't trust everyone here. You used Callum, who you know." There. That was good logic. I couldn't tell her why I didn't trust the opposite sex anymore, not now, not with my unhealed wounds.

"What are you saying then? Because all I hear are excuses, Romano."

"For looking sweet, you're a little spicy, Mack." I laughed and yanked her toward me. I gripped her hips, my thumbs dragging along her exposed skin. She was so warm. "I'll complete the challenge with *you.* No one else."

She nodded, her lips parting. Then, in a lower voice, she said, "But what if people think I'm … easy if I do one with you after Callum?"

"First off, who cares what people think. Secondly, I have an idea." Keeping one hand on her hip because it was an addicting sliver of skin, I whistled to get Callum's attention.

He had his arm around two girls, who looked like twins. "Romano, my man. This is Kelly and Kiara. Want to join us?"

"I need you to do another body shot off someone." I jutted my chin to the girls. "Or both of them."

"Wow, what a hardship. Ladies, what do you think?"

They were game. He led them to the bar, the crowd not even half of what it was before. Mack's teammates sat next to two of the baseball guys, but Ale wiggled her brows at Mack in some sort of code.

Was that code for Mack or for Ale? Girls were weird. They had to communicate in different ways because men were generally idiots. I didn't want to be that guy anymore, and I needed to know what the hell Mack was thinking. She was clearly a little tipsy, so was this… taking advantage? Fuck.

When we arrived at the bar, a few feet down from Callum, I picked her up and set her ass on the edge. I stood between her thighs, keeping my hands on her. This felt so natural, so perfect to be between her legs. Her muscular thighs were fantastic and so thick. I wanted to run my face along them and bite them, just to see how strong she was.

"Mack," I said, swallowing the thickness in my throat. "Are you sure about this? Are you too drunk?"

"I'm not drunk. I have the perfect buzz." She leaned forward, putting her chest even closer to my face. "You can't back down now, Romano. I don't understand why you're demanding it has to be me when you could have anyone, but if you're looking for excuses, my buzz is not one of them."

"You've got a mouth on you," I teased.

"I know. My attitude does tend to flare out when I have a few drinks. Or when I'm on the field. Only places this Mack Attack shines."

"Mack Attack." I smiled. "Makes perfect sense."

The bartender returned, an annoyed look on his face. I slid him a hundred, and that frown shifted to a smile. "Another round?"

"Please."

I gently helped Mack lay on her back. Callum and the girls were farther down, most of the crowd around them. I didn't worry about who watched at all. Lo and Luca were gone, and they were my only real concern. Not that this was even that bad.

Lo didn't care that she did one with Callum, so why would she give a shit about me? He got around more than I did.

Excuses. Okay. Spicy Mack was right. I was coming up with excuses because I was nervous. I hadn't touched a woman in months, and hell, I hadn't felt interest in one in the same amount of time. Until Mack.

She looked up at me, pupils dilated and pulse racing at her neck. I kept a hand on her hip, trying to assure her it was okay.

"Whiskey?" the bartender asked.

"Yup."

I never took my eyes off hers. The guy poured it in her belly. Goose bumps broke out of her body as the liquid started spilling over the sides. Without thinking, I licked up her side to get the spill. Then, I did the same on the other side. Then, I sucked down the liquor while my mouth was on her skin.

My ears rang, my hands shook, and my cock hardened. Mack squirmed and let out the tiniest little noise when I nipped the skin just beneath her belly, and my skin was on fire. I wasn't unfamiliar with lust, but after not having it for months, touching her skin felt like my first time. I couldn't breathe. I couldn't think.

I wanted my mouth on hers, my body on hers, and my cock inside her.

People cheered, and I couldn't take my mouth off her stomach. My brain disappeared, replaced with a desperate horniness. I forgot we were in public, that people watched us.

Mack could spread her legs for me, and I'd go down on her right there.

"Dean," she said, an urgency in her voice. "It's done."

"Kay." I pulled back, refusing to be embarrassed. It lasted maybe ten seconds total, but holy shit. Her skin was so soft yet toned. She tasted like whiskey and smelled like heaven.

Her nipples strained against her barely-there top, and I

wanted to know what they looked like. Were they pink or darker? Did she like when someone touched them, or she did prefer biting?

I helped her down from the bar, carefully making sure she didn't brush up against my dick. It'd give me away. Luckily, I wore loose enough shorts that no one could tell.

"What was that?" she whispered as she stood between me and the bar. "You… licked me for a while."

"I was thorough. Some was spilling down the sides." I traced from her belly to her side. She shivered.

"Callum didn't do that."

"I am *not* Callum," I almost growled. "You tasted so fucking good I couldn't stop. There. That's the truth."

She swallowed loudly. "I tasted good?"

I nodded, licking the side of my mouth. "Mackenzie, it's been a while for me, and your skin was so soft I forgot we were at the bar."

"H-how long is a while?"

"Months."

"No way," she said breathlessly.

I nodded again. I ran a finger over her exposed collarbone, watching her nipples harden in real time. She liked when I touched her. "It's true."

She took a shaky breath, her hands coming up and resting on my stomach. She dug her fingers into me, like she was afraid she'd fall if she let go. "This is just because it's been a while. You're not… attracted to me."

"Stop." I stepped closer to her, not quite touching her but moving near enough for her to look up at me. "That's not why. You feel it too. I'm definitely attracted to you."

"Uh."

"Want to knock another item off your list?"

"Which one?" she squeaked.

"Grinding in pubic. Getting naughty. Whatever the fuck that one was because I want to feel your ass against me, Mack, and if we stay here, I'll be forced to behave."

"This is just alcohol. We're having fun. That's what this is. It's not real," she mumbled to herself, not meeting my eyes. "This doesn't mean a thing."

"It doesn't have to." The words were hard to say, but they were true. It was my sister's best friend and a girl who said she didn't want an attachment senior year. I sure as shit didn't want a distraction during the season. Been there, done that. No more feelings for me, but this attraction? Please, dear god. "It's checking off your summer list. That's it."

"The list." She licked her lips. "This is for the list."

"For the list," I repeated, watching the pulse race at the base of her neck. It sped up. "Now, want to head to the dance floor?"

She nodded, her cheeks pink and her eyes wide. I held out my hand, tense as hell. It felt like eighteen minutes before she placed her small hand in mine. Our fingers intertwined, and an unpleasant, sus thought hit me. When was the last time I'd held hands with someone when it wasn't leading them to the bedroom?

As I guided us to the dance floor, I went through all recent memories, and the gesture of simply holding Mack's hand had me in a spiral. Her palm was warm and her grip strong. Her purple ring dug against my skin.

The upbeat dance music pumped through the speakers, vibrating the ground and air around us. It smelled like sweat and regret, and there was hardly any light. The DJ put on an old school mix with a fast tempo, and without overthinking it, I spun Mack around and pulled her back to my chest.

Her list said to grind with someone. And to get naughty in public. We were going to do both as long as she was game.

Dancing wasn't my thing by choice, but it had a time and

place. Mack's tiny shirt left so much skin to touch, and my god, it was addicting. With her ass nudged against me, I ran my nose along her neck and shoulder. She shivered, and goose bumps exploded.

"What do you want to check off first, Mallinson?" I whispered, nipping her ear in the process. "Grind against me or do something naughty?"

She ground against me harder. "This is unreal."

"No. Very real."

I put a hand on her chest, my other one on her hips, moving us to a rhythm. It was intoxicating. She smelled so damn good, and the whiskey went down real easy. We moved to the beat, her ass nestled against my dick. I was aware of everything—how sweat dripped down her neck, how her thick thighs tensed as she danced, how fast she breathed, and how she gasped when I put my mouth on her.

"Have you ever had anyone touch you on the dance floor?"

"Uh, dancing? Yes."

"No, I meant *touch* you." I ran a hand up her hip, over her bare stomach and teased the underside of her breasts. She definitely wore no bra. "Here."

She shook her head. "N-no."

"Do you want me to?"

She tensed.

My stomach dropped. If she had a single doubt about this, I would launch her across the floor. I never fucked around with anyone unless they were one thousand percent into it and able to communicate it. "Mack—do you—"

"Touch me," she demanded. "Do it, Dean."

Don't need to say it twice.

The momentary blip of worry morphed into downright lava. This was about the list and my lust. *Getting my libido back list.* It might be for Mack to go outside her comfort zone and for me to find my groove. This wasn't serious. The erratic beat of my heart had everything to do with my adrenaline and excitement of being turned on and not at all related to the curve of her spine and feel of her skin.

I cupped one of her breasts, overcome with desire to the point I forgot we were on a stupid dance floor. My jaw tensed, and I bit down the urge to devour her. She gasped as I grazed my palm over her nipple. It was a slow form of torture to just touch her and not *see* her, but I wasn't complaining. This was intoxicating. She leaned forward into my touch, her ass digging into me harder as she urged me on.

I pinched her nipple, twisting and pulling a bit until my cock was hard as a rock. My mouth watered. My skin felt too hot and too tight for my body. The whiskey altered my brain, probably, because Mack was the absolutely the hottest person I had ever seen, ever touched.

Unable to stop myself, I licked from her shoulder to her ear, then growling against her as I bit on her collarbone. I wanted to demand answers from her. Did this feel as good for her as it did to me? Was she excited and wanting to continue this?

It still didn't mean a single thing. Our touching, attraction was for the lists. I knew that. I couldn't afford to ever let anyone mess with me again.

But *fuck*. "God, I want to lick you everywhere," I said against her skin. "Is that on your list? Can we add it?"

She giggled and rested her head on my shoulder. "I vote this as an amendment."

"I'm adding it. I vote yes."

"Great demonstration of democracy," she said, closing her eyes as she sighed.

It was a gorgeous sound, like she was content with me and that we could keep doing this. I ran my fingers over her forearm, over her elbow, and up her bicep, making her squirm.

No one paid attention to the arms and how sensitive they were. I was obsessed with how strong she was while also being soft and smelling incredible. It was such an amazing combination, and when she squirmed against me, our bodies touching was my new favorite place.

Our cheeks pressed together; our bodies molded. We weren't dancing so much as swaying and touching as much as possible. It had to be the hypnotic music and shots and lack of light because I couldn't think of a single reason why we couldn't do this all the time. There was no convincing argument from my end.

"We should—"

"There you are, girl! Girl!" Ale appeared right in front of us. She grinned, almost too much, and the whites of her teeth stood out in the dark room.

Her presence dampened the weird, mesmerizing state I was in. *What* was I doing? Hitting on Mack? Wanting to take her home?

I cleared my throat, pushing her away as reality crashed down on me.

"What is it?" Mack asked, her hand immediately going to her throat.

"Vee's ex is here and starting a fight. We need backup."

"Oh shit." Mack spun, her gaze finding mine, filled with questions and uncertainty. She eyed the space between us, and a little frown line appeared on her forehead.

Please don't ask questions. I begged, silently willing to sell my soul to not have this conversation. Questions swirled in her eyes. They were right there. I had to act first. I attacked on the field and did it well, and life was no different. "You can mark quite a few off your list tonight, Mack. Good for you."

I winked, feeling slimy and weird and disliking myself a little bit. But I walked out of the bar, leaving her with her friends because lines blurred tonight, and I had no idea how to clean them up. There wasn't a world where I could *be* with Mack. I'd never let anyone have power over me again. Jessica taught me that. It didn't matter that I trusted Mack. I'd trusted Jessica too, and she'd fucked me up mentally and messed with my game.

I refused to let history repeat itself. I knew better.

CHAPTER **NINE**

Mack

The Summer Playbook

- ~~Buy a guy a shot~~
- ~~Mixologist challenge – ask bartender to let you make a drink~~
- Skinny dipping
- Get a makeover
- Tattoo
- Take a body shot off someone
- Someone takes one off you
- ~~Grind with a stranger or someone~~
- Make out with two people in one night
- Hook up past first base with a stranger/someone
- ~~Be naughty in public~~
- Ask three guys out
- Dance on a bar
- Streaking
- Dance in the rain

- Concert
- ~~Join a game already going on with strangers~~
- Bonfire (talk to five strangers)
- Wear an outfit you normally wouldn't wear
- Dye your hair a new color
- Crash an event (or wedding for bonus points)
- Lose the cell phone for a whole day
- Strip Poker

Eyeing the list, my head throbbed with annoyance. Could I even cross out the grinding with a stranger or someone because it was with Dean Romano and not a stranger? I rubbed my right eyebrow, the headache having nothing to do with the shots from the night before and everything to do with Dean.

My fantasy. My crush. My best friend's brother.

What the hell was I doing? My chest pinched, like the small shield I grew around my heart cracked because I told myself I was over him. No more crush. No more pining.

Yet, we hung out for one week and I was a fangirl again? Stupid. Silly and stupid. I ground the coffee beans, wincing at the sound just as Luca walked out of Lorelei's room.

He wore low hanging shorts. That was it. My mouth dried up as one small inappropriate thought went through my head. Luca was hot. It was just facts.

"Morning, sunshine!" I teased. "You look well."

He grunted, walked by me, grabbed two water bottles, and disappeared into her room. Did I secretly stare at his muscles? Yes. I wasn't a hero. Lo was lucky.

My mind appreciated the momentary distraction, but it was back to my regular scheduled bullshit.

Dean.

I watched the coffee brew, eyeing the list like it was the

villain in my origin story. How could I look Dean in the eyes now, after we did what we did for the list? Nothing more than that.

No feelings, nothing else.

I wasn't made for this. My stomach cramped at the stupid idea of these challenges. I couldn't be a fun girl, no-feelings girl, no-attachment girlie. I had too many nerves and insecurities to just… be.

Coffee would help. It'd clear my head and help me think. My throat hurt from all the talking last night, and a hot cup would ease it. Vee's ex started shit, and she and the ex yelled. A lot. Then we had to talk it out, Ale, Vee, and I in an ice cream shop after. Vee cried. Ale and I consoled.

There was no reason I should be up this goddamn early after last night. The coffee finished brewing, and I poured a large ass mug, opened the patio door, and curled up on one of our chairs that overlooked the parking lot. It wasn't the best view, but it was *a* view. It had trees and a small garden instead of a back alley. I was grateful for the crisp morning air, cooler than it should be for summer. Maybe I'd go for a run to get over the hangover and regret clouding my thoughts.

Seriously. I knew better than imaging Dean would be anything other than a crush. Ugh. I'd tried for *years* to flirt with him, to see if he was interested. He'd never noticed and was fixated on the next party or the next hot girl. He was always kind and respectful but very clearly *not* into me that way. No lingering touches. No looks or flirtatious remarks.

But last night!

I closed my eyes, resting my forehead on my arm just as someone said my name. A familiar voice. One I knew well, but was I in a halfway, half dream situation? I'd heard of these. Lucid dreaming, maybe? That voice should not be here, near me.

My heart tripled its pace as I swallowed. Any chance I was still drunk?

No.

Glancing up, I found Dean Romano in our parking lot with a brown bag and a tray of coffees. He wore a backwards hat, a navy Central State football shirt, jeans, and Vans. He looked way too good for the morning. His dimples teased his cheeks, and there wasn't an ounce of shame in his eyes.

I rivaled a raccoon. He looked like a god.

"Uh, what are you doing here?" My voice came out all scratchy. It was from the damn yelling. I took another sip of my coffee and choked.

He frowned and hustled toward our patio. "You good?"

"Yeah." I coughed again. "Wrong pipe."

"Hate when that happens." He glanced from my face to my sports bra, then to my shorts.

It was what I slept in. Royal blue spandex and a matching sports bra. I wore it to run or work out, but right now, with the way his eyes heated, I felt like I was wearing lingerie.

"Uh, what are you—why are you here?" I tried again. I brought my knees up to my chest and wrapped my arms around them. "Lo is still sleeping and won't leave hibernation until eleven, at least."

"I know." He set the bag and coffees on the table in front of me. Then, he stepped over the gate with his long ass legs. *Oh, no big deal, I'm Dean Romano and can just scale fences like its nothing.* What a weird thing to find hot.

He smelled like cinnamon, soap, and cologne. The wind hit just right, and I breathed him in, memories of last night hitting me like a ball to the head. *His hands on my breasts. His hard cock against my ass. His tongue on my skin.*

"I brought these for you." He sat across from me, his brown

eyes crinkling on the sides. "I recall you losing your mind for a bear claw once."

"It's happened more than once." I pursed my lips, still very confused. "Dean. I love a pastry. But why are you here?"

"Because of last night."

He regrets it. He's going to say to forget about it, remain friends.

I mentally prepared myself for his argument, and I would accept it, gladly. I'd do it with dignity because I was a damn hero. My stomach twisted, and my throat closed up, but I faced him.

"Okay, let's talk about it."

He ran a hand over his face, sighing before one side of his lips quirked up. "I left in a bit of a weird headspace, and I was concerned how it could've come across to you."

That's… unexpected. "You're worried about what I'm thinking?"

"Yeah, exactly that." His eyes warmed. "Take a pastry, please. They are for you."

I grabbed one, my mind whirling with the notion he cared about my headspace. It was… sweet.

"So you're not here to…" I pressed my lips together, too afraid to continue.

He tilted his head and adjusted his hat. His thick brown hair was in every direction, and my fingers twitched with the urge to touch it. I wanted to run my fingers through the strands, pull on the ends. Would he like it or not?

"I hoped to ask if you're alright with everything we did." He rested his elbows on the table, his stare intense. "We had a couple of drinks, and it's important to me that you're good. I planned to text, but this seems like an in-person conversation."

"I'm okay with what happened. As you said, it's all for the list." I swallowed the ball of emotion in my throat. I didn't want it to be *just for the list.* I wanted to burn the list but then I'd lose the competition, which was also terrible. It was a lose-lose situation for me, my least favorite situation of all situations.

"Yeah, about that." He ran his hand over his jaw, the intensity somehow increasing in his gaze. "I have an idea."

"For the list?"

"Kinda." He smiled quickly and glanced inside. He wet the side of his lips, a dimple popping out for a second before he hit the table. "You want to live it up before senior year and life gets serious, right?"

Frowning, I nodded. "Yes. That was the goal."

To have all the experiences I missed out on trying to prove a point.

"Yes. Just clarifying, stay with me here. I've been dealing with some things. They don't matter. But hanging with you and doing these challenges? This has been fun as hell. I don't have time for distractions once the summer is over, and you've expressed, you're not trying to catch feelings." He paused, arched a brow. "You feel me?"

"By feel you, the words make sense together. I still don't understand." My pulse raced, the constant thud under my skin like a rippling stream. Hope had me drawing some very unrealistic conclusions that I wouldn't dare say aloud. If Dean was suggesting what I thought he was suggesting, he had to spell it out like I was a five-year-old. No offense to five-year-olds anywhere, but they knew what they were doing with simple, clear instructions.

"Here's my idea. We explore this chemistry between us. You and me. All summer. Once classes begin, we go back to being friends. No strings, no feelings. Just fun as we work through your list."

"Because we have chemistry," I said, my voice sounding muffled.

He stared at my mouth. “Yes, Mackenzie. We both feel it.”

I ran my finger over the table, avoiding the split wood to not get a splinter as I let his suggestion wash over me. We were attracted to each other—this was news. I had always been attracted to him, so he was into me *now.* I could work with that. No feelings would be hard, but what a time to try it. This would be just another new thing for me to experience.

This felt heavy, scary even, to agree to this, but I’d regret it if I walked away. This was Dean Romano offering to be my Summer Playbook buddy.

“So,” I said, smirking and ready to push him. “Making out with three dudes in one night is off the table?”

“Yeah, no. You’re not making out with three dudes if we’re doing this together. Not a fan of that.” He shook his head, dismissing the idea with tight lines around his mouth. “You do the entire list with me. Only me.”

“You want to be *exclusive*?” I asked, my voice raising an octave. What was happening? What was this?

His eyes sparkled with amusement. “If you mean we agree to do the list together and not with others, then yes.”

“List-clusive?” I repeated, combining the words like a dumbass.

He nodded, his grin growing. “Definitely list-clusive. DAMPB—Dean and Mack’s Playbook Pact.”

“Wait.” I blinked. “You want to go *streaking* with me?” My voice was worse than a twelve-year-old boy going through puberty.

His gaze lit up. “I’d enjoy it very much.”

“And skinny dipping?”

“Wanna go now?” His gaze heated. “I’d love to see you underwater.”

I closed my eyes, dizzy and overheated, and why was I wearing so many clothes? Why was June so hot already? Doing the list with just Dean…this was a fantasy, right? Could I tell the girls? Not Lo! No.

"Okay, did I come on too strong? I'm sorry. I feel so comfortable with you it's honestly jarring." He smiled, a little blush on his cheeks. "I can't tell if your silence is because you're trying to tell me no nicely or –"

Miss a summer with my crush? Get a fucking grip Mack!

This was the adventure I wanted. The thing my friends wanted me to do!

"I'm in. I am *so* in."

He grinned. "Fuck yeah, girl." He held out a fist. I hit it.

We stared at each other, like dorks, and my heart sped up like I ran three miles in fifteen minutes. (I could do it)

"Give me—"

"Should we—" I said.

Then we both laughed. It broke the weird tension between us, and I relaxed into my seat. "Wow."

"I was going to ask for your number."

"Pretty sure you said *give me* and not Can I Please Have."

"Fair." He smiled again, this time letting his gaze linger on my collarbone. He'd bitten and licked me there a lot at the bar, and now with my list… maybe do that again? I mean, going past first base was on the list for sure.

My thighs clenched together as leftover heat from last night returned. I handed him my phone. "Put your number in."

I had a million questions to ask, mainly, when were we starting, and could we make out first? I'd fantasized about kissing Dean the second I saw him freshmen year, before I became Lo's best friend. Dean and I were in the same freshmen orientation, and it was love at first sight.

Now I could kiss him this summer? Crazy. My life was crazy.

"So—"

"What's this?" Lo opened the patio door, wearing her bumblebee robe. She had sleep lines on her face and leftover makeup on her eyes.

Guilt stabbed me in the chest. How dare I lust after her brother after she shared with me that they were going through something? She told me how she had friends use her to get to him, and here I was, planning on skinny dipping with him and thinking about his mouth.

"Uh, nothing."

"I brought pastries. Figured you were both hungover," Dean said. "Plus, Mack and I are friends now."

"Yeah, I've noticed." Lo narrowed her eyes at her brother, but any of the anger disappeared just as fast as it showed up. "What pastries?"

"Your favorite. Obviously. All the berries. Blue and rasp and straw."

"You're so weird," Lo mumbled.

"Did you bring one for me?" Luca joined her at the door.

This was just fantastic. I couldn't lie for shit, and my face told my feelings like the words were bolded on my forehead. *HORNY AND GUILTY* were pretty much plastered on there now. Might as well put some neon lights and glitter on there too. I chewed my lip, my mind spinning on how to play it cool.

"Help yourself, bro." Dean ran a hand over his face, his gaze lingering on his sister as she touched every pastry in the box. "Okay, don't put your gross germs over all them."

"I'm testing the squishiness. I have feelings about the firmness."

"Yeah, but we, other humans, have to eat those, and you're dirty." Dean swatted her hand away, his tone playful. "I brought them for Mack too. Let her pick."

Lo narrowed her eyes on her brother, the flash of annoyance

returning. "Right. Everyone else comes first for you now besides me. Got it."

Lo shook her head, her shoulders slumped as she went back inside. My gut ached at the horrified, guilty look on Dean's face. His brows furrowed, and his lips parted, like he forgot how to speak at how upset Lo was. The sliding door shut, leaving me, Dean, and Luca on the patio.

"Fucking talk to her. I'm not asking." Luca pointed at Dean, his gaze darkening. "You told me you'd punch me in the face if I ever hurt your sister, and I agreed. But you know what? That goes both ways. You're upsetting her, and I'm a day away from punching you."

"You'd hit your quarterback?"

"Yeah. I'd hit my quarterback if it meant getting his head out of his ass." Luca glared, then eyed the food. He aggressively picked up two doughnuts and shoved one in his mouth. "Thanks for this."

"Sure thing." Dean sat straighter as Luca went inside, the playfulness I saw earlier disappearing. "I should go."

"Hey," I said, unable to stop myself. His gaze met mine, and his large brown eyes were filled with grief. I *hated* seeing Dean like that. I mean, I hated the fact Lo was upset more, but Dean was always the untouchable, aloof, confident badass who led the team in playoffs and had almost a million followers on social media. Seeing him sad meant the earth was out of sync. "You have people who love you. You're lucky. Not everyone has a sister like you, a team like you do, a family like you do. The point of any relationship is to be there for the ups *and* the downs. You can't pick when they are there for you or when they are not."

His jaw tightened, like he chewed gum, but his stare only intensified. "Lo is lucky to have you. You're a good friend, Mackenzie."

He hit the table softly before standing and staring over the garden. "Want to place a bet on if Luca hits me if I go in there?"

"No. I'd place a bet on if I hit you if you *don't* go in there." I pointed to the door, hard.

His lips twitched. "Spicy Mack. I like it."

"Do I need to do a countdown?"

His eyes flashed, and he stared at my mouth. His nostrils flared as he caressed my body with his gaze. I had never felt sexier than I did in that moment, all from how he looked at me. He started at my toes, letting out a little snort when he eyed my toe ring. He traveled up my legs and over my stomach, stopping on my chest before meeting my eyes again. His were like an inferno of lust. "You're my favorite kind of trouble. What are your plans tonight?"

"Tonight?"

"Yeah. I'm going to talk to Lo for a bit, convince Luca not to kill me, then shower. You want to hang out, or do you have plans?"

"I'm probably gonna hang with Lo." I shrugged, unsure if it was too soon to spend time with him. I didn't even know what I'd agreed to, per se, and I wanted a night to clear my thoughts, check in on my best friend, and breathe.

"Tomorrow."

"Was that a question or a demand?" I arched a brow, loving this banter between us. I'd seen the way girls fawned over him. Sure, I had a crush that was epic and dangerous, but every time I challenged him, his eyes got dark and his voice all deep. He never did that with other girls. He liked it, and I enjoyed pushing his buttons.

"Could we do something tomorrow?"

"Is there a please in there?"

"You." He laughed, the sound magical. "You are fucking trouble, and I am here for it."

I tilted my head up toward him, pursing my lips in confidence. “I might be able to move things around for you tomorrow. Maybe.”

He walked toward me, rubbing his thumb over my bottom lip. “Move things around. *Please.* I’m not a patient person, and I really want to kiss this mouth.”

He winked, let go of my face, and walked inside the apartment.

CHAPTER **TEN**

Dean

If I channeled my inner Callum, I'd joke this entire thing off and make my sister laugh. If I was Luca, I'd just grump and provide her one-word answers. If I was Oliver, I'd give a pro and a con list and then have her set up a meeting with me to discuss afterwards. I wasn't any of my teammates though. It was Lo and me.

Twins.

Best friends.

Athletes.

Once, roommates.

And I'd hurt her.

She wore her hair in a crazy bun with curls all over the place, and she had on one of Luca's T-shirts and some running shorts. She seemed the same, like my sister, but her expression was like a knife in the gut to me. She was a ray of sunshine, always happy and hilarious, and now…she looked sad. Her shoulders were slumped, and her eyes didn't have the same smart-ass light they always did.

"Thanks for coming to talk to me today," she said, running her finger over the crack in their coffee table. "I'm sorry I was passive aggressive to you on the patio. That wasn't helpful."

Luca and Mackenzie had gotten the fuck out of the apartment once they realized Lo and I were going to talk. It was just us. Nowhere for me to run to escape the truth. My thighs ached from how tense I grew in the silence. I'd been on Lo's side of this situation, the hurt one. The one who wanted an explanation and apology, and to be honest? It wasn't any easier being the one who fucked up.

The guilt and ache that grew in my gut sucked. No other way to put it. I didn't even know where to start. That was the problem. I couldn't just… say sorry and tell her how a girl had messed with my entire future, my entire life, and I couldn't move on from it.

"Dean." Lo steepled her fingers together, sighing as she looked at me. "Are you sick?"

"What?" I reared back. "No."

"Then what in the ever-loving shit is going on with you?" She stood, the sadness shifting to pissed off real quick. "I am sick of tiptoeing around you. I'm sick of my boyfriend knowing everything about your life when I don't. I'm fucking sick of worrying! Tell me. Tell me right now what's going on, or I will call Mom. I will call Grandma. I will post on your social medias that you sleep in the fetal position and suck your thumb. I swear to—"

"Jessica fucked me up, okay!" I shouted, pushing up from her couch. "I really liked this girl; it was going well, and I was really into her. For the first time, I wanted to be exclusive with someone and *try* this whole relationship thing. Only, it was a lie, and she tricked me. She told me she was pregnant. She got me excited about maybe being a dad, even though it would change my life. I got *excited about it.* Then, she said she lost it.

That the baby didn't make it. It *gutted* me. Then! I find out she lied about the whole thing, actually cheated on me, and was pregnant with someone else's baby. Okay? That happened. That fucking happened, and my life hasn't been the same since, and I don't trust *anyone* anymore, but how could I?" My voice cracked. My hands shook. My stomach ached, and I swallowed down the urge to vomit. I couldn't face my sister. I turned toward the wall, gripping the edge of my hat. "I've been so angry, Lo. All the time, I am just… I'm so mad. It's not fair. I feel the loss of everything even though it wasn't real."

My eyes stung.

I didn't hear her, but suddenly, my sister was in my arms, tackling me into a bear hug. She smelled like she always did, lotion crap, but it reminded me of home and safety. I hugged her back, tight, and closed my eyes. I leaned onto her, suddenly feeling so foolish that I'd never opened up to her.

"It's a good thing you didn't tell me," she said into my chest.

"Wait." I coughed, shaking my head. "What do you mean?"

"I'm too young for murder, and Dean?" She looked up at me, her dark brown eyes swirling with venom. "I'm going to *kill* her. Who is she? Who is *Jessica?*"

"Yeah, not telling you that." I smiled, finally, a chink in the armor around my soul. I felt lighter after telling my sister. "Please, *please* understand it was never about you. I was ashamed, horrified. I let someone do this to me. If I—"

"You *what?* No. Don't do this shit my presence. She made her choices. Her actions are why this happened, not anything you did. If you blame yourself for one second, I will knock out a tooth, and I know how vain you are about your teeth."

"Have you always been so aggressively threatening?"

"Yes. I've gotten worse in the last few months you've ignored me."

"Touché." I swallowed and put my hand on her shoulder, squeezing. "I am sorry I hurt you while dealing with my own shit. I hate that I hurt someone I love."

"I forgive you. I'll always forgive you, but Dean, you *have* to talk to someone about this." She rubbed her lips together, a sad sigh escaping. "That is a lot of trauma for one person to deal with. Even if you think you're the coolest, best, most laidback—"

"No. I'm messed up. I can't trust anyone anymore. Besides you and Mack, I'm keeping women away from me."

"Mack?" Her eyebrows rose until they disappeared into her hairline. "What does my best friend have to do with any of this?"

"Her list. I like her dumb list." Guilt had me pausing, but I powered through. "It's helping me put myself back out there too." *Lo doesn't need to know about the secret part where it's just Mack and me. Not yet.*

"You have your own list?" She tilted her head to the side.

"Yeah, kinda." Kinda meant I wasn't lying.

"Dean, I love you and have your back always, but if you're going to be friends with Mack, be careful. She is the most loyal, kindest, goofiest person you'll meet, but she wears her heart on her sleeve and gets attached easily. You don't. You also went through something really fucked up and need to work on yourself. Do you see the problem?"

"We're having fun, not getting involved." I forced a smile. "I can be myself with her, and she makes me laugh."

"She's hilarious and the best person I know. I understand how she can suck you in and make you feel okay. She's our entire team's emotional support person. But I can't… look, this makes me a hypocrite because I'm dating your tight end, but please don't get involved with her unless you absolutely mean it."

The guilt grew, then doubled in size, then tripled. It was like the opposite of the Grinch here. Instead of my heart growing, it was my guilt, and it crept up my throat to the point I had to clear it. "Understood."

"Good. I won't mention it again because I truly do get it. She's the easiest person to be around."

"And I trust her. I think, to me, that's what broke. I don't trust anyone besides my team, you, and Mack."

"That's a scary place to live, Dean." She squeezed my arm. "Will you consider talking to a professional about this?"

"Consider is a strong word."

"You need to get your shit together before senior year and the draft. If you won't talk reason, then I'll talk football. You think you can lead a team if you're a hot mess inside? You can't. Sports are all mental, and you know this. If you're not mentally strong enough to carry the weight of a team, you'll lose."

My jaw tightened. "Fuck."

"Yeah. Fucking go see someone." She sighed before yanking me into a hug again. "Thank you for telling me. Thank you for being my brother. I love you, and if I ever learn where this Jessica chick is, I will get arrested for what I will do. Save a chunk of your money to bail me out."

My lips quirked up. "That Get Lo out of Jail Card has been around since we were six and you tripped Ben headfirst into the lake."

"He was an asshole."

"He was, but I've seen your sadistic side. There's always been a fund to bail you out. I've even invested in it."

"Wow, look at you." She smirked, but the sparkle dimmed in her eyes. "You'll get through this, yeah? It might be hard, but you will. You'll learn to trust again. This is just a bad season you're in. It's not forever."

"Thanks, Lo."

I felt lighter telling her the truth, not keeping it from her and having Luca dance around it. But knowing she was right still weighed me down. I had to deal with my trauma before the season. Opening up this much was enough for one weekend, so I told myself I'd research the next week. For now? I wanted to party with my housemates and convince Mack to hang out with me. Because one thing was for sure—she and I could do her list without getting involved. I'd make sure of it. She helped me forget about all this shit, and I had an addictive personality. I didn't just *like* something. Things consumed me. And right now? Her smile and attitude were an addiction, and enjoying her for the summer was the perfect distraction.

Dean: make out or streak

Mack: ummmm hi who is this?

Dean: Jesus, it's Dean. We exchanged numbers? Yesterday?

Mack: I meet so many men it's hard to remember. Dean… who?

My lips quirked. *Funny girl.*

Dean: Mm, okay Spicy Mack. Answer my question. Make out or streak.

*Mack: Those are my ONLY two choices? What about skinny dipping? *eyes emoji**

Dean: I didn't want to start off too strong. But I'm down. I am SO down.

Mack: How would this work? What do we tell people? How would we get naked?

Dean: How about you come outside, and we talk it out?

Mack: You're… here?

Dean: Yup. Sure am.

Mack: Be right there.

I smiled, pocketing my phone as I waited at their front door. Luca and Lo were at his grandma's place today, a few hours away, so I knew Mack was alone. Anticipation burst through me. The only comparable feeling was the pregame jitters I got every single time. My pulse elevated, my skin seeming a bit too snug as my mouth dried. It was ridiculous because this was my sister's best friend, Mack, who I'd seen hungover, throwing up, and crying within the past three years. There was no reason to be nervous, but I felt different after telling Lo what happened with Jessica.

Nothing had changed in the last twenty-four hours, yet butterflies tackled each other, all left unprotected as I watched the front door handle twist open. Mack stepped out and damn. Just… damn.

Her long blonde hair was twisted into braids, her purple tips tucked into the ends. She wore high-waisted, cutoff shorts and a cropped top that barely covered her boobs. My jaw tightened at how edible she looked. Her face was clean of makeup, but her lashes stood out against her blue eyes, and my fingers made fists at my sides. The inch or two of skin showing had me wanting to trace it with my finger, to see how many goose bumps I could give her before she shivered.

"Is this how it's gonna be? You just show up?" she asked, crossing her arms. She arched one of her brows and smirked.

"To be fair, I did text you." I grinned, honestly just happy to be near her. No worrying about saying the wrong thing or having her stab my back. "You think about our choices?"

"Streaking or making out?" She tapped her pointer finger against her lips. "Get over here and kiss me so I can go back to what I was doing."

I couldn't tell if she was joking or not, and I was mildly insulted. "What the hell are you doing?"

She blew a raspberry with her lips and opened the door. "Come on in, I'll show you."

I followed her, inhaling her perfume and orange scent. The aroma was incredible and subtle enough to not overwhelm. It reminded me of the night at the bar, her body against mine, the feel of her… I coughed into my fist. She had a ring light set up on her table and her phone on some holder. "What's this?"

"I'm starting an OnlyFans account."

Fuck. I sucked in a breath, gasping for air to the point I choked. Her knowing smirk was devilish. Evil. What a witch.

"God, your face. Ha! That was worth it. No judgement to those on there, earn that money, but damn." She threw her head back and laughed, the jovial chuckle echoing in the kitchen, and I wanted to keep the sound.

It was carefree, unattractive, and beautiful all at the same time. My lips twitched as I fought my own smile. "Think you're funny?"

"Mildly so." She sat on the chair and waved her hand in the air, indicating the whole setup. "I'm nowhere near your status of social media fame, but I do live sessions twice a week and answer questions about what it's like being a D1 soccer player. My fan base has been growing lately with the rise of attention on female athletes."

"I love that. And my followers aren't following me to talk about football. They want to see my persona, the life they all wanted. It's a façade, for sure."

"Yeah, I know. The guy I know as Dean Romano is very different than you are online." Her words were kind, but there was an undertone in the sentence that had my spine stiffening.

"What does that mean?" I sat next to her at the table. My thigh touched hers, and her warmth radiated into me. It took a lot of effort to not run my hand over her skin because damn, I wanted to.

"You've been a playboy and a flirt the last three years, for sure, but you're not just some womanizing footballer. You volunteer with the team. You tutor the younger guys. You lead by example. None of that is shown on your social media. You just post photos of Central State Gear, cute women, fans, and the team."

"Well yeah, they aren't following me for anything other than my jersey number." My face burned, and I frowned. "They don't give a shit about my views or goals, just wins. It's not like you. You can be yourself and speak up, and people want to listen to you. That's cool as fuck."

"Don't you get to control what you post, what you speak about?" She tilted her head, a little wrinkle forming between her brows. She looked at me like I told her dogs should wear pants.

"I mean, sure, but they want the quarterback life." I scratched my chest, hoping that would help the unsettled feeling behind my ribs. I came here to kiss this girl, and now we were having a heart to heart. "Mack—"

"Pretty sure you're the boss of your own life and your own narrative, Romano." Her eyes flashed. "Now kiss me quick so I can get back to this."

"Using my body then kicking me out? Wow. You do have this professional athlete lifestyle down," I teased, thankful as hell that the conversation turned to one more in my domain.

Flirting. Kissing. Seducing. I *used* to be incredible at this, and it felt good to flex those muscles again without freaking out. Sure, my mind went to Jessica and her face and the lies, but I could shove the images away faster now.

"I gotta practice before I'm playing professionally. I'll just be going through men like takeout. Use them, kick them out."

That… no. Didn't love that image.

"That was a joke, Romano. Don't judge me with those eyebrows of yours." She laughed again. "If you don't plan on kissing me, then do you mind waiting around for a few minutes? I'll finish this round, then we can go hog wild and streak."

"I'll wait until you're done." I leaned back in the chair, the idea of watching her perking me up. I'd love to see what she said, how she interacted with her growing fan base. Mack went viral a few weeks ago, and since then, her following had grown fast. All sorts of people watched her account now, and I'd lie if I hadn't followed her and watched a few of her posts myself. She was engaging and endearing.

"Okay, cool. I need to finish answering these questions that were submitted, then we can get naked, kiss, get face tattoos, whatever."

"In that order, yes, please."

Our gazes met, and a warm, pleasant feeling replaced the uneasy one, and there was no other place I'd rather be than right here. Nothing sounded better or more entertaining that spending time with Mack.

With the ring light on, she adjusted her phone and smiled into it. "Three more questions for today. This one is from Melodie Smith. How can we support women's sports more? I'm a huge fan, but I don't know what else to do. Great question. First, thank you for being a fan. Large markets often say that men's teams drive in more revenue, so that's always the reason why they don't give women's teams the most coverage, but y'all are missing out." She laughed and leaned onto her elbows, looking cute as hell as she continued. "Talk about your teams. Buy gear. Tag accounts when you're watching. Be loud and proud of the teams you support. If you can't afford going to a game or buying gear, you can post and be creative online.

Owners need to know there is a fan base at the ready, so the more engagement there is, the more likely money will funnel toward those teams."

She paused and hit the stop button. "Okay, two more."

"You're incredible," I gushed. "I love how your voice gets all high and excited when you talk about it."

She eyed me. "I can't tell if you're making fun of me or not."

"Not at all, Mack. I like learning this side of you." I reached over and squeezed her forearm. "You're captivating."

"Hm." She twisted her lips, like she didn't believe me. "Too many compliments means you're hiding something or you feel guilty. What did you do?"

"Wait, what?"

"Yeah, you're being too nice to me, so that means you want something or you're compensating for a past mistake."

"Actually, it means I think you're sexy as fuck, and I'm enjoying watching you talk about things you're passionate about. That's it. Now, finish your questions because I've been patient and nice, but I stand by what I said earlier. I need to fucking kiss you, and you're stalling."

I pointed to the camera, fighting the urge to yank her into my lap. Her cheeks reddened, and her pulse raced at the base of her neck. "Record."

Mack pushed my buttons for fun, but I could do it right back, making her flustered. She licked her lip, and the little action sent a bolt of lust to my core. I wanted Mack, and I was gonna do whatever it took to kiss her. OKMM—Operation Kiss Mack Mallinson was in full force.

This summer fling was the best idea *ever.*

CHAPTER **ELEVEN**

Mack

Besides Lo occasionally being around for the videos, I wasn't used to having an audience while I recorded. Instead of being nervous though or awkward, it felt empowering. Dean stared at me with awe in his eyes, like I impressed him, and with all the talk of kissing me…I wasn't sure of his end game, but I wasn't letting myself care. He wanted us to have a summer fling and explore this chemistry, and even though I was a hot mess of anticipation, excitement vibrated through me.

"And that's it." I finished the third video, answering a question about a practice schedule while balancing school. The questions I received were generally good and interesting. It felt inspiring to have younger athletes and fans care about the collegiate lifestyle. I told myself if even one person went into soccer because of me, it'd be worth the effort. *And another secret fuck you to Coach Emily.*

It didn't make sense to me, how one person had told me I'd

never amount to anything, and I let that get under my skin. I was twenty-one, for fuck's sake, and her words still bothered me. Her disdain fueled me to work harder *and* to be the best person I could, so at least I could thank her for that?

No. I'd never thank her. She'd planted seeds of doubt that grew into full ass trees in my confidence and soul. I tore those trees down, but the roots remained, never quite disappearing.

I took a sip of water as Dean studied me with a half-smile on his face. His eyes twinkled with amusement, and my stomach somersaulted. It had been a long time since any guy had looked at me with this much interest. Plus, when Dean focused on you, it was blinding. Nothing else mattered.

"Are you thinking about attacking my face now that I'm done?"

"Always thinking about your face, yes." He snorted. "It was cool watching you. Thank you for trusting me."

"Oh. You're welcome." I frowned. That was a weird thing to say. "So, now that I'm done, what are we gonna do?" My voice shook as my nerves came to the surface. I wanted to be the cool, chill, composed girlie. The one who wasn't flustered and could hang and banter with Dean Romano, but deep down, I was a nervous nellie with a million questions.

The battle of wanting to be cool and asking my questions was a full-out war. *Banter with him. Ask him what this means. Make the first move, impress him. He'll never be impressed since he's been with hundreds of girls. Hundreds? Thousands?* "Oh my god, have you hooked up with thousands of people?" I blurted out.

His eyebrows disappeared into his hairline, his lips parting as he chuckled. "Thousands? Mackenzie. Come on."

"I don't know your life. You get around." I pushed up from the chair, my legs shaky as I busied myself picking up the camera, light, and cords. This was a silly idea. Us, kissing?

Hooking up? Bah! I couldn't compete with his past hookups! I was a tomboy, too athletic, too busy. That was what past boyfriends said. *But this is a fling!*

I felt more than heard Dean approach me. He smelled the same, a dangerous and delicious combination of soap and cologne. Placing a hand on my back, he spun me around so we faced each other. My hands were filled with my stuff, acting as a protective barrier, and I swallowed hard as he frowned at me.

"Why are you nervous right now? Am I making you nervous again?"

I chewed my lip. "Um, yes and no."

"I need more than that, Mackenzie." He slowly took the stuff from my hands and set it on the counter next to me. "We've been hanging out a lot the last two weeks. I thought we were good."

"Dean." I pinched my nose, hoping the lack of his scent would clear my head. He was so close. Heat radiated off his body, and his mouth was right there, his lips absolutely perfect. He had some scruff on his face that I wanted to feel on my mouth, scraping my skin and reddening it. I clenched my thighs together as an aggressive want overtook me. I wanted this man, in every way, but my brain was halting progress with unhelpful comments.

"Mack," he said, one side of his mouth twitching up. "We don't have to do anything you don't want to. I thought we were vibing and flirting when I suggested streaking, but please know even if you wanted to hang out and talk, I'd still be here."

"Why? Why would Dean Romano, hottest guy on campus want to hang out and *talk* with me? I don't understand." I licked my lips, the lack of moisture having to do with him sucking all the air around us with his presence. "I'm just a dork."

"You're not a dork. You're…" He stared over my shoulder, a dark look crossing his face before he met my eyes again. The darkness was gone, and instead a warm, heated gaze caressed my face. "I can be myself with you. Do you know how freeing that is? You make me laugh. You drive me crazy with your sassy ass comments. Hanging with you reminds me I'm normal, and I really need that."

"You want a normal, boring girl?" I said, hurt lacing my voice.

"You're only listening to part of my words here, and that's pissing me off. Stop picking up on the words that could be taken out of context. Why is it so hard to understand I like spending time with you?" He ran a finger over my ear, down my neck, and over my collarbone.

"Because you've never noticed me before," I whispered.

"I noticed you," he said, slowly, softly. His finger moved from the base of my throat, up my face until he cupped my chin. "I saw how you treated your friends, how you played like a boss on the field, how you inspired younger athletes in a way that makes me ashamed I don't do enough. I've noticed how thick your muscles are and how loud you laugh—it's contagious. Now, are you nervous about kissing me? We can go slow. Or is it something else?"

My eyes fluttered as that damn finger kept caressing my face. Suddenly, I was back at the bar, his hands on me and his mouth on my neck. My body heated, and my nipples tightened with need. A soft moan escaped from my mouth. "I-I don't know."

"Your body is reacting to me." He ran the finger down the center of my chest, swirling it around my pebbled nipple. I sucked in a breath, and he repeated the process on the other one. "Mm, I love the feel of these."

"I'm in a sports bra," I said, like he couldn't see with his own eyes. "Not sexy."

"Uh, hard disagree." He continued his slow teasing as he

grazed over my breast and to the strap. He dug his finger under it and slid it onto my shoulder. "This is super fucking sexy, knowing you don't have anything on underneath it. I can see the outline of your nipples and how they tighten every time I do this."

He ran over the tip again, this time tugging over the fabric.

I arched my back, needing him closer. My body was on fire with need, want, and desperation. We were both fully clothed, yet he looked at me like I mattered, like he really did think I was sexy. "Dean," I said, my voice gravelly and throaty.

"Yeah, Mack?" He licked his lips as his hand dropped to the skin beneath the crop top. He teased the waistband of my shorts before he met my eyes. His pupils were so large his eyes were black.

His gaze darkened with need, and I felt drunk on power.

"Is this… for the list?" I couldn't decide if I wanted it for the list or not. I was too overcome with the need for him to touch me, and I didn't care what the hell he said. "What… what are we doing?"

"I'm showing you how sexy you are and how fucking into you I am." He kept his slow caress going, moving over my stomach and up my sides back to my neck. He repeated the process, driving me mad without doing more.

I bit my lip hard. This was out of my element. Could I touch him? Could I tackle him? I wanted to, but fuck, his touch felt so good, and the list remained in the back of my head. Make out? Or more than first base?

"You're thinking too much. I can hear your brain." He laughed, the deep vibration hitting me in my core.

"This is for the list," I said, swallowing the lump of unwanted, messy emotions in my throat. I wasn't going to freak out or overanalyze this. This was supposed to be fun, goddamn it. I was using my shenanigans list to put myself out there. "We're knocking off the list."

His eyes narrowed for a second before he nodded. "For the list."

His gaze dropped to my mouth, and I couldn't take it another second. I fisted his shirt and yanked him against me in the most uncharacteristic Mack action of all time. I never took charge off the field, but no more. It was *my* turn. He let out a little oomph before I slammed my mouth against his, finally kissing the man behind the fantasy. Fireworks exploded from head to toe, my scalp tingling with an aggressive, delicious want that had me ignoring everything.

I forgot my name, who I was, what breathing was. I just needed more of *him.*

The scruff tickled my face. His full lips had no business being that juicy and perfect as they parted and devoured me. Dean's hands moved toward my hips as he groaned into my mouth, the growly, deep vibration setting me on fire. He tasted like mint, the light burn of his gum tingling my tongue. Dean didn't just kiss, he owned. He didn't just hold me, he gripped me like his life depended on it. His fingers pressed so hard into my hips that my skin burned, but I welcomed it.

He sucked my tongue once, twice, then swirled his tongue deep into my mouth, kissing me blindly into oblivion. My heart pounded against my ribs, his erratic beat as fast as mine. One hand moved behind my head, holding my head in place as he tilted me back. "Your mouth. Fuck."

He licked my neck, biting my skin as he said, "Perfect. Your mouth is perfect."

I shuddered as he picked me up and wrapped my legs around his waist to set me on the kitchen table. He ground into me, his erection pressing against my warm pussy. "Dean," I moaned, my eyes about rolling into my head. Everything was on fire. My mind, my lips, my pussy. My core throbbed with need, my body begging him with an unsaid *please, please, please.*

Placing a hand on my chest, he pushed me down as he continued kissing all parts of my exposed skin. He nipped at my neck, collarbone, my exposed stomach. His deep satisfied groans made me hotter as I gripped his shirt and ran my fingers through his hair. "I love your hair," I blurted out.

"Pull it. Do what you want. Just keep making these sounds, Mack." He leaned up to meet my gaze, his eyes all black as he ran a finger under the crop top. "Past first base, yeah? That's the list?"

I nodded, unable to form words. I wanted a home run. I wanted a goddamn grand slam right now, a stadium clearing, walk-off hit grand slam. My mouth dried up, and I arched, wanting him on top of me again. My ideal weight was having Dean Romano on top of me.

"Use your voice, Mack." He teased the underside of my breasts again, his lips parted and his eyes wild. "Say it."

"Yes."

"Yes, what?" he demanded.

He licked his lips as he stared down at me, the expression a totally new one on his face. I'd never seen it, and it seemed like hunger. Like he was hungry for me.

"Touch me."

"For the list?" he repeated, his nostrils flaring as he flipped up the band of my crop top. My nipples pebbled at the cooler air as they were fully exposed. Dean stared at them with want radiating off him. His hands shook, and his jaw tightened as he whispered, "Gorgeous."

"They're small," I said, needing to remind myself that this was Dean. He wasn't *into* me. This was helping me out for a list, that was all. I wasn't like those supermodels and gorgeous girls he usually dated. Not me.

His gaze flashed to mine, anger swirling behind them. He cupped each breast, squeezing them together as his thumbs traced my areola. "Have you ever come from nipple play, Mackenzie?"

I swallowed and shook my head. "Wh-what? No."

"Mm." He licked his lips again and jutted his chin. "Sit up for me."

He guided me up to sitting, his jaw set in a determined line. "Raise your arms."

I obeyed, lost in lust. He kissed my neck as he carefully removed my crop top and stared down at me with an intensity that made me even wetter. He ran a hand over his face as he stared and stared, lost in his own head. "Dean?"

"Sorry, your body is insane. I'm committing it to memory right now." He smirked before running his fingers over my nipples but not quite touching them. "New rule for us."

"Hm?" I leaned onto my elbows, my body way too hot and on edge. He wouldn't stop touching me. His hands went up and down my ribs, stomach, around my nipples and repeated. His hands were rough, calloused, and the roughness made it feel even better.

"Never talk about your body in a negative way," he said, voice firm. He waited for me to meet my gaze before grinding into me again. "Does this feel like your body isn't perfect? Do you feel how much I want to bury myself inside you and have your thick ass legs wrapped around me? I need to eat you, Mackenzie. But not today."

"Wh-why not?" I trembled now. His erection was huge and thick against his shorts, and his muscles strained as he pulled himself back.

"Because your list requires more than first base, and I want to give you a nipple orgasm. Be your first. I'm competitive like that." He grinned, a wicked gleam in his eyes as he sucked in a breath as he stared at me. "Your body… I plan to lick every inch of you."

"Lick me then."

"Oh, I will, Mackenzie. In time." He smirked and ran his fingertips over my breasts, circling and teasing and approaching the tips without touching them. "Oh, you like it when I do this."

I squirmed at the tension. I wanted him to bite and suck me. Sweat beaded on my forehead as he teased me for minutes, not saying anything but watching my reactions. "Dean."

"Are you wet for me?" He hummed.

"Find out yourself," I ground out, thrashing at this point. The orgasm was growing, building slowly behind the scenes as he teased the ever-loving fuck out of my breasts. "Touch me."

"Show me." His eyes flashed dark. "I'm going to keep teasing your perfect tits while you push your panties to the side and show me."

"Holy shit." I trembled with want as I slid my shorts off, staying in my black cotton boy shorts. They weren't sexy by any means, but how Dean stared at them? He made me feel like I was in lingerie. The weight of this whole thing hit me as nerves hit me. Dean Romano was teasing my nipples and wanted to see my bare pussy. What…

"Don't get shy on me." He leaned forward, licking the tip of my nipple before biting my mouth. "You want me, and I want you. Don't make it more than that. Now show me how wet you are."

I whimpered as I slid my panties to the side and exposed myself. Dean hummed in approval.

"Good girl. Now touch your clit for me. Go in small circles, yeah?"

"Fuck, Dean." I closed my eyes, the sensation almost too much. "I'm close."

"Keep your eyes open. I want to see what color they are when you come for me." He *finally* fucking touched my nipples, pinching and pulling both of them. The pain matched the rhythm of my finger, and I bucked. "That's my girl, fall apart."

He bent down and sucked one breast into his mouth, biting and nipping the tip for a full minute before swirling his tongue around it. It was so sensitive, every swish of his tongue sending my nerves on edge. His teeth closed on it, and he tugged, hard.

"*Dean!* "I moaned, releasing my hand and gripping the table.

"Yes, Mack," he urged, moving toward the other breast, repeating the process. "Do you like my mouth on your tits?"

I couldn't speak. I couldn't move. He pulled my nipple so hard the sting made my eyes water, but his hand never left my other one, and he did the opposite, caressing and teasing. The pleasure and pain line blurred, and *holy shit.* The orgasm consumed me, head to toe, tingles and fireworks exploding off in a rhythm through my core. I violently shook as the slowest burn, most aggressive orgasm started at the base of my gut and floated to every limb.

Pleasure unlike anything I ever had consumed me, making me blind as I drifted out of my body. Dean hovered over me, fully clothed, as he continued using his tongue in wicked ways on my chest. His own moan vibrated my skin as I came down, and the dark heat in his eyes was terrifyingly beautiful.

He looked half-human at this point, tensed muscles, dark pupils, and perfection. He was so gorgeous, and *what just happened?*

I panted, making awful sounds to breathe again as I pushed up. "What the shit was that?"

“That was a nipple play orgasm.” He looked smug, way too smug as he ran his hands down my ribs and toward my thighs. “You’re gorgeous when you come.”

“Jesus, Dean.” I blushed hard and looked away. “Are you always so… extra with your hookups?”

“Yes.” He grinned, kissing my stomach a final time. “Now, where is your list? Let’s check this one off.”

CHAPTER **TWELVE**

Dean

I was hard as fuck. My body trembled for release, all the blood resting in my dick, and god, it was challenging to breathe. She lay there, naked and satisfied and vulnerable for me. Mackenzie Mallinson. Soccer star and tomboy and girl who'd taken me by surprise. I licked my lips as I grinned at her, content for the first time in half a year. "Where is the list?"

She laughed softly and pushed up. "You might be more into this list than I am, Dean."

"We're competitive. It's a whole thing." I adjusted my cock in my pants, my eyes blurring with how horny I was, as I moved toward the small living room area. The paper sat on the coffee table, and I picked it up, scanning it. "Hm." I struck out the two we could check off, wishing I could write *my* name in there.

It'd be foolish. I wouldn't do that to her or my sister, but damn, I wanted to insert myself into her plan, officially. "You're not making out with other people in one night."

The Summer Playbook

- ~~Buy a guy a shot~~
- ~~Mixologist challenge – ask bartender to let you make a drink~~
- Skinny dipping
- Get a makeover
- Tattoo
- ~~Take a body shot off someone~~
- ~~Someone takes one off you~~
- ~~Grind with a stranger or someone~~
- Make out with two people in one night
- ~~Hook up past first base with a stranger/someone~~
- ~~Be naughty in public~~
- Ask three guys out
- Dance on a bar
- Streaking
- Dance in the rain
- Concert
- ~~Join a game already going on with strangers~~
- Bonfire (talk to five strangers)
- Wear an outfit you normally wouldn't wear
- Dye your hair a new color
- Crash an event (or wedding for bonus points)
- Lose the cell phone for a whole day
- Strip Poker

"How do we get around that one then, since I've only made out with you, one person?" She came up behind me, her clothes back on. The blush still covered her face and neck, her nipples perfectly tight and hard under her sports crop top. Her eyes seemed bluer, lighter, and I ran a hand over her shoulder. Her skin was magnetic, pulling me toward her. She responded to my touch in a way I wasn't used to. There was no performance, just pleasure, and I clenched my jaw to stop from groaning. Today was about *her.* Not me.

Plus…nerves still existed deep in my gut. They weren't gone by any means, but Mack helped settle them down. She wasn't out to get me. She wasn't selling my story or lying or tricking me into anything. She wasn't here to play me.

She leaned into my touch, and fuck, I liked that. "Make out with me again. Then it's two times," I teased, already back to the list where I plotted to make more of challenges happen between us. Strip poker? Yeah, that was just with me. Dyeing her hair? I loved the purple bits in them, but she'd probably want to do that with her girls. Losing her phone for day? We could drive out to the lake an hour out of town.

Fuck, that sounded perfect.

"Dean," she said, her voice all throaty and deep. I stilled, instantly snapping my gaze to her. Her teeth grazed her bottom lip, and her eyes grew large. My voice stuck in the back of my throat with how heated her gaze was.

"Yeah?" I croaked out. Her fingers danced up my arms, over my chest and down my stomach. She took a shaky breath, her cheeks turning pink again. What I would give to know her thoughts. A million dollars? Yeah. Probably that.

She moved her fingers the waistband of my pants, and I sucked in a breath, going absolutely rigid. The tips of her fingers grazed my cock, and holy shit, her touch was a blast of lust. I stilled her hand, my heart beating so hard it couldn't be healthy. I felt every thud through my body, from my toes to the top of my scalp as she moved closer. My eyes fell shut as her lips grazed my neck, her breath tickling the sensitive area beneath my ear. "The deal was we'd go through the list together."

I swallowed, my skin heating. It had been *months* since my

body reacted to a woman, to anyone else. I'd spent a lot of time with my hand, and now this beautiful girl was touching me. Breathing was hard. I wanted everything, everywhere all at once. I craved her mouth, her spread thighs, her sounds, her touches. I said none of that and closed my eyes, and when she ran her hand over my length, I moaned.

"God, Dean." She stood in front of me, her breath hitting my face as she teased my cock again. She fisted me, and my eyes snapped open. Her cerulean blue eyes were wide and heated, staring at me with the same want reflecting back at me. "You need to move past first base too."

"Mm," I said, taking a shuddering breath. "Take my dick out and stroke it, Mackenzie."

She gasped before licking her lips. *She likes my dirty talk.* I smiled, groaning as she did as I said, "Keep your eyes on me."

She obeyed, and I couldn't stop myself from saying, "Good. You listen well."

Her lips parted as she stroked my cock head to base, my length too long for one hand. She fisted me with both, a little sexy sigh leaving her mouth.

My head tilted back as she stroked me tenderly, like she didn't want to hurt me, but I wanted *more.* "Harder. God, your hands feel so good."

I leaned onto the couch, needing to sit down for this. My limbs lost control, and my balance was shit at how fucking good it felt for her to touch me. She kneeled now between me, her gorgeous face right in front of my dick. I gripped the side of the couch, needing to hold onto something as she pumped me. Closing my eyes, I groaned as I bucked my hips forward.

"Eyes on me, Romano. I want to see your face when I make you come."

Fuck me. The bossy tone, the attitude—I was hot as fuck for

her. I snapped my gaze to hers, and she smirked. "That's a good boy."

I shuddered. She was perfect. The tone. The face. The stroking. She didn't let up. She bit her full swollen lip as she pumped me, her face set in a serious expression.

"Jesus, Mackenzie," I swallowed as my thighs tensed. "I'm gonna come."

She pumped me harder, using one hand to tug on my balls as I came *hard.* My vision blurred, my body hummed, and pleasure steamrolled through me, knocking me on my ass as ecstasy flooded my veins. *So good. So damn good.* I panted, trying to make the high last longer because holy shit. I spilled all over her hands, my stomach.

That was incredible.

It was a hand job, that was it, but Mack kneeling between me, calling me good boy, her triumphant grin made this… everything. "Kiss me, now."

I cupped the back of her neck, needing to kiss the smile on her. I wanted to taste her joy and suck it out of her mouth. She moaned into me as I slid my tongue into her mouth, claiming her, thanking her, desperate for her to feel how much this meant to me without words. She helped me gain parts of myself back, and I would never forget this.

"Dean," she said, laughing as she broke apart our kiss. "I need to uh, wash my hands."

I made a mess on her, and *fuck* that was a new fantasy to add to the list. I wanted to come on her body and smear it over her. *Dude.* That was new. I sat back, more content than I had been since the fall, and I couldn't stop the grin. "Is it wrong to say you look fucking hot all messed up?"

She shook her head, blushing. "I-I like it too."

My eyes widened. "I'm thinking we're gonna need our own

list that includes all sorts of things we can do before the summer is over."

She didn't respond to my comment, but she stood up and stared at me with an unreadable expression. "I'm gonna change and wash my hands. Then I was gonna probably go for a run."

Disappointment hit me right in the chest. Was she kicking me out right after we got off? *God,* how many times did I do this to girls? It sucked. I kept my voice even, unaffected. "Were either of those invitations for me, or do you want me to go?"

"You gonna help me change my outfit?"

"I sure can. I'm a big fan of you taking off your clothes," I teased.

The sparkle returned to her face, the playful curve of her lips a welcome sight. Things were weird for a second or two, but it felt good now.

"We could run together. I also found this new protein shake I plan to try tonight if you're up for it."

"I'm down."

I was so down for this girl; it was good we had a timeline. I thrived on a time clock and left everything on the field every game. This was no different. I'd go hard, enjoy every second, but when the buzzer went off, I'd walk away.

Our football workout schedules for the summer were set by mid-June. Skill positions tended to have morning workouts; linemen were in the afternoon. Going into my senior year meant I didn't have to take a summer class, but our coaching staff insisted that the younger guys take one either online or in person. It felt amazing to not worry about school this summer. I could focus on working out, preparing for the season, and *hanging out with Mack.*

Last year, I partied every weekend, hooked up just as often, and was an idiot. I met Jessica at the Fourth of July party, which fucked up the next four months of my life. Never again. I ran a hand down my face before going back to the machine. Morning workouts today helped wake me up and set the tone for the day. But… I missed helping Mack with the soccer camp. They were back at the girl's stadium today now that they were done with the seeding, but I loved doing that. I sent her a quick text for an update on how it was going, secretly hoping she'd want to hang after.

Even after working out with her and having dinner, I woke up wanting to see her again. It was wild, but hey, it was a new summer for me. My summer of getting back to myself. I had researched some online counselors to talk about what happened. I hadn't scheduled anything yet because it made my skin crawl, but I looked, and that was a good step.

"Hey, is Coach running summer camps again?" I asked Callum as he worked on his thighs. The dude was a tree trunk as he grunted, lifting a few hundred pounds with his legs alone.

"Yup. He has the sophomores running them thankfully. I did it last year, and it was tiring as hell." He pushed the machine again, his face straining. "Why?"

"I helped Mack with the soccer camp last week, and it was more fun than I thought."

"Ah, yeah, you never had to run camps, you bitch." He laughed. "Damn specialty positions never experienced the hazing. It wasn't too bad but a lot."

"You ever think about the younger generation?" I wrapped a towel around my neck, holding each end of it as it rested on my chest. I'd already run a few miles, did my rotations of full body lifts for the day, and now I avoided going home to the empty house. "Lo and Mack do all this shit to spread awareness and reach out to other generations, and what do we do?"

"Post thirst traps because that's what our fans want." Callum did a few more reps before getting up. "People don't follow you for anything but your arm and your face and championships."

Jesus. I fisted my hands. That was what my friend thought of me?

"Dude, don't look at me like that." Callum narrowed his eyes. "I don't feel that way. I know you're a great person and the main reason the team is as successful as we are. You're a good fucking leader and work your ass off. What I'm saying, is your image online is curated for the fans, not for *you.* If that's bothering you, do something about it."

He shrugged but then his attention moved over my shoulder. He squinted, and I followed his gaze until it landed on our new athletic trainer. She wore black glasses and had long black hair tied up with a bright pink hair tie. She hurried toward a group of guys working out in the back, and Callum studied her until she was out of view.

Interesting.

"Anyway," he said, shaking his head. "You don't think I'm aware of what my image is? Playboy? A little bit of a whore?"

"A little?"

Ha laughed. "Fine. A lot of a bit. I'm a risk based on my reputation and image. I'm cool with it. I don't have the same pressure you do being the QB, but I control my image for me. I love being the untroubled, no-feelings guy. I'm about having a good time, and people know what to expect with me. They lower their expectations, and it works out."

A twinge of pride and jealousy mixed together. I wanted to be that sure of myself, that confident. I felt that way on the field, but off? I used to party hard, have a good time. I also used to train so much my coaches told me to chill. It was like Callum and Luca had a weird love child, and that was me. Not quite falling into Callum's carefree world and not finding a spot in Luca's pure determination and focus.

Then Jessica came in and fucked it all up.

"How are you so confident in who you are?"

"Dude. I have three older sisters. I basically had four moms." He laughed and put his hair in a half bun thing on his head. "They made me feel like I was the coolest person in the entire world. I started believing it at one point and never stopped. Try it. You're legit, man."

He slapped me with his towel before the girl with the glasses came back into view. His entire posture changed, and his nostrils flared. There was a story there. "Who's the new girl?" I asked.

"Ivy Emerson. She's one of the athletic trainers this season."

"Did Coach introduce her?"

"No." He frowned, running a hand over his jaw. "Why?"

"Curious how you know her name. I've never seen her before." I fought a smirk. Was this the moment Callum had his first feeling? I wanted a front row seat. "She's kinda cute. I might—"

"No." He glared at me. "You keep pretending you're not into Mack. Don't get involved with Ivy."

"Is this you getting into Ivy?"

"*No.* I've known her most of my life. She was my best friend for over a decade."

"And why the hell haven't we met her? Did she just transfer?"

"No." Callum's jaw tensed as Ivy spoke with Xavier, one of the newer guys on the team. She laughed and pushed her glasses up that had slid down her nose. "There's a reason I haven't brought her around you guys. Now, I need to finish working out. We can catch up later."

He stared at her for a long second when her gaze caught his. Her eyes widened, her posture straightening. Then, she looked away. *Weird.* That wasn't how best friends treated each other.

Very interesting. I needed to text Lo about this so we could dive deep into what this meant. Even knowing I could message her again made me smile.

Dean: Callum and Ivy. You know about this?

Lo: His childhood friend? I think he mentioned her once.

Dean: how TF did you two gossip about this?

Lo: When Callum and I became wallmates.

Dean: Well, she's working for the team this season.

Lo: Oh, this is gonna be FUN. HA.

I still had my phone in my hands when Mack texted me, and you would've thought it was my first time talking to a girl with how much my stomach swooped.

Swooped. Like I was teenager lusting after Harry Styles.

Mack: It's supposed to rain tonight, AND I found a concert. Want to come with me? If not, no worries, I'll go alone!

Like hell.

Dean: I'll be there.

Mack: I'm wearing something I wouldn't normally wear too ;)

God, this girl was gonna kill me.

CHAPTER **THIRTEEN**

Mack

There was something about country music in the summer. I preferred rap or heavy rock while prepping for a game. The fast bass and energy of the songs pumped me up before showtime, but when there wasn't soccer or a physical competition looming, country it was.

Songs reminded me of laughing at the lake, getting sunburned, running with sparklers on the Fourth of July, and now, there'd be this perfect image of Dean Romano swaying his hips side to side with a bandana folded into a thin line and wrapped around his head.

He held up his phone so it mirrored a lighter and put his arm around me as we swayed to the song about whiskey and women. He smelled like sweat, sunscreen, and spicy cologne that created the perfect combination.

"This is the best date ever," he said, lowering his face so his lips grazed my ear. "You're a dream. This is a dream."

I blushed. Dean had a few shots before we left, and tipsy Dean was my new favorite. He spoke his mind, unfiltered thoughts running together. But the biggest difference was he seemed genuinely happy. He carried himself lighter. I wasn't foolish enough to think it was *me,* but if I kept earning those smiles with this damn list, then I'd never stop.

Five more weeks.

Football took off in five weeks, and that was the end of this… thing that we were doing. *Unless we finish the list first.* My stomach soured, and my heart beat harder at the fact I was already in too deep. How could I not be when Dean touched me like this and said things like that?

"Why aren't you smiling, Mackenzie?" He tilted my face toward him, his brows drawn in concern. "You're frowning."

"What? No." I shook my head hard.

"Yes. I've been staring at you a lot the last few seconds, and you're not wearing your smile lines." He traced one finger along the side of my eyes, then down to my lips. "Do you need something? I can run to the concession stand."

"No. I'm great. I got caught up in my thoughts." I smiled, my body warming at his concern. He pulled me tight against him, our chests pressed together as he wrapped his arms around my shoulders. "Uh, Dean?"

"We're dancing. Just hold onto me."

I buried my face into his chest, breathing him in as the song ended and moved into a slower one. It was about summer love, regret, and living in the moment. *How fitting.*

Dean hummed, and the vibration from his chest soothed me. He was a decent singer—who knew? I loved that I got to hear this part of him. Dean Romano liking country music? That went against his image.

"I like the bodysuit, by the way." He ran a hand over my spine, the back of the suit almost nonexistent. It had an American flag on it, dipped low in the front, and I paired it with short, cutoff white shorts I found. This exposed so much of my skin and made me nervous, but the second Dean saw me, his eyes never left me.

It was his idea for us to both wear red bandanas in our hair. We looked like a couple, and he touched me like one.

"Seriously, Mack, this outfit is sexy as hell." He ran a finger under the strap.

I shivered.

"I want it to rain so we can check off dancing in the rain. You? Wet? Please. Yes." He laughed at his comment and ran his nose along my neck. "You smell delicious."

This man made my head spin. I didn't respond before he sucked the spot right beneath my ear.

"You're mine all summer, Mackenzie Mallinson." He lifted his head, meeting my gaze with a hard and serious look. His face was set in determination, and his eyes heated with intensity.

Was he expecting an answer to that? I swallowed and found my voice because I couldn't let him have the last word. "Actually, You're *mine*, Dean Romano."

His answering grin told me that was the right thing to say. Laughing, he guided us away from the dance floor and toward the entrance to the venue. He held my hand hard, our fingers intertwined. Something about seeing our limbs all tangled up made it seem more intimate than a summer fling. My breath caught in my throat as Dean ordered us two shots of tequila.

"Country makes me think of shitty beer and tequila, and honestly, I have no idea when I'll get to do this again, so let's live it up, baby." He handed me the neon pink plastic shot glass. "God, you're gorgeous."

Something was different about him tonight, and I couldn't figure out what. He complimented me with more intensity and made me wish that we were real. That this was legit. Even though I knew our time would end in heartbreak because our sports would always come first.

He jutted his chin toward the shot, and I took it back, wincing at the harshness of the liquor as he pulled me into him. There was no time to stop as he kissed me. He gripped my chin, forcing me to glance up as he devoured me. The taste of tequila lingered on his tongue, and he groaned into my mouth, the sound deep and sexy. I squeezed the edge of his red, white, and blue shirt, needing to ground myself because this wasn't just a kiss, it was a devouring.

He swiped his tongue inside, his hand tightening on my throat and the other on my ass as he took the kiss deeper. His groans grew. His tongue went faster, harder. He stole the air from me but then breathed into me when something hit my head.

My eyes flew open, and Dean stared back at me, not stopping the kiss at all. My stomach swooped again just as the same weird feeling repeated itself.

Wait.

"It's raining. Fuck yes," I shouted against his mouth. "Dean. It's raining!"

"Sure is, Mallinson." He settled both hands on my shoulders, and we looked up at the sky as I laughed.

"Top ten moment," I said, my face hurting from how hard I smiled. "The music, the company, the rain. I'll never forget this specific snapshot of life. The list might've been dumb, but this is magical."

"I'll never forget it either."

His voice sounded off, and I glanced at him, only to find him watching me with hooded eyes. His nostrils flared, and some strands of hair escaped the bandana, so they stuck to his forehead. Water dripped down his neck, over his chest and forearms. He was a real-life wet dream of a human.

"If the football team ever needed to raise money, you could do a calendar of you guys in the rain." I took a shaky breath. "You look so sexy right now, Dean."

"I can't stop watching you." He licked the side of his mouth, his gaze heating as he looked me up and down. "I want to peel this outfit off you and trace every part of you with my tongue. That's all I'm thinking about. What does your skin taste like here?" He caressed my stomach. "Or here?" He moved down to my waist. "Or here?" He tickled my inner thigh as he shuddered.

"Don't forget, Romano, that this goes both ways." I touched his chest. "I want to run my tongue and teeth over here, down your stomach." I ran my finger down, resting over his abs before dipping a finger into his waistband. "Then down here."

"*Fuck*." He closed his eyes. "Is hooking up in public on your list? I need to touch you right fucking now."

"Already did." I laughed as his hands shook. "How about we finish dancing in the rain then we head back and do all the things we want?"

"Yes. Whatever you want, dream girl."

"I don't know if Lo is home," I whispered, standing outside the door to my apartment. Nerves choked me. How could I be so stupid? "I didn't think about this."

"Fuck." Dean ran a hand over his face, the guilt etched on his mirroring mine. "Can you sneak me into your window? I'm not walking away from you tonight. Don't ask me to."

"Okay. Shit. I could… let me go in and see? I'll text you."

"You have two minutes." He cupped my face and kissed me hard. "You're soaking wet in a bodysuit, danced on me for hours, and my dick can't take it anymore. Put me out of my misery."

I snorted. Me? Making Dean miserable? I loved it.

"Wait here. I'll text you."

He rolled his eyes as I went inside our place. The lights were out, but sometimes Lo went to bed early. My heart thudded as I scanned for signs of her. There was nothing out of ordinary. Perfect.

I tiptoed to her room and almost cheered in relief when her door was wide open, and the room was empty. Hell. Yes.

I sprinted to the front door and flung it open. Dean's eyes widened as I gripped his shirt and yanked him inside before jumping on him. He laughed as he slammed me against the door, kissing me hard.

"Fuck yes, Mack. Arch those hips into me."

I had never been attracted to anyone so much in my life. I thought I would burst and die with how turned on I was. My body had never felt so alive, so on fire in the best way. I couldn't get enough of him. I clawed at his back, ground into his erection, and kissed him with everything I had.

He returned the urgency and walked us straight to my room. He kicked the door shut before tossing me onto the bed. He ran a hand over his face, pressing his eyes for a second before he opened them and said, "You're unreal right now."

"Then stop staring and do something about it."

"Fuck, you're perfect." He breathed hard, panting, and he bit the middle of his lip. "I have… I have this fantasy right now."

"Oh?" My skin heated even more. "What is it?"

He undid the bandana in his hair, the same serious, sexy expression on his face. Like I was the most important thing he'd ever seen. Like I was an item from the playbook. "I want to tie your hands with this."

Heat flared through my body, my core pulsing. Dean planned to tie me up? I'd let him do whatever he wanted to me. I nodded.

"Use your words, Mack. I've never had this urge before, but seeing you lying there, nipples poking through your outfit and wet hair everywhere… I want to tie you up as I taste you. Do you want that?"

"Y-Yes." I gulped.

Dean grinned. "Arms above your head, baby."

Baby. Dead. I was dead. "Wait, the bodysuit—"

"It's staying on."

He kneeled next to me, the summer smell of rain and sweat filling me as he leaned over with the bandana. I sucked in a breath as he kissed each wrist before tying the fabric around them, binding my hands so I couldn't move them apart.

Once it was secure, he leaned back, and his eyes were on fire. No other way to describe how dark and big his brown eyes got. "Look at you, Mackenzie." He shook his head, a ghost of smile on his lips. "You're gorgeous like this. All tied up and waiting for me."

"Didn't know you were into this kink, Romano." I squeezed my thighs together, the lust in Dean's gaze making me even hotter.

"I wasn't until you." He bit his lip again as he traced the outline of my nipple with his finger. "Mm, I love your tits."

I shuddered.

He kneeled over me, one thigh on either side of my legs as he bent forward and tugged my earlobe with his teeth. "I want you to fall apart. That's my goal, have you screaming. Is that okay?"

I nodded.

"Words. If we're doing this all night, I need explicit words, Mack." He licked down my neck and over my chest, around my nipple, and sucked me through the fabric. I bucked up, the sensation so hot I moaned.

"Yes, please."

"Thatta girl, always using manners." He chuckled as he slid down my body, his hands stopping at my shorts. "I'm a big fan of these shorts. I stared at your ass most of the night."

"I'm thinking about keeping them."

"Oh, you absolutely should." He undid the button and zipper, sliding them down my legs as he stared between my thighs. "This *snaps?* Holy shit. Why is that even hotter?"

"Are you gonna stare at it or undo it?" I said, knowing how he'd react.

He sucked in a breath and ran a finger over the soaked fabric. "All this for me?"

"Eh, could be the rain."

"You little tease. You like giving me attitude, don't you?" He undid the snaps one by one, his eyes never leaving mine. The crack of the metal snaps echoed in my room as his nostrils flared.

He undid the bodysuit, and his eyes widened when he realized I was bare underneath it. The ragged breath sent a flutter of anticipation through me. I had never felt so powerful in the bedroom. The tequila helped ease any self-doubt that Dean Romano couldn't possibly be into me because the way he stared at me, his mouth parted and eyes wild? He was into me. *So* into me.

He ran his hands up and down my thighs, his fingers shaking, as he lowered himself to the ground. "Put your feet on my shoulders, Mack, and don't move your arms."

CHAPTER FOURTEEN

Dean

My entire purpose in life was to please this woman, in this moment. It was clear by the way she thrashed beneath my touch, the way she sucked in a breath when all I did was blow on her inner thigh. Mack kept her restrained hands above her head, and right before I flattened my tongue against her, I met her gaze.

My heart thudded twice, the same way it did right before I ran onto the field every game, and I used the same mental energy and focus on her that I did as a quarterback. Gripping her thighs, I slowly teased her pussy, gently tracing along where she wanted me most. She arched her back, letting out a desperate grown.

"Patience," I whispered, before licking her again. I fucking loved how her thighs tensed, her thick muscles clenching. Her legs were gorgeous and strong, and after I made her come once, I'd bite into those thighs. My finger shook as I kneaded her skin, while my focus was on her wet pussy. "I can't decide between dragging this out or letting you come."

"Please, Dean. My body is on fire."

"We can't have that, hm?" I lowered my mouth again, dragging my tongue over her clit in slow, rhythmic flicks. I never changed pace as I licked her, and after a full minute, her body trembled. After hearing her come before, I needed to see it again, this time from my mouth.

Next time will be my cock because one thing was for sure: I was nowhere near done with her. A blip of worry pinged in the back of my mind, but it disappeared as her body flew off the bed as she moaned. "*Yes, Dean!*"

I continued my rhythm as she came on my mouth. Going down on a girl wasn't something I usually loved doing because it required a level of trust and intimacy I never had with hookups, but with her? I'd do it every day. The way her ass jiggled in my grip, her muscles clenching, her nipples pebbling for me? It was an addicting sight. "That's it, come on my tongue."

"Fuck," she groaned, her deep satisfied sighs hitting me right in the chest. She wiggled and let out the sexiest sounds until she stilled. Her chest heaved, and the pulse at the base of her neck beat erratically.

"You're so sexy." I kissed her inner thigh. "I love seeing you like this."

"A hot mess with my hands tied up?" she said, her eyes still shut. "That was the best orgasm I have ever had, Dean. I don't want it to get to your head, but holy shit. You kept going slow, and it annoyed me, but damn, the buildup was wow. My pinky toe is tingling from how good that felt."

My ego grew four sizes. I grinned at her while the ridiculous competitive urge that was deeply ingrained in me went *we can do better.* "Too bad *come hard on a football player's face* isn't on your list."

"I might add it just to cross it off."

I snorted and spread her pussy, eyeing it as my cock twitched. Usually, hookups were a means to an end. With her though… I was in no rush. Despite pre-coming so hard my shorts had a wet spot, there was no urge to get off. Instead, I hoped to give her an even better orgasm, to use this to show her how much fun it had been hanging with her. "Roll over onto your stomach."

She flicked her eyes open. "Oh?"

"Yup." I grinned at the uncertainty in her eyes. "Mack, your ass is insane. I want to play with it before getting you off again."

"Play with… my ass?"

"I'm not going in it today." I rolled my eyes, the thought of doing that some night though enough to have me stroking my cock and groaning. "Someday, maybe."

She gulped. "Do I untie my hands?"

"No. Not yet."

I helped her roll over to her stomach, her head tilted to the left while I stared at her spine where her tied hands rested. The suit hadn't been lifted over her ass yet, so I slid it up higher and higher until I could spread her thighs and see everything. *Fuck.* She was soaked, and I ran a finger through her.

She hissed and wiggled her hips.

"Your ass is my *favorite.*" I dug my fingers into it, rubbing the thick, strong glutes. She had a huge ass, but it was solid. All muscle. All earned. I gripped both cheeks before running my tongue over one and biting down. I sucked on her skin.

"Did you bite me?"

"Yes." I kissed softly over the bite mark, hoping to ease the sting. "You're delicious everywhere I licked you."

"You're wild, Romano. Wild."

"For you, yeah." I laughed against her ass, licking and kneading all over her. I wanted to bury my face in her ass, tease her entrance to see what she'd do, but I didn't want to push her. A part of me knew I was focusing on her so much because there was still a flicker of hesitancy of sleeping with her.

It wasn't her. It was me. The ghosts of the trauma I hadn't gotten over.

With one hand on her ass, I used my other to play with her clit again. She let out a throaty moan as I played with her. I bit, licked, then stroked her clit, over and over until sweat pooled on her lower back. With a swipe of my tongue, I licked that up too as she bucked against her bed in slow movements. "You want me to fuck you someday?"

"Jesus, yes."

"You want my cock in you right now?" *I can do it.*

I hadn't slept with anyone since Jessica, and the thought of actually doing it had me more nervous than I cared to admit. My pulse thudded, and my stomach twisted.

"Please, Dean. I *need* it. I'm so hot I'm gonna burst if you don't fuck me. If you won't, get my vibrator then. Please. I am begging you."

Holy shit. The perfect answer.

"You have a vibrator? Show me." Damn. My voice came out all husky and deep, like I was on my last thread. I kinda was. "I want to fuck you with it. Where is it?"

"Middle drawer."

I leaned over, opening the drawer and pulling out a sleek purple vibrator. "You use this a lot and think of me?"

"Yes."

Hell yes.

My skin buzzed with her answer. The thought of her using this while thinking of me was enough to have me panting with need. Every touch sent a current through me. The way she lay there, spread open and trusting and gorgeous? Beautiful. "You're so wet."

I nudged the vibrator at the tip of her entrance, teasing her and slowly inserting it in. She stiffened for a second before relaxing. Her muscles unclenched, and she sighed, contented and loud as I gently fucked her with her toy. Switching the vibration on, I watched as she writhed like an unhinged woman.

"Dean, shit, wow, okay, *wow.* I'm so… so sensitive already I-I-I…" She ground her hips into the bed as I continued pulling it in and out, not rushing or giving it to her hard. The toy buzzed in my hand, and there was a real chance I was gonna lose it.

Her juicy ass jiggled as she ground her hips. The toy's high-pitched vibration and her throaty moans filled the room, and then she bit down into the sheets as she screamed. I couldn't handle it.

I had to stroke myself.

I kept one hand on the toy, fucking her, while I unzipped my shorts and took out my cock. I was beyond control at this point, barely breathing as Mack fell apart a second time. Her legs twitched as she rode the orgasm out, moving left to right, arching her hips and taking the toy deeper. Switching on the higher setting, I angled the toy to get her clit, and she cried out my name over and over. My cock was hard as steel, and I stroked hard. Pleasure zinged through me. After hours of foreplay, I was a live wire, ready to burst into flames. The sound of her saying my name was still in the air as I groaned, fisting myself. It barely took a minute before pleasure exploded through me like a hit to the chest—it was a slow tingle then bam, the absolute force of a truck having me arch forward. The orgasm blinded me, my hands shook, and my legs froze as wave after wave of pleasure roared through me.

"God, you're sexy," I panted, pulling out the vibrator and setting it on her nightstand. I used my T-shirt to wipe myself clean, then tossed in on the floor to deal with later. Kissing the base of her spine, I undid the bandana and helped her roll over. Her face was flushed, bright red, and her eyes *sparkled.*

I had to kiss her, just to get a taste of the joy she radiated.

Gripping her chin gently, I leaned forward and kissed her softly. "Your wrists okay?"

"Um, every part of me is okay." She grinned and ran a hand down *my* face. She traced my eyebrow, then my cheek and over my jaw.

It was pathetic, but the gesture made my throat close. It was so intimate. So… sweet. *Jessica used to touch my face too.* The intrusive thought barged in, unwanted, and I tensed as I pulled away.

Mack frowned, but she hid it just as fast. "If you were worried, the second orgasm was definitely better than the first one. I might need to be tied up every time I get off now."

"We can arrange that." I picked up her hands and stared at the red skin where the tie had been. "Let's get you ice, just in case this hurts."

"It's totally fine." She tore her hands from mine, a shield coming up on her eyes. She was so expressive. Each emotion she wore like a book. Her happiness was all smiles and light eyes, competitive was narrowed eyes that darkened with each look, and lust well… I'd grown accustomed to that. This though? She was unsure. Nervous.

It was my fault. Her simple touch to my face made me act like an idiot. She had no idea about my past issues, and it wasn't her fault. None of it was on her at all. If anything, she helped bring me back to life. My stomach soured, hating the fact my micro-action upset her even a little bit.

Fix this.

"Come on, Mallinson." I stood, held out a hand and waited for her to take it. "I think we need a snack."

"Wait." She gulped; eyes wide as she remained on the bed. "What if Lo is back? We can't go out there."

Did I want my sister giving me shit about this? Right after we talked through our issues? No. I didn't. Things were great now, and she'd warned me about getting involved with Mack, but I had to remove that look from Mack's eyes right now because the thought of her pushing me away or hurting caused a terrible pang in my chest. "Cyberstalking," I blurted out.

"I'm sorry, what?" She tilted her cute head, her lips pursed.

"Socials. Lo posts every day, numerous times. Let's see where she's at tonight."

Proud of my choice, I found my phone and quickly pulled up her feed. Her and Luca had a fun date planned and *boom.* They were at the football house. "Not coming back here tonight."

I showed her the phone, and she arched a brow. "Well done, Romano."

"I'm not just a pretty face, despite what people say. I use my brain." I tapped my temple a few times. It was easier to make fun of yourself.

"No one thinks you're *just* a pretty face, Dean. You're the coach on the field, the leader of the entire team. Everyone knows the success is largely in part of your quick thinking and split-second decisions that affect the game. Your looks are simply a bonus." She rolled her eyes as she stood—not taking my hand—and stretched her arms over her head. "Didn't realize you needed an ego stroke, big guy, especially after I told you I had the best orgasms of my life."

She snapped the bodysuit back as she pulled out an oversized shirt and slipped it on. Her comments rooted me to the spot, my heart racing for a different reason than seeing her naked. Did she view me that way? My frown was set, my face twisting in hesitation. I wanted to ask her to explain more, but that would make me look stupid, needy even. Swallowing, I took a small breath when she met my gaze.

"Dean," she said softly, her eyes narrowing as she chewed the side of her lip. "Do you think people assume you're just… pretty?"

"No," I scoffed, my skin feeling too tight for my body. "I mean, sometimes. It's not a big deal. Callum hinted at it once. I should've… I made a bad joke."

"Self-deprecating humor has a time and a place, but after hanging with you a lot the last few weeks, I can tell something is bothering you. Lo has been worried too, but she's never shared, if you're concerned. D-do you want to talk about it?" She reached a hand out but then pulled back.

I wanted her touch.

I was supposed to comfort her, remove that uncertain look on her face, and here she was, trying to comfort me. Man, I sucked at this. Jessica made me forget how to be a good partner, good lover, good *anything*. Pressing my lips tight together, I took a deep breath. "I'm not sure."

She laughed, the sound wonderful and fixing the worry wedged in my gut. "That, I understand completely. Well, maybe we can talk about it, or maybe we can have a snack to soak up all the leftover tequila."

"Yeah?" Hope burst through me. She accepted my *maybe* answer? Most people would dig deeper, demand to talk now. Everyone always wanted a piece of me, but she didn't, and fuck. I ran a hand over my chest, the pang in there growing. This girl, with her hair still wet from the rain and makeup smeared on her eyes, was really getting to me.

"We all have our own hangups, but truthfully, we never really understand how others view us, so we have to focus on how we see ourselves. Because at the end of the day, we spend the most time with our inner thoughts." She winked and left her room.

What did I do? I followed because what else could I do? This damn girl, who happened to be my sister's best friend, who also put her sport first and was just as dedicated, had pulled me in. Five weeks with her was gonna change my life, that was for damn certain. It was a good thing we planned to walk away because it was clear, things with her could get serious, and I refused to do that ever again.

CHAPTER **FIFTEEN**

Mack

Something haunted Dean. Between Lo complaining that he shut her out and the tension between them, something was off. They had handshakes and routines, and those were forgotten since she started dating Luca, and that was her worry. But it was clear to me that this wasn't a Luca thing. I couldn't pinpoint why I knew that. Maybe it was the fact I'd crushed on him hard for three years, and he acted differently now? Or maybe it was the dark look and insecurity on his face tonight.

I knew what it was like to have self-doubt. I'd lived that most of my life. I was too athletic, too tall, too focused, too much of a tomboy, too silly for dreaming of playing on the USWST. People were haters. They loved being cruel to those different than them. I had a great group of friends and teammates who were my chosen family. My parents were fine, but since they were best friends with Coach Emily, they weren't exactly my go-tos for advice. Having real friends you could trust, who built you up when you were down, made all the difference in the world.

Friends I'm lying to about Dean…

I swallowed down the thought and busied myself with making a snack. Those feelings would be ignored for the time being and revisited… never. This fling was short, and once it was over, I'd share as a fun anecdote. They didn't need to know now and tell me how much of an idiot I was being. They'd warn me to be careful, to not get hurt, and I'd agree and do it anyway. This fling with Dean was just like this Summer Playbook—a summer fling that ended in August. It'd be one last adventure before the final year of college took over.

After using the bathroom and wiping the makeup from under my eyes, I felt better and focused on making Dean more comfortable. It was strange that in the bedroom he seemed so in charge, and I loved it. My life was pure focus, and having him tell me what to do? It was hot. I wasn't the one making the decisions for once.

Yet when the moment ended, he pulled away from my touch and shared he believed people just thought he was a pretty face. The cocky guy I met freshmen year would never have said that about himself. Something had to have happened for the shift. I also wasn't one to stick my nose where it wasn't my business. I hated being on the receiving end of other's nosiness, so I rarely asked too many questions myself. Plus… this was a fling not… real, so were feelings even a thing we spoke about? I was winging this whole experience, half motivated by lust, half adrenaline.

"Okay, Romano, I have pretzels, hummus, vegetables, popcorn, or trail mix. We also have Gatorade and water." Bringing the attention to my favorite thing ever, food, seemed like the right idea.

"Pretzels are great," he said, his voice a little scratchy.

I grabbed the bag and two waters and set them on the small coffee table. He sat on the couch, legs spread because he was so large, and I positioned myself on the floor with my back resting against our small recliner. "Snacks of a champion."

"Why aren't you asking me what's wrong?" he asked, before shoving one of the sticks in his mouth. "Most people would."

Direct. Like in the bedroom. My face heated, but I used the pretzel as a distraction as I shrugged.

"Because I know what it's like to doubt yourself, and it's not helpful to talk when you're not ready."

His eyes widened, like my response surprised him. Then, they warmed, and he stared at me like I was the answer to a question I wasn't sure of, and it made my nerves flutter.

Change topic. Blinking fast, I scanned the room for a single item that would help this scenario and landed on the paper in front of me.

"Oh, the list! Let's update it!"

The Summer Playbook

- ~~Buy a guy a shot~~
- ~~Mixologist challenge – ask bartender to let you make a drink~~
- Skinny dipping
- Get a makeover
- Tattoo
- ~~Take a body shot off someone~~
- ~~Someone takes one off you~~
- ~~Grind with a stranger or someone~~
- ~~Make out with two people in one night~~
- ~~Hook up past first base with a stranger/someone~~
- ~~Be naughty in public~~

- Ask three guys out
- Dance on a bar
- Streaking
- ~~Dance in the rain~~
- ~~Concert~~
- ~~Join a game already going on with strangers~~
- Bonfire (talk to five strangers)
- ~~Wear an outfit you normally wouldn't wear~~
- Dye your hair a new color
- Crash an event (or wedding for bonus points)
- Lose the cell phone for a whole day
- Strip Poker

"Not too bad of progress with about five weeks left of summer, huh?" I held up the sheet. "Not sure how to handle asking three guys out though."

"Ask *me* out on three dates, Mackenzie."

"Well, hey, I asked you to the concert tonight. That counts."

"You didn't really *ask* though."

"I sure did, buddy." I rolled my eyes and enjoyed how he smiled again. "There is a lot of nakedness on this list. My friends suck."

"We'll find a way to knock those out for sure." He leaned back onto the cushions and closed his eyes. He let out a long sigh, and I swore I could feel the tension on him.

I wasn't sure how to comfort him. We weren't together, not really, and when I tried touching him earlier, he didn't like it. It put me in this weird spot. Did he want to leave and not know how to say goodbye? Ugh. My stomach soured at the thought, but I didn't want him to feel pressure. "Hey, if you want to head home, you won't offend me."

His eyes snapped open. "Do you want me to leave?"

"That is not what I said." My face heated. Shit. My question made the hard look come back on his face. "Dean, I can tell something is bothering you, and I'm trying to help, but I don't know how. You don't want to be touched, so I can't do that. Even though my love language is definitely physical, so figured you might want to—"

His eyes narrowed, his lips parting in shock. "I like it when you touch me."

"You flinched when I put my fingers on your face."

He closed his eyes again, groaning. "That wasn't you. I like your hands on me, Mackenzie. I'm… fuck. I hate being like this."

"What? Honest?"

"Yes." He snorted, the sound crude. "Weak."

"How is this weak, you sharing what you're going through? Explain that to me, please, because I don't understand."

"Sometimes you stare at me like I'm the coolest thing ever, and I don't want to ruin that. I like how you look at me, okay, and if I seem weak… your opinion might change."

"That's ridiculous."

"It's not though. Not to me. I love seeing your face light up when you see me."

"Well, Jesus." I cleared my throat, making a mental note to chill the hell out. The last thing I wanted or needed was to be a stage five clinger where my crush on Dean became public and pathetic. When only I knew the depth of how much I crushed on him, that was fine. Everyone else learning it? Nope. No fucking thank you.

He snorted and placed a hand on my shoulder, massaging it with his rough fingers. "Your blush never gets old."

"Not to you, but to me, yes it does. So anyway, you like how I have no chill? Cool. Cool."

"It's a compliment. You have a great face." He winced, like

he realized how dumb that sounded. He ran a hand over his head, groaning. "How am I making this worse?"

"Maybe stop talking?" Laughter threatened to sneak out. I *loved* seeing him like this.

He cackled, and the joy radiated in his eyes. "I like being around you, Mallinson. You make me laugh and feel normal, like myself, and safe. God, being on the football team seemed like a fantasy the first two years. I partied, acted like a dumbass god. But the truth is, everyone wants a part of you. Someone begs for tickets to a game, a jersey, a selfie, a way to claim they knew me before I went big, or money. Everyone wants money, but you're not like that at all."

"Hm." I chewed on the outside of my lip, letting his words wash over me. That sounded heavy. Lo told me girls used her all the time to get to her brother, so I was sure that element of it bothered him too. That was a lot of weight to carry.

"That one syllable felt like pity, and I don't want that either. It's…" He pressed his lips together tight, steepling his fingers into a triangle as he stared out the window. "I'm working through something after trust was broken in the worst kind of way. I want to share it, but I don't know how to yet. Is that okay?"

My chest tightened. Reaching out to rest my fingers on his forearm, I paused, waiting for the slight turn of his lips, before placing it on him. His skin was warm, perfect, and I gently ran a circle with my thumb. I traced the corded muscle bulging along the side. Did I want to lick it? Yes. Not the time though. "That is more than okay. You don't have to share anything you're not comfortable with, Dean."

His entire body relaxed; his shoulders slumped, the lines around his eyes softened, and the pang behind my heart grew. How was this beautiful, strong man so nervous about sharing his thoughts? Lo talked about her feelings every second of every day. I knew how she felt when she woke up, if she had to pee, or if she had her period. She wore her heart on her sleeve where her twin was the opposite.

The pang shifted to guilt, the gross feeling sliding down from my chest to deep in my gut with the lies I kept from her. Did she know about Dean feeling this way about something? Would she be horrified that we snooped on her social media to see if she'd be back? I wasn't a liar, at all, and keeping this from her felt like part of my heart was cracked. Chewing my lip, I glanced at my watch.

"I should leave, yeah." Dean stood abruptly. "It's late."

"Hey, I wasn't—That wasn't—I wanted to see the time. It wasn't a way to have you leave," I said, not wanting to be alone. There were a lot of thoughts racing in my mind, dominating for the top spot. If he left, I'd obsess over everything.

"Nah, it's not you." He smiled, but it didn't meet his eyes. "Luca would call me out if I didn't come back."

"Right. Sure." I forced my lips to curve, mirroring his grin. Both seemed forced, fake, and awkward. The twist in my gut pulled as he walked toward the door. He'd showed a different side of himself tonight, and so much felt uncovered. As he walked out the door, he paused and glanced back at me with lips parted.

Would he ask to stay longer? To end this?

I gripped the edge of the chair, breath in my throat. But he didn't say a thing. He waved and shut the door. Not two seconds later, my phone buzzed.

Dean: Lock up tonight.

Dean: Thank you

Why did that thank you feel worrying?

Mally, Vee, Ale, and Lo sat around our favorite booth at the bar as Mally pulled a napkin out of her purse. "The agenda, ladies. I spent time on this so appreciate me."

"You're a goddess," Lo said, smirking.

Ever since she shared Luca called her a goddess, she dropped the word every chance she had. Rolling my eyes, I elbowed her side. "Enough of you."

"Luca is pissed at me, thanks to you all."

"Anger sex is fun though," Vee said, arching a brow. "Especially with him, I'm sure. He could just throw you around all angry."

"Why is he upset?" Mally asked.

"The tattoos. I told him we were going with Callum." Lo snorted and took a long swig of her mojito. "Not sure if its jealousy or what, but I offered to have him come along too."

"He doesn't want one of the matching tats? Lame."

"Still can't believe we're doing it this week," Mally said, looking at me. "Speaking of tattoos and this list, Mallinson, you've made progress, and I need every single detail. Who did you go further with? You did all this? Danced in the rain?"

My face heated as my teammates stared at me. I'd prepared for this moment. I'd practiced in the mirror, but sweat pooled on my hands. Glancing at Lo, I cleared my throat. "Uh, well, I told y'all Dean wants in on the list too?"

"Dean Romano?"

"The quarterback Dean?"

"*Her brother* Dean?"

I nodded. "He said he's been in a funk and wanted to have his own list to break him out of his head and so we decided to join forces. What I do, he does. So, he's the person who is my witness to all these."

There. That's not a lie. He was the witness… and the person I did them with. Totally okay. I swallowed. "He can vouch for them."

"What concert?" Lo asked, her brows set in a hard line. That line meant confusion, which was better than anger. Or accusations.

Progress.

"Last night, outside the fair."

She ran a finger over her stress wrinkle, wiping it away in the process. Her large brown eyes, so similar to Dean's, softened as she gazed at me. "He seemed really happy this morning. He even whistled while we had breakfast over there."

Swoop. I couldn't stop my smile if I tried. My lips curved up so high my cheeks ached, and the warm, gooey feeling in my stomach grew. "Yeah? Did he…talk about it?"

"Oh no. Mack." Vee rubbed her forehead. "You know better."

Mally elbowed Vee in the ribs. "Shut up."

"What? Can we not talk about it?" Vee sighed as she stared at me, a knowing look in her eyes that had that swoopy feeling turning to lead.

Ale winced and adjusted her bangs, a clear sign she was nervy.

"Not about *what*?" Lo said, her tone hesitant.

"Dude, you know your brother. He's hot as sin to most of us, but he's nothing but heartbreak. A friend of a friend, I don't really talk to her anymore, but one of her girls dated him this fall, and he turned out to be a total dick to her. I've never really brought it up here because I know y'all are close, Lo—"

"You don't know the entire story," she fired back. "And half that shit isn't true."

"I'm sure I don't, and your brother is generally a good guy, but this girl was fucked up after they ended. Transferred schools, I heard. Mack's eyes are all heart-eye emojis right now, and it makes me nervous. I'm gonna mention it even if it's awkward."

Lo fisted her hand on the table. "Someone transferring schools is their own choice. Not Dean's. Let's stop that bullshit rumor right now."

My throat closed up. Sweat dripped down my back. This was worse than a penalty kick to end a game. I wanted to ask her about the friend of a friend who Dean was a dick to, but that showed too much interest. Also wanted to pretend this wasn't happening because what if Lo accused me of using her? I would never. And I wasn't totally heart-eyed emojis, right? If Vee saw it…then everyone probably did.

My face had to be fire-engine red as I felt them all staring at me. I ripped the straw wrapper in half, then repeated the process as the silence grew to one, two minutes. What would I say? Nothing. I had nothing.

"Look," Lo said, clearing her throat and putting her arm around my shoulder. "Dean is complicated. I love my brother, but he can definitely be an idiot at times. Most dudes are. I love the fact he's happy right now, and if he needs Mack's Summer Playbook to help him with whatever is in his head, then I'm game for it. We're here to talk about our agenda, and was my brother on there?"

I loved that she was standing up for her brother.

"No, but I have the right to add anything as the secretary. It's in our guidebook."

Lo rolled her eyes. "Okay, fine, but I have the right to veto it since I'm still chief this month, yeah?"

I snorted. "We're so *lame,* and I honestly love it. Who else makes rules about meeting? We do. Totally dorks."

"Oh for sure. My mom thinks this is hilarious and asks me about it every Wednesday. I'm proud of how consistently we've done this and stuck to our goofy rules." Vee winked and kneed me under the table, softly. "Mack, I love that you're going outside your comfort zone, and it makes me so happy to see the little mischief twinkle in your eye. If Dean is helping with it, then so be it, but be careful. His playbook is one-night stands and yours is love."

"Mm, I don't know if its love," I said, my brain whispering *liar.* "I'm also not interested in catching anything before senior year. I don't have time for *love* or feelings, to be honest."

"No one has time for it. It's exhausting and takes work," Vee said, laughing. "But it's not exactly your choice if you fall for someone. As much as I wish we could control feelings and tell them to calm the hell down, we can't. So, be careful. That's all I'm saying. I don't want my girl hurt."

"I'm fine. I won't be hurt." I forced a smile and thought of the way Dean said thank you as he left last night and the fact he hadn't reached out today. We agreed on the summer, but every day felt like it was the last. "Now, can we talk about the tattoos we're going to get?"

"Yes!" Lo leaned forward, pulling out a sheet of paper. She'd scribbled some designs, and I wanted to hug her. We'd have to have a conversation about her brother at some point, but I'd rather wait.

Because if Dean and I were going to part ways in a few weeks, was it even worth it to mention it to her? Nothing would change. With as much effort as possible, I shoved thoughts of Dean away and focused on my teammates. They were easier to deal with than my growing feelings for the complicated quarterback.

CHAPTER **SIXTEEN**

Dean

"Romano, over here."

Coach jutted his chin, and I jogged toward him at the end of the field. He had me and the backup QBs run some plays and watch film to analyze, and the others had already headed out. Brady was gunning for the starting spot, just waiting for me to mess up and get injured, but it was Jayden who I thought was the next starter. He was a sophomore, but he carried himself the way a QB should. He led with his brain, not his feelings, and wasn't afraid to make a snap decision.

"What's up, Coach?" I rested my hands on my hips, breathing in the smell of summer. Humidity, grass, sweat and sunscreen. Throw in a little stale gear and it was the perfect combination. Nostalgic in a way too.

"I've been around a while."

"You're not that old."

He laughed, the deep sound echoing off the empty field. He

clapped my shoulder before his face returned to his normal expression: hard lines on his forehead from years of squinting into the sun, eyes so blue they looked like ice, and a mustache that moved when he spoke. Coach Benson was tough as shit, and everyone in the Midwest wanted to play for him. "Thank you, but not what I was going for. My wife keeps me young."

I smiled and rocked back on my heels. Things were going well this summer, and my stats last year were great. Agents couldn't talk to me until after our last game, but enough had been around and at games that I was confident I'd find representation before entering the draft. I had my eye on two in particular who fought hard for deals and took care of the athletes. But that meant I had to have a hell of a senior year and continue my stats. *And not be distracted.*

Jessica's face, followed by Mack's, entered my mind, and I cleared my throat to get rid of them. This was not the moment.

Coach narrowed his hard eyes, taking his time staring before he nodded. "I want you to pick the captain this year."

"Wait. What?" My jaw hardened.

"You heard me. I want *you* to think about who should be captain this year. Being the captain means different things to different people, and we both know you're the leader on the team. You lead, they follow. You've had that swagger since freshman year, son, and it's not going away. My job is to win championships, prepare men for what's next, and to build a community."

My stomach bottomed out at the thought of not being the captain myself. It wasn't something I dreamed about or thought about often. It was kind of assumed I would be, and that was on me. Nothing in life was handed to you, so there was no reason I should've expected. Coach had captains keep an eye on everyone and call people out when they weren't following one of our core values: integrity, passion, and teamwork. Was it a hit to my pride not being offered the role?

A sting, not a hit.

"Okay, Coach. I'll think about it." I nodded, unwilling to show my internal reaction. "We have some good options."

"You're not upset?"

"Coach, if you think this is best, then I'm on board. I'm leading the team regardless, and if being the C helps boost another player, then I'm for it." I nodded, closing my eyes as I smiled. "That's it, huh? The responsibility of the letter, and the pride, will help another player more than it will me."

"You're departing after this season, leaving a huge gap of leadership. It'd be a disservice to this program to not grow the next leader. I want you to pick the captain and mentor them. The team looks to you as their guide. Who else should share the news of who will lead them with their character? Titles are meaningless unless people are brought into your vision. I truly believe that, and I have a feeling you do too. Now, think about it for a few weeks, and next time we're both free, we'll chat."

"You got it, Coach."

He held out a fist, and I bumped it. He strutted toward the other side of the field where some other coaches lingered, all laughing and staring at a phone. Summer vibes were different than the fall, where there was more relaxing and less pressure. Never less focus. Not with Coach Benson driving the ship.

I ran a hand through my hair, the water from the shower not drying with this humidity, and I had this restless energy that started in my chest and wiggled its way down to my legs. Did I want to run? Or walk? Or work out again? Or… what? I didn't have a job, and I didn't have anything I had to do, and I wanted something to help me work out my complicated feelings.

Mack.

The answer was so easy, so obvious, that I smiled. It was noon, hot as heck, and a perfect time for a swim. *Skinny dipping* was on her list, after all.

Dean: You busy today?

That sounded like a booty call, and after we parted a few days ago, I didn't want her feeling that. She'd been so patient and kind with me, and my chest tightened. I'd definitely avoided her the last two days, trying to get my shit together and exploring more online counselors. I even had an introductory call to just…work on my shit. But ghosting her for two days after that concert was a dick move. I scrubbed my face with my hand.

Dean: My coach dropped some weird news on me, and I need a distraction. A naked one.

Dean: Damn it. I meant to say NOT a naked one. Unless you wanted it to be? Shit. I'm making this worse.

Dean: I'd love to hang out with you if you're not busy. Whatever you want to do. List or no list. I missed seeing you the last two days.

Mack: You've lost your touch, Romano. Is this flirting? It's horrible.

I grinned, hard. Yeah, I'd fucked up the texting because I didn't want her feeling like a hookup, because she was more than that. It was a summer fling *only,* but she deserved to know I liked being around her for more than how hot she was.

Dean: It wasn't horrible. It got you to respond.

Mack: Out of PITY.

Dean: You're so selfless—put me out of my misery and spend time with me

Mack: So, we don't talk for three days and then you wanna hang?

Damn. Had I hurt her? I wanted to give her space after that

night felt heavy. Plus, I was embarrassed. It was about me, not her, but fuck. She could've easily taken it that way.

Dean: I'd like to explain in person if you'd let me. I'm sorry I upset you.

Mack: I'm about to dye my hair neon green if you want to help?

Dean: I'll be there in ten.

Neon green? She would. She'd look good too. I scratched my chest as I walked toward my car, my body already lighter knowing I'd talk to Mack. She reserved all judgement and actually listened to me when we talked. So many people listened just to respond to me. They weren't actively hearing what I said. They were so worried about their response that the conversations weren't real. They wanted to impress me or say the right thing or get something out of me.

Mack said whatever she wanted and was thoughtful in responding.

It'd be good to see her. It'd settle this unnerving feeling that had grown the last few days. It rivaled the same sensation of being on the field after a few days off.

I parked near her place and sprayed cologne on my neck because I wasn't a Neanderthal. Plus, she said she liked how I smelled, and I wanted to hear it again. Compliments from her hit different. No other way to say it.

After knocking on her door, my stomach fluttered like pregame nerves. Nerves were an expression of passion and wanting to do right. Rationally, I knew why I got the flutters before a game, but now? Was I nervous to see Mack?

The door flung open, and she stood there in a… trash bag?

"Hi?" I tilted my head to the side, checking her out. Her legs were on display, and that was it. "Are you naked under there?"

"No." She ushered me in.

I walked past her, breathing her in, and without overthinking, I ran a hand over her face and collarbone, admiring the racing pulse at the base. She stared at me like I mattered and *not* just because I played football. Her full lips were curved up, her cheeks flushed, and her eyes…. they sparkled at me.

"I'm sorry I disappeared for a few days. Last time I was here, I felt exposed with things I'm not used to talking about, and it made me feel really weird. I should've communicated it better with you, and I don't like that I probably upset you."

"Thank you for the explanation, but it's fine." She shrugged, the sparkle dimming before she leaned into my embrace. Her words didn't match her body's movements, and it carved a hole out of my chest seeing the conflict on her face.

Is she using her body and not her heart? The thought of that being true sent an alarm through me, besides the fact that I did the same thing. It was all about the list, that was it. *So why did I want it to be more on her end?*

She licked the side of her lip, totally keeping her hands to herself, before she glided down the hall. She didn't just walk, and she didn't strut. Mack glided with her strong legs and quick feet. "Want to help me with my hair?"

"Yes." Any reason to touch her? To be near her? Yes. Duh.

"Great. I'm just doing the tips, so it won't be too bad. I just mixed the dye, but it's hard to get the back of my hair, so having another person will make it easier."

JTT. Just The Tips. God, I was a fucking idiot.

"Where are you doing it?"

"Bathroom. I have a station set up. When we do this, talk to me about your coach."

Right. I texted that. Damn it. I didn't want to talk about me. I wanted to discuss her and why she seemed different. Did ghosting her for three days make a huge difference? Fuck, I hoped not.

She sat on a stool in front of the sink and had a paintbrush and foil things in front of a bowl. "Stand behind me?"

I moved behind her. The bathroom was kinda small, so it meant I touched her back. She met my gaze in the mirror, and the usual kindness was there but not the warmth I looked forward to. I swallowed. "Hey, are you okay?"

"Yeah." She frowned. "Why?"

"Did I hurt you?"

Her gaze shuttered, and the worry lines around her face deepened. Mack had a face for smiling and joy, and the frown and apprehension made everything seem off. I hated this look. Fucking despised it, and it was a sucker punch to the chest knowing I'd caused it.

"I'm struggling with a few things. I'll work through them, but the short answer is… a little. The long answer is no."

"Fuck, I'm so sorry, Mackenzie." I put a hand on either shoulder, massaging her neck with my thumbs. "What can I do to make it right?"

"I'm not sure. Honestly? I don't know what happens to us when the list is done or the summer ends. Do we stay friends? Pretend this never happened? We never really hung out before, Dean. We would be in the same place, but we didn't hang before the last month, so it seems weird to just pretend this never happened and then you disappear for a few days."

"Hey," I said softly, hating the words coming out of her mouth. "This summer is about having fun and experiencing things we can't because once the season starts? You and I won't have time to worry about anything but our sports. You'll be so focused on working out, games, tapes, and leading your team that you won't be worried about me."

"And you won't think about me because you'll have

football. Yeah." She sighed, and that little sound was a knife wedged between my ribs.

She sounded *disappointed.*

The worst of all emotions. Anger meant passion. Annoyed was temporary. Disappointed meant I wasn't living up to her standards she set for me. "No, I'll always think about you because you helped bring me back to life in a way."

"And people say girls are dramatic. Jesus, Dean." She snorted and shook her head, the tension gone from her face. "You're right though. I'm sorry. I always think too far ahead, and this summer is about fun and living in the moment and the list! The whole reason I'm dyeing my hair booger green."

"You'll be a hot booger if that helps."

And just like that, we were back. No more sighs or weird glances. She smiled so wide it was hard to look away. Every time she laughed, her nose scrunched, and there was a tiny dent between her nose and forehead, and damn, I loved that dent.

"Now, how do I help?"

She guided me through the steps to grab some chunks of hair at random at the tips and put the goo on them. There was no rhyme or reason to how she applied the color. "Just, whatever feels right."

"Mack, I need a playbook for this. What do you mean just *whatever feels right*?"

She laughed, the sound absolutely obliterating any worries that remained in my gut. This girl was pure joy and sunshine. "Pick up a few strands. Then paint them."

"You're wild."

"Wait until you see the tattoos we're all gonna get. I'm a new woman."

"Why is Callum going with, by the way? He won't shut up about it, and his comments are pissing off Luca."

"Then you have your answer. Callum is chaos. If it annoys

Luca, he'd get a face tattoo of Lo for fun. Callum, Lo, and I really became close this past year. He's a sensitive soul with a party animal personality. It's a strange combination, I know, but he's one of the girls, honestly."

"You trust him?"

"Yes. For sure."

I didn't like that. I held her silky hair in my gloved hand and dabbed the goo on it before she handed me a foil strip and instructed me on what to do. The combination smelled like chemicals and… sweet.

"Talk to me about your coach."

"Ah." I found a rhythm of taking a few strands, putting the goo on them, then using foil, and it crossed my mind that she could definitely take over at this point. She could reach this part of her hair, but I didn't want to stop. I liked doing this for her. Our gazes would meet in the mirror, and a tingling sensation would zip down my legs. "He wants me to pick the next team captain."

"Like, after you leave?"

"No." I smoothed the foil down over a chunk of hair and made sure it stuck before letting it hang on its own. "For this season."

She chewed the side of her lip, her face deep in concentration. "That's…a choice. How are you feeling about it?"

"Mixed emotions, I'm not exactly sure. It's like…I get what he's saying about me already being the leader on the field with or without the captain role. It's hard not to be when you're the quarterback."

"What else did he say?"

"That his job is to build a legacy, and with so many of our seniors leaving after this season, there isn't as much leadership remaining to continue the same driving force. He thinks, or he said at least, that me picking the captain will have more buy-in from the team."

"I have a question for you." She waited until I met her gaze, then she sighed. It wasn't a disappointed sound, but it was a resigned one, like she accepted whatever feeling she had going on. "Would being named captain change a single thing about what you'd do with the team? Would you still push them when they needed it? Call them out if they were acting like assholes?"

I nodded hard. "Hell yeah, I would."

"Because you're naturally the leader. People follow your attitude and guidance. Now, think about someone younger who has potential."

My thoughts went to Gavin or Peter or Jayden. *Jayden.* The sophomore with the grit and focus that could rival Luca. The kid was ready for whatever was next, but the team… they wouldn't respect a sophomore.

"Someone came to mind for you, I can see it on your face. But why the frown?"

"He's a sophomore."

"So? Weren't you the QB freshman year? Who the hell cares if they're in their second or third year playing? If he has the potential to be what the team needs, it's an easy choice. Now, if this sophomore was chosen as captain, would his attitude or demeanor change? You clearly don't need the C, but what would they do?"

"He'd probably be more assertive, get out of his comfort zone. He'd take the responsibility seriously and live up to it in every way. Some guys would give him shit, but he'd win them over. He's sharp as hell and fuck." I ran a hand over my face. "My ego took a hit a little bit when Coach said this, but it kinda makes sense."

"Everyone has an ego, and typically, they are good. But you, Dean Romano, don't need the C for leadership. You need to show up on the field, and the team will follow you. You have the chance to shape the next season by guiding this sophomore. That is absolutely amazing. Lo and the girls and I are hoping to find a buddy this season to mentor to do the same thing, but this? Your coach must have the utmost respect for you for him to ask you to do this. Did you ever think about that?"

I shook my head, absolutely hung up on every word coming out of her mouth. Mackenzie Mallinson spoke with conviction, with confidence, and it was hard not to believe everything she said. "So, it's not because he doesn't think I can do it."

"Not at all." She spun in her chair, staring up at me. Her blue eyes had flecks of gold and brown around the pupils, and how had I never noticed the freckles dancing along her cheeks?

"Dean," she said, her voice soft. "I'd be upset too and questioning it. Honestly, Lo could be named captain over me this year, and I'd be really upset, but at the same time, she brings so much to the table. Not being named captain won't hurt your chances of getting drafted. How you react to this will. How you lead will. Have your feelings, but you are incredible. When you play, it's clear everything else disappears and it's just you and team. You play hard and use your brain, and you're fast as hell. Watching you play—"

I kissed her. I had to. I needed to take her air and breathe her in with the words she said so confidently about me. She gasped against my mouth, the little intake of breath fueling the growing need to be as close as possible with her. "You're…" I couldn't find the words.

She was everything in this moment. The biggest cheerleader I'd ever had? The most mature college athlete I'd ever talked to? Someone who I trusted? My hands shook as I cupped her face, tilting her neck back to kiss her deeper. She tasted like mint, the tingling sensation as our tongues clashed making the kiss even better. My stomach swooped when she moaned into my mouth.

"Can I touch you?" she whispered.

My heart broke in two. She asked because she knew I struggled. *Fuck,* this woman was something else. "Yes, baby, touch me *please.*"

I picked her up, so she sat on the bathroom counter. Her legs spread, her hair in foil, she stared up at me with lips parted.

"You're gorgeous, my god. I love looking at you."

She snorted before grabbing my shirt and yanking me toward me. "You're talking to me and not your reflection, right, Romano?"

I barked out a laugh before she kissed the hell out of me. She clawed at my chest, a desperate growl coming from her as she sucked my bottom lip into her mouth. The aggression sent a bolt of lust through me, my cock swelling as I thought about her tight, strong body. God, the idea of her thick thighs clenching around me as she rode me?

I was gonna pass out from how much I wanted it.

Our kiss was teeth and groans, and I sucked her neck, wanting to feel what I did to her. She arched her back, her hands finding my waistband when the sound of a door shutting stopped me.

I stilled. Heart pounding, stomach bottoming out. The door. It meant I should stop. Door meant… *my sister.* Mack's eyes darkened, like she was mad I stopped, but then we both heard my damn sister.

"Mack! You here?"

When reality hit Mack, she sat up straighter. Eyes wide, mouth swollen and parted. "*Shit.* Fuck. She can't know we did this. No. Not after last night. Goddamn it." She slid off the counter, running a hand over her face. "Okay, okay, we have to dye your hair green too."

"Um, what?"

"Why is my brother's car here?"

God, be subtle, Lo. I groaned, trying to get my cock to settle down as my sister approached the bathroom door. She'd ask, and I had no answer besides I loved being around her best friend.

Never in my life had I ever hooked up with one of Lo's friends. It was an unwritten rule. She never hooked up with any of mine until Luca, and while it was weird at first, it made perfect sense. But the fact Mack and I hid this from her felt gross. Lo and I had just gotten to a better place after I told her what happened, and I wasn't sure how she'd react.

"Sit down. Sit on the bench now." Mack shoved me onto the stool, her cheeks pink. "We're dyeing your tips." Mack hit play on her phone, music filling the area with some old-school song my parents liked.

"Booger green?"

"You said you wanted my list, Romano. Now shut the fuck up and play along."

My lips quirked just as Lorelei joined us in the bathroom.

"What is going on?" Lo said, her gaze moving from the foil in Mack's hair to my face in the mirror. "Uh, what?"

"I told you he wanted in on the list too, even if I tried to tell him it was a terrible idea. I'm changing my tips to neon green, and now I'm adding some frosted tips to his."

"Green?" She chewed her cheek, staring at me with a million questions. "You're dyeing your hair, that is all over campus and social media, green."

"Just the tips." I shrugged, trying not to laugh. "It's for the list, Lolo."

"Right." Lo pursed her lips for a beat, a thoughtful, dangerous look in her eyes before she smiled. "I wasn't expecting this when I came home to grab lunch."

"Want in on it?" I asked, smirking at her. "Could you imagine Luca's surprise?"

"He'd find a way to compliment it even though I'm really questioning both your choices. Also, don't love the fact y'all are becoming close. Am I getting pushed out?"

"Did you and Luca push me out?" I said before Mack could respond. I regretted it immediately because Lo's face fell, and that wasn't what I wanted. I winced. "Wait, that came out wrong."

"No, it's a fair question. I'm at work all day, and you two are spending time together." Lo swallowed, her expression still upset. Call it twin shit or the fact we knew each other well, but I'd hurt Lo with that comment.

"Lolo, hey, I'm sorry. Really, that came out wrong. What I meant was to say that you and Luca didn't push me out when you got together. You include me in everything to the point it annoys me. Mack would never do that to you, you know that, and I'm just a lonely idiot who she's taking pity on."

"You're not an idiot." She sighed and punched me in the arm. Her eyes spoke for her, the concern in there swirling. We hadn't talked about Jessica since I told her, but Lo's fury and thirst for revenge would never end. Her focus went to Mack, who remained frozen. "Who would've thought this list would make you and my brother friends?"

"Honestly, not me. Never in a million years, actually. This is still weird to me too, okay? But we really do enjoy hanging out." Mack shrugged and ran a finger over her jaw, like she was nervous.

"Yeah, I can see that. You both seem happier. That, above everything, makes me happy." Lo smiled, any hint of distrust disappearing.

"Look at us, all happy and shit," I said, easing the tension. It was clear Lo knew more than she let on, but she wasn't gonna question us on it. "Want to grab lunch tomorrow near your office? We can try that salad place."

"You and me?" Lo asked, hope on her face. "I'd love that. We could play our game. It's been a while."

"What game?" Mack asked, her cute head tilting to the side.

"The make-up-stories game or the dare-and-eat game?"

"Either one. Let's see how creative we're feeling that day." Lo's eyes sparkled, the idea of a challenge spurring her on.

"Sick." I held out a fist, and she bumped it. "Now excuse us, we have some tips to frost."

"You're both ridiculous." She grinned, her and Mack communicating without words. Girls were wild with their telepathy. "Anyway, I'll let you get back to this. I need to grab my salad and go. Be ready for that tattoo tonight, Mack."

"I'm born ready, baby. Summer Mack fears nothing." She puffed out her chest.

"Obviously, because why else would you do *green?*"

"The list said a weird color!"

"Why not rainbow then?"

"Oh." Mack deflated. "Fuck. That's a way better idea."

Lo winked. "You could always add in more colors, just saying. If you bums don't have anything to do… go get more."

She tapped the doorframe before she left, and I swore both Mack and I held our breath. Her footsteps thudded into the kitchen, then out the front door. "Jesus." Mack gripped the edge of the counter, bending over and sighing for a full minute. "I hate this."

"Lying to her?" I stood and rubbed her back.

"Yes. Keeping this from her. I should tell her, but I don't want to upset her or hurt her. She's said so many people used her to get to you, and even though I had a crush on you at one point, she knew I never friended her to get to you. That's…I would never. We never even talked!"

"Wait." *Crush on me.* I knew she thought I was hot, most girls did, but a crush? "Tell me about this crush right now."

"Oh." Her face caught up to her head, and just like that, she was red as a tomato. "I said that. Shit. Uh, it was minor. Just a little thing I had."

I grinned. "Doesn't sound minor."

Had. I'd address that later.

"Dean, please."

"Did you say that to yourself and touch yourself, thinking about me? How big was this crush, Mallinson?"

"You *suck.*" She pushed off the counter and shoved me away. "It's not there anymore, okay? It's gone. I got over it when I realized nothing would ever happen because you're out of my league. It was silly."

"Wait. No. Stop." I held up a hand, her words slowly taking root. *Out of my league. It's not there anymore.* "I'm not out of your league, Mackenzie. Do you believe those words?"

"Dean. You're the hottest person on our campus! You're on billboards! I've seen how you flirt and work a room. You have hundreds of girls ready to be with you if you so much as breathed. You didn't see me that way for three years, so it's a safe thing to assume I'm not in your league."

"Mackenzie," I barked, using a tone I hadn't with her before. Her words pissed me the fuck off. More than I would've guessed. My adrenaline spiked, and I clenched my hands in fists to channel it somehow. "Never put yourself down like that in front of me again. You are fucking incredible, and I'm honestly pissed right now."

I walked out of the bathroom and into the hall just to pace and use energy. My breathing came out hard, like I sprinted, but *fuck.* She saw me that way. She thought I was some guy who would never pay attention to her, even when she was the best.

"Dean, it's not a big deal. I'm not upset or anything. It was just the silly crush I had."

"Having a crush on me is silly? That's what you're saying?"

"Thinking I used to have a chance with you in any capacity was silly." She swallowed. "That's what I meant. I had to stop my crush because its hard liking someone who never paid you any attention. You are very crush-worthy, if that's what has you angry."

"I'm not angry about *me.*" I pulled on my hair, hating how my words wouldn't form the sentences I needed to communicate this. All these thoughts and emotions all tangled together, and it sucked. "This is hard to say, and I don't know the words. Just... Mackenzie, I think you're great. If we weren't who we were, with our senior seasons on our shoulders, with Lo between us, I would want to *be with you,* but we know we can't. We are in the same league. You are ... anyone would be lucky to be with you. That's why this summer is so awesome —is because of *you.*"

I crouched down, heart racing, desperately needing her to understand how important she was to me. She'd helped me get over Jessica. She made me laugh and find joy, got me to talk about feelings more than surface level. She was *everything.*

"Hey."

A soft voice appeared next to me, like she kneeled by me.

"I have an idea."

"What?" I snapped, regretting it. She was right there, freckles and scrunched nose and patient eyes. "Sorry. I'm... what's your idea?"

"I say we go to the store and get more colors. I want to be a rainbow. Want to come with me?"

"Why are you being nice to me right now? I'm a jackass."

"Because I lied earlier." She smirked, her eyes getting that mischief sparkle again, like she enjoyed razzing me.

"About what?" I stood, wanting to learn the reason behind her smirk. "Are you a little liar, Mallinson?"

She nodded, biting her lip to prevent herself from smiling. "The crush never went away. I still very much have a huge crush on you."

The physical affect her words had on me was intense. My whole stomach flipped over, like I went down a hill too fast in a car, and my heart slammed against my ribcage over and over. *She likes me. She likes me. She likes me.*

My mouth dried up, and my palms sweated. My chest ached, like she removed a part of my soul with those words. All because she said she had a crush on me. She stared at me, her brows furrowing with the long silence, but she had to know those words rocked me.

She saw me be vulnerable. She saw me talk about things that made me weak. I shared parts of myself with her that I hadn't with anyone else, and she *still had a crush on me* despite the bad.

"Hey, if it isn't clear, my crush has nothing to do with the fact you can throw a football a decent distance. American football isn't as cool as European soccer, but it's fine, I guess."

My lip twitched, and I had to change the subject, or I was gonna propose to her. I believed her when she said she didn't care about football, and fuck, if that wasn't the hottest thing ever. "Okay, let's make a rainbow."

"No other comment?"

"Other than that, I fucking have a huge ass crush on you too?" I pulled her into a hug, kissing the top of her head. "Yeah, you made my day, Mack. Now let's get more colors because I'm not doing booger green."

"But Lo—"

"No booger green. That's where I draw the line. Now, let's get this weird UFO hat off your head and buy more. My treat."

"Settle down, or I'll fall for you more with this sweet-talking."

"That's the plan."

I had it bad for Mack. There was no other way about it. I had no idea what the fuck I was gonna do at the end of summer because one thing was certain—I was addicted to this girl.

CHAPTER **SEVENTEEN**

Mack

Tattoos were never my dream. I loved seeing ink on other people, but the thought of a needle touching my skin made me shiver. The loud buzz, the smell of cleaner… the pain. I gulped. The parlor's walls were covered with photos of ink, and loud rap music blared from the speakers. This was it. The damned list.

"What are we getting, ladies?" Callum put his arm around me and Lo, his fresh cologne a welcome scent compared to the cleaner. He ran a hand down my arm, squeezing. "You nervous, Mack?"

"She hates needles." Lo smirked. "This list is about getting outside of her comfort zone and to live a little."

"I'm living. I'm uncomfortable."

They laughed as Vee held up the idea she had. It was a small heart with a number drawn into it. "We are teammates for life, even you, Callum. I say we all get the heart with our soccer number on our wrists."

"Oh, that is so cute." Lo squealed before elbowing Callum

in the ribs. "You could have yours be a football instead of a heart?"

"I could do that."

A very large man with long hair and green eyes crossed his arms over his massive chest as he stared at us. "You all want the heart with the numbers?"

Lo's eyes widened as she stared, and I couldn't blame her. This dude was just… big. "Yes, please."

"Who wants to go first?"

"Mack does," Lo said, winking at me. "No backing out now."

Okay. I can do this.

"Love the hair," the giant man said, smiling at me. "Follow me."

"Th-thank you."

Dean and I had finished dyeing it, and the tips were rainbow now. It looked awesome. I snapped a photo and glued it to my journal. I had my Polaroid with me here too and would capture evidence once we were all done.

I took a giant breath, nervous as shit, and Callum squeezed my hand one last time before I let go. It was me and the giant man now. Just the two of us.

"First tattoo?" he asked as he gestured for me to sit in the chair.

"How can you tell? Are my nerves showing?"

He chuckled. For as intimidating as he was, he had a kind face. "You'll be fine. This is a simple tattoo. Should be fast."

"How quick are we talking?" My heart raced. Each pulse sent a warning through me, like my body knew the needle was a predator. But once I settled down the freak-out, a flicker of pride weaved its way in there. *I'm getting a tattoo.* The athlete. The tomboy. The never-break-the-rules girl who always focused on soccer and nothing else.

I could do this.

"Ten minutes, max."

He prepared all the materials, putting on gloves and scooting a small tray near us. "You want it here, yes?" He touched under my wrist.

I nodded.

"Mack Mallinson, huh? Pretty cool I get to give you your first ink."

"Wait, how do you know my name?"

The needle touched my skin with my number 12 right there. The buzzing grew, and shit, it stung. Like a million little beestings.

"I know our star soccer player, who will probably go play pro and hopefully make the national team someday."

Our eyes met, and I laughed. My first real smile. "Ah, soccer fan then."

"My whole family is. I have three sisters who play. We're fans of yours." He continued doing the heart, pausing so he could write the number in.

"Wow." My entire body relaxed. "Thanks for the support."

"Of course. Women rule the world, and my sisters will freak out if I don't take a selfie with you. When I'm done, can we?"

"Yes!"

It wasn't unheard of that someone knew who I was, since I was kind of the face of the team. Lo was also talented and good, but she wasn't trying to play after senior year. She gave it her all but would end after this season. Ending wasn't a choice for me. I was constantly posting about the future, getting young girls excited about the sport, and being an advocate to change the narrative around female sports. But to have this huge man who scared the shit out of me say he was a fan? That was so cool.

I can't wait to tell Dean.

"You're all done, Mack." He applied some plastic thing over the ink and left a list of instructions. "Leave this on a day, do not itch it, and put some cream on it if it cracks. It has been an honor giving you your first tattoo."

"Thank you so much." I hopped off the chair, grinning so hard my face hurt. He got his phone from his pocket and came to my left side as we took a selfie.

"Thanks. I might be grown man, but anything to make my sisters jealous is still fun."

I snorted. "Of course. Do I just… go pay and send someone else in?"

"Yup. Shirley will take care of you and send whoever is next back. Nice meeting you, Mack Mallinson."

"You too."

I strutted out of that room, a huge smile on my face, and ran into *Dean*? "What are you doing here?"

"Let's see it." His eyes sparkled with mischief. "I heard these vultures made you go first."

"They did." I frowned, trying to read Lo's face as to why her brother was here. She just smiled at me like it was planned. "Um, what—"

"Shirley—we gotta put a photo up of me and my girl, Mack Mallinson. I just sent it to you. Can you print it?" the giant man said, winking at me.

"Sure, Gabe." The woman with bright red hair nodded.

"Want me to sign it?" I teased.

"Please.

"Who is that?" Dean asked, moving closer to me. His tone was curt, and he lost all the playful edge he had seconds ago.

"Gabe. He did my first ink. He's also a huge soccer fan too, which was awesome."

"Come here, rainbow." Gabe ushered me toward the counter.

Vee, Ale, Mally, Callum, and Lo all stared with lips parted. Ale whispered *he's so hot, oh my god* as I walked up. Gabe was appealing in a lot of ways, that was certain. But my skin prickled with Dean's stare.

I glanced over my shoulder at Dean, who looked pissed. His eyes were hard, his jaw clenched, as he stared Gabe down. A flutter of giddiness lifted me up. Dean seemed…jealous. Which… there was no way. Right?

"Sign this for me." Gabe handed me a photo that Shirley printed. "We have a favorite wall, and I want to put this up."

"Ah, yes, so when I'm famously famous, you can reflect on this moment." I took a sharpie he handed me and signed my name and number. "You're welcome."

He chuckled. "You're fun to watch on the field and in person. Dangerous combination."

"Remember that."

His eyes heated for a second before he righted himself. "Okay, who's next?"

"Me! Take me!" Ale said, not even trying to hide her enthusiasm. We all laughed as she followed Gabe to the room, and I stared at my wrist, grinning.

"You look happy." Callum nudged my hip with his. "Nice work."

"Thanks. I feel so cool, which is so lame."

"Not lame. The whole point is to push yourself. Isn't asking some dude out on your list? You should totally ask Gabe out."

"Wait, what?"

"I was thinking the same thing!" Lo said, her eyes dancing with evil. My best friend was adding fuel to the fire. "Don't you think that would be a great idea, Dean? He was into her. She should ask him out. What's the item on the list you need with a stranger?"

"Oh uh, I don't… remember."

Shit. *Shit.* A muscle in Dean's jaw tightened, and his hands were fists at his sides. The same hands that helped me dye my hair today, the ones that gently caressed my collarbone as he spoke to me about his worries for the season. I wanted to spend time with him for as long as he let me. Not… Gabe.

"Sure you do. Come on, we could slip him your number." Callum nudged me.

I shook my head, my stomach twisting with all the secrets and feelings. Dean was pissed, that was certain, but I didn't know what to do. I didn't want to give Gabe my number. It was a perfectly fun interaction that ended here in the shop. My friends took things too far sometimes, but I wasn't sure how to escape this without giving Dean and I away.

Guilt clawed at me, scraping me inside out at how horrible of a friend I was to Lo. I shook my head, opening my mouth with the hopes the words would come out. Instead, I looked like an idiot who's face tingled with blush.

"Or we could acknowledge you're making Mack uncomfortable and let her have this moment. She got a tattoo, and she's terrified of needles. That's fucking big." Dean held out a fist, and I bumped it.

Gratitude washed over me. He understood.

Lo frowned, her entire face falling as she chewed her lip. "Dean is right. I'm sorry, girl. You and Gabe had tension though, so I wanted to play on it. You freaking hate needles, and look at you! You got a tattoo!"

"I sure did!" I held up my wrist and did a wiggle. "I know you guys are teasing me, but just… I want to savor this moment."

"Yeah, we went too far. I'm sorry." Lo pulled me into a half-hug. "We're gonna have matching tattoos for life."

"Yeah, we are." I leaned into her, breathing in her familiar perfume. I loved Lo, and the unspoken lie between us grew heavy. I had to tell her. I made a vow to tell her as soon as we were alone. "Can't believe Callum is getting one too."

"Lo, come help me decide on this. Do I do a heart or a football? Or do I do both? I'm comfortable with both, but what's sexier?"

"Jesus." Lo broke the embrace and stood next to Callum as he doodled on some paper. Vee was with them, and that left Dean and me.

"I want to see it," he said, softly.

I held out my arm, showing him the underside where my tattoo was, and he gently touched me. He grazed a finger over the plastic, his lips turning up in a cute little smile. "I love it."

"Thanks. I'm a badass now."

His eyes warmed. "Sorry I crashed. Callum texted me to come and get a tattoo with him, and I knew you were here…"

"So you came."

"So I came." He smiled at me, a soft, gentle one that made butterflies swarm my gut. Whenever he was near, life outside the two of us disappeared. He captivated me, like he always had, but my attraction to him was deeper. How the hell would I survive the end of summer?

The butterflies shifted, a wave of unease ruining the moment. My smile faltered, and Dean noticed immediately. "What's with the face?"

"Oh. Nothing." I waved my hand, pushing the thought away. *Change the subject.* "Are you really going to get a tattoo?"

"Sure. Always wanted one. What should I get?" He shrugged, like having a death needle on your skin was no big deal.

"You're so casual about this. A tattoo is forever. And it hurts. Gabe was quick—"

"Fucking Gabe." He rolled his eyes. "I don't like him."

A snort-laugh escaped before I could stop it. "You're jealous."

"He made you blush *and* smile. I like doing those things." His eyes searched mine, bounding from my left eye to the right, like he was looking for something. The lines around his eyebrows deepened, the serious set of his lips contradicting the warmth in his gaze. "I want all your cute blushes and smiles, Mackenzie."

His voice came out low, raspy, heated. His breath tickled my face, and I wanted to slam my mouth on his. We hadn't fooled around after Lo ran into us earlier. We focused on the hair job, and the urge to kiss him overtook me. This moment felt heavier than what it was. Heavier between us, like something had shifted.

"For five weeks, right?" I whispered.

He nodded, but longing remained there.

"Gah! Look at this. Gabe, you're a dream!" Ale cheered, shimmying her way out of the room. Her entrance broke the moment, and I jumped back, blushing head to toe at my thoughts of Dean.

"Let's see," I said, my voice cracking. She and I were the first ones to follow through. I'd seen enough TV shows to know my friends could back out, but I was proud of this tattoo. I loved soccer, and I was always 12. It was my birthday, December 12, and it always brought me a lot of luck.

"Holy shit, why am I afraid my parents will be pissed at me?" Ale said, eyes wide. "I'm twenty-one years old, and I'm worried about my mom. She'll hate it."

We laughed.

"It looks beautiful on you." Gabe smiled at her before his gaze moved to me. It lingered, long enough for Dean to clear his throat. "Who's next?"

"Shit. Okay. Me. Gah!" Lo shimmied and clapped, pumping herself up. "I can do this. I can do this."

"You got it, girl," I said.

She fist pumped the air and disappeared into the room with Gabe. Only Vee and Callum were left.

"Did you bring your list with you, Mack?" Vee asked, joining Dean and I near the photo wall.

"Of course." I reached into my back pocket and unfolded the paper. It was falling apart, and some of the words were blurring together. *Save it.* Frowning, I made a mental note to redo it somehow to preserve this.

"Let's see it." Vee gave me a pen, and I crossed off *tattoo.*

The Summer Playbook

- ~~Buy a guy a shot~~
- ~~Mixologist challenge – ask bartender to let you make a drink~~
- Skinny dipping
- Get a makeover
- ~~Tattoo~~
- ~~Take a body shot off someone~~
- ~~Someone takes one off you~~
- ~~Grind with a stranger or someone~~
- ~~Make out with two people in one night~~
- ~~Hook up past first base with a stranger/someone~~
- ~~Be naughty in public~~
- Ask three guys out
- Dance on a bar
- Streaking
- ~~Dance in the rain~~
- ~~Concert~~
- ~~Join a game already going on with strangers~~

- Bonfire (talk to five strangers)
- ~~Wear an outfit you normally wouldn't wear~~
- ~~Dye your hair a new color~~
- Crash an event (or wedding for bonus points)
- Lose the cell phone for a whole day
- Strip Poker

"Shit, Mack." Vee rested her head on my shoulder. "You're almost done."

My heart sank, and my gaze jumped to Dean. He had his hands in his pockets, focus right on me, but his face didn't change. If anything, he looked relaxed as hell. *Maybe he doesn't care?*

"There's like eight or nine left." I swallowed, forcing a laugh. "This summer has gone by fast."

"Fourth of July is next week." She groaned and ran a hand through her hair. "Ale and I are going back to visit my sister in Missouri. You have plans here, or you wanna come with?"

I chewed my lip, my stomach souring at the fact I only had nine things left to complete with Dean. I knew we said until summer was over, but if we did all nine of them in a week… then would we stop hanging out? I had to preserve them. Which meant I wanted to leave for the weekend to not complete the list, but that contradicted with the fact I wanted to hang out with Dean as much as possible because we didn't have much time.

"Uh, I think I might stay here," I said, snapping my attention to Dean for a second. He gave me a small nod. That had to be good.

"No worries. I figured. Lo is staying here too. I think her and Luca are visiting his grandma for a night. Will you be alone then?"

Alone. No Lo.

I was a horrible person. My first thought about Lo being

gone was that Dean could sleep over. Rubbing my temples, I shook my head. "Nah, I'll find something to do."

"Callum and I will steal her for the day," Dean said, his usual charming voice and easy smile obliterating any tension. "I've been wanting to go to the lake for a while. His family has a house."

"Oh." I rubbed my lips together. "That sounds like a lot of fun."

Dean winked. "Yeah, if you're game, we'll just do that."

"The lake with Dean Romano and Callum? Hell yeah. You better go. Shit. Maybe Ale and I should stay back and go too?"

"You're more than welcome. I mean, I'm inviting on behalf of Callum, but shit, we could make it an event."

"Hm. Let me talk to my family about it. I love my sister, but this sounds more fun." She smiled and nodded at Dean. "You're alright, my man. Wasn't sure about you at first, but you're okay."

"Wow, thanks for the weird compliment." He snorted.

It was such a simple exchange, but this moment had me thinking fantasy things. A reality that wouldn't happen. Dean *fit in* with my girls. He fit into this side of my life, which was super important. If this was real, and we were together, it would be simple. He could hang with my girls.

"Anytime, Romano. Lo is still my favorite, but I'm loving these blue tips. What the hell happened?"

I couldn't stop myself from laughing. Dean had followed through on his part of the list, and I dyed the tips of his hair blue. He looked ridiculous but still pulled it off.

"Ah, this look?" He ran a hand through his hair, the motion causing the tendons in his arms to tighten, and *mmm* he had great forearms. "Mack hooked me up. She's a rainbow, and I did blue."

"It's annoying that you still look good," I said, giving him a pointed look. "No one should be able to pull off blue tips that well."

"It's a gift."

I rolled my eyes just as Lo came out. Our attention moved to her as she proudly held her arm in the air.

"I'm inked. Gabe was my first." She turned to him. "Thank you, sweet man, for making my first time gentle."

"Jesus, Lo," Dean said, groaning.

She laughed and high-fived Gabe, who just grinned at us. "Look, I already told Mack Mallinson this, but our family is a huge soccer family. Could I get a photo with all you ladies once you're done? To quote Lo Romano, if I'm your first, I'd love it documented."

"Of course!" Ale said, giggling with Vee.

"Fucking dork," Dean said under his breath. I elbowed him. "What?"

"Should've dyed your hair green after all," I teased. "Your jealousy is showing."

Something between a groan and a growl rumbled in his chest, and I leaned closer. "At least I know I *could* use Gabe for one of the items on my list if you ditch me for three days again."

"You wouldn't dare. We made a deal, Mallinson." His eyes flashed with warning. "It's you and me, all summer."

"Or what?"

"Then I'm gonna mark you as mine. Right here." He ran a finger over my throat before narrowing his eyes. "Don't tempt me, Mack, or I'll make sure he and everyone knows you're with me this summer."

And what about when it ends?

Worry about that later.

My brain was at war, but I pushed the negativity away. This summer was about having fun in the moment. Dean was that:

fun. It took a lot of effort, but I smiled and said, “I think I’d like being marked, Romano. Maybe that should be on my list.”

“Fuck, you’re gonna kill me.” He leaned his head back and laughed. “Just wait until the next time we’re alone, Mack. Just you wait.”

CHAPTER **EIGHTEEN**

Dean

The morning after watching the girls get tattoos, it hit me that I hadn't thought about Jessica in days. There were no reminders of thinking I was a father, then not, then being lied to. The ache in my chest eased a little, and breathing wasn't as hard. I went through some exercises the counselor suggested, where I wrote out what was in my control and what was out of it. It was freeing in a way.

As I ate cereal and wasted time on social media, I could legit feel my muscles loosening as I jumped to Mack's page. She posted all the time with her series of information. She had thousands of followers and was so damn cute. A recent one caught my attention because of her rainbow hair.

I clicked on it, and she went into five ways to stay hydrated if you were playing outside in the summer. She then shared her favorite post-workout drink recipe. It was clear she loved doing this, speaking to younger players, and pride ballooned in my chest.

"When are you telling your sister?" Luca joined me at the

breakfast table, his usual face set in firm lines. "This is the second fucking secret I've had to keep from her, and it's getting old, Romano."

"What do you mean?" I asked, playing dumb. Using my looks to feign lack of intelligence helped from time to time.

"Shut the fuck up with *what do you mean,"* he growled, dropping down at the table with a loud thud. He then scooted the chair forcibly, so he was closer to me.

Okay, so Luca knew.

Guilt swirled in my gut as I closed my phone, Mack's voice disappearing. "What am I supposed to do, Luca? Mack and I are having fun, and it's no big deal. It's just a summer thing. It won't last, it *can't.* So why bring drama into it?"

"Because you're fucking around with Lo's best friend, who has a massive crush on you. You ever think that you're going to break her heart? You're a player, dude. I love you like a brother, but you break hearts. How do you think Lo is gonna feel if you kept this from her intentionally, then break her friend's heart before their senior year? After you've held her at a distance, and you just made up. She's never gonna forgive you."

I frowned. He was right, and it sucked. "That's not… I'm not a player anymore."

"Doesn't work like that." Luca pinched the top of his nose. "Lo is not an idiot. She knows about Mack's crush, and thank you for finally telling her what went down with Jessica. But you're walking a fine line of assholery right now. What's really going on? I want to understand it."

"Mack makes me feel worthy of shit, okay? She's a breath of fresh air. She doesn't give a shit that I play football, and I needed that after all that with Jessica and the previous hookups. She's fucking smart and way too mature for her age. She makes me laugh. Dude, I like being around her. And she's the first woman I've been into since that went down. It'd been *months* before her."

Luca's eyes widened, and he placed his hands on the table, intervention style. "Dean, this isn't just a summer thing. What you just said? That's how I feel about your sister. That goes deeper than a fling."

"Nah, it's just the list she has. We're completing it together, then parting ways as friends. We talked about it." Even as I said the words, they felt wrong, shallow. Did we truly talk about it? Mack alluded that she wasn't in my league, which pissed me the hell off. Did I need to revisit it to make sure we were on the same page?

Probably. Yeah. I should, to be safe. We couldn't continue because football had to come first for me, soccer for her. She told me she didn't want a boyfriend, and I sure as hell didn't want a relationship. Not for a long ass time.

"Fuck, you're annoying. I'm telling you I went through this same shit with your sister. It's not going to end well. I know you went through some horrible stuff with Jessica, but please don't hurt your sister. I can't…Lo matters in this."

"Of *course* Lo matters in this. Don't twist my words. I'd kill for my sister, and I appreciate you looking out for her, but what do you think is going to happen? Mack and I are on the same page." Anger and pride flared beneath my chest, warming me. He was protecting Lo, which I loved, but not at my expense.

"You're gonna be a dumbass, and Lo is gonna side with her best friend, and I'm gonna side with Lo. So, this shit better be worth it because at some point, the three of us and probably Callum are gonna be pissed at you."

"You're flirting with being dramatic right now, Luca," I said, gritting my teeth. "I don't like it."

"If this is real with Mack, then *tell her.* Tell Lo. Let me go back to being the guy who doesn't care about feelings. It's exhausting caring so much."

My lips twitched. "Lo does that to you, makes you feel all sorts of things, huh?"

"It's annoying, but I'll do anything she asks."

"Hey," I said, kindlier. He met my gaze. "I'll figure it out with Mack so no one is hurt or upset. I promise."

"Good. Because I've seen you be a dumbass before, and I'd hate for you to hurt yourself or Mack in the process." He tapped his fist on the table. "Good talk. Now leave me alone."

"You approached me, bro."

"Shut up."

Grinning, I watched my tight end walk away, shoulders bunched, and I couldn't stop myself from laughing. He was such a sucker for my sister. He was right though, and the thought unsettled me. The idea of hurting Mack or my sister caused me physical pain in my chest. That was the last thing I wanted. Reminding Mack, and myself, that we had a timeline would help.

I took another bite of cereal and checked my calendar. Coach wanted to meet after the holiday weekend, but besides some gym time, I had nothing. All I wanted to do was call Mack and see if she needed help with something, like one of her Insta stories or coaching younger kids. The urge to see her 24/7 was new for me, but it was nice. My teammates were busy this summer with family, working out, or jobs, where I needed a new bud. Sure, she was hot as hell, and I knew how she sounded when she came, but she was still my buddy. It was normal to want to hang out with friends all the time.

Once school started, I wouldn't have a spare moment to think about her. I spun my phone on the table, fighting the urge to text her when my phone buzzed.

The inexplicable swoop of my stomach was annoying when her name popped up.

Mack: I FOUND A WEDDING.

Dean: Mm what?

Mack: To crash. We must crash a wedding. My aunt is in town, and I went to see her at her hotel, and there is a big event there tonight. I've seen the signs! I also stalked their wedding website, and it's formal. So you gotta look good.

Dean: I always look good

Mack: yeah, yeah, yeah, fine you're hot. Are you in, or do I need to ask Gabe?

What the fuck?

Not funny.

Dean: you devil woman.

Mack: I don't see you saying yes. I'm going with a date. If it's you or not…

Dean: Do you want me to bite you?

*Mack: *shrug emoji**

Dean: What time?

Mack: website says it starts at seven, so want to pick me up at 6:45?

Dean: Wear something red. You look fucking sexy in red.

Dean: Never threaten me with Gabe again.

Mack: Then be a good boy

Shit. I loved spicy Mack. My spirits soared, and I eyed my watch. Only ten more hours until I could see Mack.

You're into her for real, Luca's words repeated back at me. I brushed them off. I was having fun, and after the mindfuck Jessica put me through, I was enjoying the moment. This didn't have to be serious.

Nerves danced down my spine, my heart racing like it was a major play in the final quarter. I'd been to prom and all that shit. I went with a different girl every time because being a dumbass like I was, I loved bragging about that. *Different girl every dance.* Never caught feelings. It was such a point of pride when I was younger, but now my foolish choices made me roll my eyes.

This wasn't a dance, but I wore my nicest suit and found a red silk pocket square in Callum's room. I looked good. I smoothed my hands over my chest, took a deep breath, and knocked on Mack's door. My heart was about burst in my throat as I waited. I wanted to make her pay for the Gabe comment. She told me Lo wasn't home, so it wouldn't be weird, and I knew that was a conversation I had to have soon. However, tonight was about me and Mack and the Summer Playbook.

The doorknob twisted, the wind brushed the hair on the back of my neck, and I tensed, waiting to see her. The sun hit just right off her hair so the blonde streaks looked angelic with the fun colors at the bottom showing her true personality. She wore a deep red dress that dipped low in the front, the fabric hugging her round tits. Her long, toned legs peeked out of the slit in the dress, and her toes even matched the red. I scanned her up, stopping on the red gems in her ears and the red on her lips.

She looked *delectable.*

"Jesus, Mallinson. You went all out."

"It's not every day I crash a wedding, Romano. If we get caught, I'm looking good while I do it." She smirked and stepped closer to me, her perfume surrounding me. She smelled like cookies and sex, a weird combination, but it was incredible.

"What I like best about this dress is this spot right here." I ran a finger over her exposed collarbone. "Remember what I said about your comments about Gabe?"

"You going to *mark* me, Dean?" Her eyes sparkled at me. "Do it then."

"Ah, you're in a fun mood tonight. Saucy. I like it." I walked into her, putting a hand at the base of her spine and backing her up into her apartment. Once the door shut, I lowered my nose along her neck. "You smell fucking good."

"So do you." She dug her nails into my neck, holding onto my shoulders as I nipped the spot at the base of her ear. She wiggled against me, and I used the movement to wrap her legs around me.

She was so strong, and her thighs clenched as I wrapped them around my waist. "Mackenzie, I'm marking you, and you'll take it."

Her response was to arch her back, giving me more access to her neck. It was an open invitation, all her smooth skin laid bare for me. I dragged my tongue from her neck to the center of her throat. Then I inhaled, breathing her in. The scent of her drove me crazy. The glorious combination of sweat and spice, it made me think irrational, wild thoughts. Like how I would never get sick of this smell or her or her body.

The perfect spot was on her muscle, where the tendon raced with her pulse. I bit down on the skin and sucked. She moaned when I flicked my tongue on the sensitive area, her grip tightening on me as she ground into me. "*Dean.*"

"Yes, my name," I said, my cock stiffening. "Fuck Gabe."

"You're insane." She laughed and tilted my chin up with her red-nailed finger. Her eyelashes looked twice as long, and her blue eyes were the color of the sky in the middle of summer. Just her gaze had me feeling safer, nostalgic, happy.

"Your skin looks good with my teeth marks."

"Wish I had *get bitten* on my list."

"Let's add it." I winked.

She swatted my arm as I slid her down, carefully letting my hands run over her as she landed on her feet. The silky dress was so soft and smooth. I wanted to cover my body with her in this damn dress. She reached out and ran a hand over my jaw, her eyes softening. "You are gorgeous, Romano. Seriously. If I still had my crush, which I don't, it would come back."

"Cute." I pursed my lips and ran a hand over her neck, then down the center of her chest. "If we weren't us and could be together for real, I'd take you on nice dates all the time just to see you in red."

A clouded look crossed her face, but it didn't last long before she blushed. "Thank you. It was fun getting dressed up."

"I mean, it is a wedding after all. Fancy attire is required on the invite."

"You prepared to run if we get caught?" she asked, mischief twinkling in her eyes yet again. "We could get into trouble."

"I'm fast."

"So am I, but it's an everyone-for-themselves moment." She licked her lips, and I had to know what they tasted like.

I dipped my head lower and kissed her once, twice, then a third time. Her pillow-soft lips were so welcoming, like she knew I was battling this urge and took pity on me. She opened her mouth, her tongue sliding against mine and *cherries*. She tasted like cherries. I didn't know how or why, but fuck, I loved it.

I always loved cherries.

"Why does your mouth taste so good?" I said between kisses. I probably had lipstick all over my face, but I didn't care. She laughed softly, the sound resonating right in my chest where it remained.

She chewed the side of her lip as she stared up at me, using her finger to wipe under my mouth as her gaze softened. This felt intimate. Special. I cleared my throat as she dropped her hand, and I jutted my chin toward the door.

"Are you ready?"

"Sure am. Let's crash!"

I helped her into my car before putting on a punk playlist. She sang every word as she crossed one leg over the other, the slit showing so much of her skin. It hit me then that I never did this. I didn't take women on dates. I couldn't even remember the last time I took a girl in my car. Jessica and I would meet up places, generally hers, but never *this.* Before her, I'd usually meet somewhere and go back to one of our places to hook up. Even in high school, if it wasn't a dance, I never wanted to drive girls around. Working my jaw, I swallowed down the uncertainty about why Mack felt so right.

Was it because I knew this thing between us had a timeline? Or because I trusted her to not fuck me over? She looked perfect in my car, wearing that red dress, doing this list with just me. Fuck. I ran a hand over my face, leaning on my compartmentalizing skills to focus on the now. Game time.

"You just groaned. Are you nervous? We don't actually have to crash a wedding. Wait, oh no. Dean! I didn't even think about what it would mean for your season. We can't do this!"

"What? No. That's—'

"Let's just go to dinner. A really nice dinner. If you want. Not like a date, no, this isn't… we don't…date. We list. We do the list. I think, maybe, we can add a date? If you want. Not a real one, you don't do that." Her words blurred together, her cheeks pink as she waved her hands in the air everywhere.

Guilt ate at me. She'd picked up on my tension and spiraled. "First, I would love to take you on a date. A real one."

That wasn't a lie, and if this was her *not in my league bullshit,* I was gonna be pissed.

"But no, my groan wasn't about getting caught. We're crashing this wedding, Mallinson, no backing out. Understood?"

"Okay. But what if you get in trouble? Would this prove to your coach about the captain thing?"

"No. We won't get caught, and we won't get arrested." I chuckled and put a hand on her thigh squeezing. "Are *you* nervous?"

"I wasn't but then you seemed tense."

"I was, for other reasons. Being around you is easy, Mackenzie, and it made me realize I haven't… I never really dated seriously or been committed to anyone before. It's weird, yet I feel so comfortable with you."

She gave me a shy smile and intertwined our fingers on her lap. "I feel the same with you."

"You've dated though. You've had boyfriends. You know what this should be."

"Sure, but being comfortable with someone is a sign of trust. It's not easy to have, Dean. It can take months or years to trust someone, and I think because of Lo, we have a foundation of it already."

Trust. I nodded. "That must be it. Plus, since we know this is just for summer, I'm not worried about football, which also helps."

"Yeah," she said, softer. She stopped tracing my knuckle with her pointer finger, glancing out the window with a serious look on her face.

I wanted to know what was going on in her head, so badly. My gut tightened, concerned I'd said the wrong thing.

Reminding us this was temporary was essential. *We* felt too real, and with the timeline, the reminder made things easier. She had to understand that.

"Mack—"

"What's our plan tonight? Bride or groom? Second cousin, you or me?" Her smile returned, eyes bright, and there wasn't the trace of unease that was there a few seconds ago.

I followed her lead. "Team bride, for sure."

"Great. Online says their reception starts at seven and dinner is done at eight, so we can't sneak in until after dinner. Just dancing and drinks. Figured we could scope out the hotel bar first."

"And grab some food. We get our date after all, Mack." I winked, loving how her cheeks pinkened whenever I complimented her. "Because tonight, you look gorgeous, and I'd be honored to take you on a date."

"Alright, enough with the lines, Romano. I'm already here." She rolled her eyes, but she gripped my hand tighter.

The pang in my chest retuned, only it was warm and fuzzy this time, like my heart wanted me to hold Mack close and never let go.

CHAPTER NINETEEN

Mack

I never thought much about the wedding I wanted, but walking into this reception made me realize what I didn't want. There were at least three hundred people here. So many decorations, and yes, they were beautiful, but this had to cost the price of a small house. "Holy shit."

"It's a buffet." Dean kept his hand on the base of my spine, guiding us into the reception. His breath hit my neck, causing an explosion of goose bumps all along my body. Lines had blurred between us. That was clear. With the chat in the car and how he always had to touch me, this *summer fling* might be temporary, but the feelings were real for me.

"What do you need, Mack? You should eat. If we're going to drink, I want to make sure you have some food."

"Taking care of me, huh?"

"Yes." He shook his head, like the idea of questioning it was crazy. "Of course I want you to be okay. Now, they have chicken. Want a plate?"

"Where will we sit though?"

"I have an idea," he whispered, dropping a kiss under my ear. "I say we go look at the welcome table and see who hasn't picked up their card with the table assignment."

"Oh my god, Dean, that's… a great idea."

He laughed, the sound hitting me in the feels. I loved his laugh. It was deep and sexy and fuck. Why did we agree to do this? Panic caused my heart to flutter. It was like it knew it was going to experience a ton of pain in a few weeks, and there was nothing I could do to stop it.

"Ah, look at this? Mr. and Mrs. Ross aren't here while everyone else is sitting. Would you care to join me, Mrs. Ross?" he asked, grin wide and eyes sparkling at me.

"I'd be honored!"

We looped arms, the cards in our hands as we found our way to table forty. Forty. There were at least sixty tables in this room. It was *wild.* My pulse raced with the notion of getting caught, but with so many people here, who would even know?

"I would never want this number of people at a wedding," I said, not really putting stock into wedding talk. Getting married wasn't for years for me. I had goals, and those would come first. *That's why you need to end this fling.* "You thought about it at all?"

"No." Dean's brow wrinkled. "But this is way too many. Honestly, I'd want my woman to be happy. That's it. If she wanted this, then I'd do it, but this isn't intimate. My life is in the spotlight, so the less people there, the better. You never know who might leak details or photos."

We took our seats at table forty, where another couple in their sixties sat on the opposite side. I smiled in greeting as Dean pushed in my chair. "Good evening!"

"What a gorgeous couple, aren't they, Frank?"

"Yes. You are," the older man said.

"Thank you. It's all her." Dean kissed my cheek as he sat next to me. "She's radiant."

"Stop." I blushed, my skin prickling. "I'm already here with you, no need to go overboard."

"There is a need. I don't want you thinking for one second that you're not incredible and the most beautiful person ever."

"Mr. *Ross,*" I said, shoving his side. "There is a thing as going too hard."

"Never. I always want my woman to know how I feel." He winked and with that motion, stole the last part of my heart I guarded.

I was foolishly in love with him now. My crush was nothing compared to how I felt now. This…whole-body, heart-fluttering feeling was overwhelming. My hands trembled as I picked up the fork, my skin heating as I took a few deep breaths.

I was rational. I made hard decisions on the field all the time and was in control of my body. This was no different. Just, feelings instead of soccer. I focused on gaining control as we ate and laughed with the older couple. They were old friends of the groom's parents from a decade ago and had been married for forty years.

"Best marriage advice we can give? Never go to bed angry, kiss every time you say goodbye, and pick each other. There are going to be distractions and battles, that's life for ya, but *picking* each other is a choice you're always going to have to make a priority."

"My wife is right. My dad told me marriage is easy, but he'd been married four times." The man chuckled. "Marriage is hard. Relationships are. You have to work at it, and anyone who says otherwise is wrong."

"My parents always told me the same thing." Dean leaned back into his chair, his arm resting on the back of mine with his fingers dangling on my shoulder. He swiped them over my skin.

"You should marry your best friend, someone to laugh and cry with. Intimacy is rooted in trust. My parents laugh more than anything, and that's something."

"You're right, young man. Being with your best friend is the best gift in the world." The woman leaned into her husband's embrace, and my throat tightened.

For a casual dinner, this felt… heavy.

We finished eating and chatting about nonsense things, but the weight of that conversation stayed with me. Marriage always seemed so far away for me, like the next part of my life, but there was something magical about this. The music, the flowers, the laughter, the older couple laughing and acting like they were on a first date despite being married for decades.

"Care to dance, beautiful?" Dean asked, standing and holding out a hand for me. He wore his signature cocky grin, where half his mouth turned up and the other playfully remained unmoved. I'd dreamed of him looking at me like that, and here I was, living my fantasy.

"Oh, wow, how formal." I swallowed down the butterflies and placed my hand in his. His palms were cool and his fingers calloused. Where my shins and feet wore the bulk of my dedication to soccer, his hands showed his.

"You are stunning. I'll never forget this summer, Mack." He led us to the dance floor, pulled me close so our chests were pressed together, and lowered his lips to my ear. "When you're famous playing in the World Cup one day, I can say I danced with you here, when you looked like this."

"And when you're on ESPN doing interviews for winning the Superbowl, I'll get to say I completed my list with you," I whispered back, hoping the hushed tone hid my shaky voice. It annoyed me that my emotions were getting the best of me. Why couldn't I live in the damn moment, instead of thinking about how much this would hurt later?

"Yes, you will."

He hummed the popular slow song and spun us around with more rhythm than I would've expected. People smiled at us, and for a moment, I forgot we were at someone else's wedding. The bride and groom were chatting with all the couples, and I tugged Dean's jacket. "Let's go toward the back."

"Already on it."

He guided us further from the couple, but the bride studied us, brows furrowed.

"Dean…she might be onto us."

"You know, I had another idea up my sleeve anyway." He kissed my temple before guiding us off the dance floor and to the open bar. "We're each getting two shots, then I have a plan."

"One that doesn't have that bride figuring us out?" I nervously glanced over my shoulder, but they weren't in sight. Too many people filled the gap. Definitely a perk of crashing a three-hundred-person reception.

"Oh yeah." Dean had his phone out, his hand never leaving my back as we waited for the bartender to get to us. I kept looking at the dance floor, but the bride and groom were swarmed with other guests. Maybe I was paranoid, but I swore I could feel her staring at us.

"Four shots of vodka, please, with limes." Dean pocketed his phone and tipped the guy twenty bucks. Nudging me forward, he handed me the glasses. "To the best summer playbook of all time."

"All time?"

"Yes. Nothing will top this summer, Mack." His voice deepened, and his eyes darkened. A moment passed, our breaths syncing when he glanced over my shoulder. "Okay, take the shots and march out the door."

"Are they coming?"

"Shots. Now."

I downed the two and forwent the lime, my adrenaline spiking at getting caught. Without a backward glance, I marched toward the exit, Dean right behind me. He grabbed my hand and went toward the elevators. Every beat of my heart was like a bass drum coursing through my body. It was terrifying, but I had never felt more alive.

"Come on," Dean mumbled, hitting the up arrow over and over. He craned his neck, his jaw tense.

I glanced back to search.

"I don't see them following us, but still, that was close." He coughed.

"What are we doing going up? Shouldn't we run out?"

"Fucking finally." Dean led us into the elevator. We stared in silence at the hallway, and I exhaled when the doors finally shut.

"Holy shit," I said, leaning my head forward. "That was exhilarating."

"Ha, agreed. I don't think they would've done anything but ask us who we were. That got my blood pumping."

"Me too. That was…" I smiled, closing my eyes. I faced up toward the light and laughed. "Worth it."

When I opened them, Dean stared at me with so much longing that words I should never say crept up my throat.

"You're amazing." Dean cupped my face. "I have to kiss you. You're so happy, and I want to taste it."

"Then kiss me."

He did.

Gripping the side of my dress, he yanked me against him as he devoured my mouth. He groaned, loudly, as his other hand ran up and down my side, settling on my ass as he nipped my lip. "Fucking." Kiss. "Perfect."

The elevator dinged, and he straightened, a nervous, almost

shy look crossing his face. He ran a hand through his hair as the tips of his cheeks pinkened. "Okay, uh, I had an idea that sounded romantic, and now I'm nervous."

"What is it?" I frowned, confused why he would be unsure about me. I'd love anything he'd do. He had to know that by now. "What was your idea?"

"We checked off crashing a wedding from your list." He chewed the inside of his cheek, his gaze darting down the hall. "I got us a hotel room that's next to the pool. I figured we could… skinny dip and run back to our room. Late, of course. We don't want to be caught. But only if you want to. Damn. You're not smiling, so it's stupid. Terrible idea."

"Wait. No." I shook my head. "You want to spend the night here, with me?"

"And lick you head to toe? Yes. I don't want to worry about my sister or my teammates. I want to focus on *you,* and selfishly, I have so much fun with you that I hate leaving." He swallowed, his throat bobbing as he lowered his gaze to my mouth. "So, you want to skinny dip with me?"

"Oh my god." It was my turn to kiss him. Were we real? No. Would this end? Yes. But was this the best night of my life? Without question.

I jumped onto him, wrapping my legs around him as I kissed down his neck. "Yes, to all of it. You are the best, Dean Romano. Let's get naked."

He laughed against my mouth. "I need my phone, baby, to get into the room."

"Are you sure?" I tugged his earlobe with my teeth, loving how his whole body tensed. I did it again, taking in every movement. The way he sucked in a breath, the way his pulse raced at the base of his neck, and the way his grip on my ass tightened. It was all amazing, and I wanted to remember it forever.

"One second." He reached into his pocket and removed his phone, the smell of vodka still on his breath, and I traced the outline of his mouth with my tongue. "Damn it, Mack."

"You surprised me with a *hotel room.* No one has ever done that for me before. I'm excited!"

"I'm glad you are." He walked us toward a room at the end of the hall. "Here we are."

He scanned his phone to the device, and the door clicked. He pushed it open, and once it shut, his eyes darkened. "I want to give you so many other firsts, Mallinson."

My breath caught in my throat.

"It's ten." He undid one of his cuffs. "The pool closed already. So, here's what we're going to do."

"God, your bossy voice is hot."

"Yeah?"

"Makes me want you to tell me what to do and call me a good girl."

His eyes heated, and his nostrils flared. "Are you wearing a bra?"

"No." I smirked and slid one of the straps down. "I can't with this dress."

"*Fuck.*" He shuddered as he undid his other cuff. "Are you wearing panties?"

"Maybe." I fought a smile as I undid the other strap of the dress, letting the silky material fall on either side, exposing my breasts to him. My nipples tightened with need and cold, and my breathing only increased from his stare. "Why?"

"Take off your dress, now." His focus was on my tits as he undid the rest of his shirt. The front of his pants looked a little bulged, and I took my time sliding my hands toward my waist.

"Are you getting undressed too?"

"Don't ask questions, Mack. You're doing what I say."

"Yes, sir." I let the rest of the dress fall to the floor and stood there in my heels and red laced panties. They left nothing to the imagination, and they were already soaked.

"You're making this list hard to complete. I want to fucking lick you until you scream. God, the way you look right now…" he trailed off, his voice going low as he stepped near me. "One taste."

"Are you telling or asking?" I teased, willing to do anything he wanted.

"Saucy girl. Spread your legs." Dean kneeled in front of me, and holy shit. This was a wet dream come to life. His shirt hung unbuttoned, his chest on display as he ran his nose along my inner thigh and over the damp fabric.

I didn't have time to feel self-conscious, not when he groaned and gripped my ass in his hands. "If you only get *one* taste, make it count."

"Mouthy. God, that's hot." He tongued my clit over the fabric, the deep growl coming from his chest making me wetter. It was like he was enjoying this as much as I was.

I gripped his hair, guiding him to stay right between my thighs. "You look good on the ground for me."

"I need to fuck you." He slid the fabric to the side, tonguing me bare and sliding into me.

I shuddered at the sensation. It was so raw, so dirty, so *right.* He didn't just tease me with his tongue, he probed me, sending every nerve into a frenzy. "With your mouth?"

"Everything." He groaned into me. "Your pussy is derailing my plans."

I closed my eyes, enjoying the feel of him touching me everywhere. My ass, my pussy, his breath on my thighs. "Hate it when that happens."

He chuckled before sliding a finger inside me, not stopping his continual stroke of my clit. He sucked it into his mouth, releasing it with a pop that had me shuddering. "I'm a guy who wants to stick to a plan," he said, moaning as he slid my panties back in place and moved to sit on the edge of the bed.

He looked manic. His pupils were dilated, his jaw tense, and his lips wet from *me.* "It took heroic strength to stop right now. I want that noted."

"And why did you stop? I want your tongue on me, in me," I said, hoping his reaction would be worth it.

He hissed. "Fuck, Mackenzie. Okay, we have all night. Let's knock out skinny dipping."

"Or… we could do that at the lake house next week?"

"No." He licked his lips and palmed his cock through his pants. "With everyone around? No. They don't get to see you."

"Ah, selfish and possessive." I walked toward him, watching the way he eyed my tits and almost drooled. I straddled his thighs and ran my nipple over his lips. He shuddered before taking it in his mouth. "Yes, Dean."

"What do you want, devil woman?"

"You," I said, being the most daring I ever had been in my entire life.

"But the list—"

I pushed him onto the bed, his shirt spread open and his delicious chest warm and sweaty. He panted, and his jaw tightened as I stared down at him. "If we have all night, then we can do that later. Don't you want me, Romano?"

"More than anything."

"Then take me."

CHAPTER **TWENTY**

Dean

I remembered the first time my parents bought me a football. I remembered the call that I received a full ride to Central State. I also remembered the first beer I had and my first kiss. This moment—with Mack straddling me and looking at me like I hung the moon, all wet and hot for me—was something I would never forget.

"Take you?" I repeated. My hands rested on the mattress as unparalleled energy blasted through me.

"Yes." She kissed my neck, my chest, swirling her tongue over my pec before dragging her teeth over my stomach. "You are a fantasy come to life, and I want to experience all of you."

She undid my belt, her eyes blazing with want *for me.* She chewed her bottom lip as she slid my waistband down with jerky movements. It was like she couldn't get me naked fast enough, and her desperation fueled my own fire. This was messy and genuine and perfect. This wasn't for show. I had no worries her phone secretly recorded us or that she'd poked a hole in a condom.

Shit. Condom!

"Mackenzie," I said but growled when she stroked my cock with her warm hands. She pumped me a few times before dropping to her knees. She kissed both my thighs.

"Dean?"

"Yeah, baby?" I saw freaking stars just from her hands on me. My chest almost lifted off the bed with how horny I was.

"Can I suck your cock?"

"Like you have to ask."

"I do though." She pumped me again, her voice firmer. "Your consent matters too, Dean."

My chest tightened. My thoughts almost went to Jessica, but they didn't have time. She took me in her tight warm mouth and holy shit fuck balls. I arched my back, the pleasure almost overwhelming.

"You're so thick." She wet her hand and stroked my base as she took me to the back of her throat. I saw stars. Time lost meaning. My cock was in her mouth as she sucked me hard. Sweat beaded on my skin as her perfume lingered in the air. I wanted her. I wanted this all the time.

"Mack," I moaned, needing to touch her. "Get up here now."

"Make me."

This girl. She released my cock from her lips, and I wasted no time hoisting her up onto the bed and lifting her knees to her shoulders. "You're fucking soaked again. You like my cock in your mouth? You like feeling it hit your throat?"

She nodded, her eyes dark blue with lust.

"God, look at you." I ran a hand down her chest, to her panties and over the wet fabric. "These need to go."

"Agreed." She wiggled to remove them, but I stopped her.

It was something intimate to remove her red panties. I had never done that before. Usually the girls went commando for easier access, or they rushed to get naked. This felt special. "Heels stay on though."

"I knew you'd like them." She licked her lips, her gaze heating again as I trailed my fingers over her calves. They were perfect.

"Love them." I kissed her left calf, then her right, before reaching into my wallet and grabbing a condom. I bought it myself and knew it was fine. She sucked in a breath when I ripped it open.

"I'm so ready for you, Dean." She pushed up onto her elbows, her lips plump and her eyes simmering. "This is the best night of my life."

"Mine too." I smiled, slid the condom over my cock, and leaned over her. I wanted her to know, without words, what this night meant for me. It was a breakthrough. Jessica hadn't ruined me.

This was it—the first time since *then.* Mack stared at me, eyes wide and trusting, her lips wet and parted for me. My heart thudded against my ribs as my stomach twisted, but it wasn't just with nerves. It was with anticipation because I wanted this girl so damn much.

I slid into her, groaning against her neck at how good she felt, and all remaining tension disappeared. She was tight and warm, her muscles clenching around me forming my own personal slice of heaven. "You." I kissed and thrust. "Are. Perfect."

She nipped my ear as she wrapped her legs around me, digging her heels into my back. "Your cock is huge. You feel so good."

"So do you."

I wanted everything all at once. I wanted to watch her face as I fucked her. I wanted her sounds, and I wanted her pussy to clench around me while she came. But I focused on one thing at a time—making it feel good for her. I lifted her hip, giving myself a better angle to hit her G-spot. She bucked underneath me, her pleasured sighs fueling me to be gentle.

I rocked my hips in a rhythm, not wanting to rush this. I kissed her collarbone, her neck, her face. "You're beautiful."

"Fuck me harder, Dean. You're being too gentle."

I stilled, staring down at her. "Excuse me?"

"You heard me." She smirked and smacked my ass, digging her nails into it. "We can go slow later. Right now, I want it hard."

Fuck. "You're…" I lost my words at how gorgeous she was. "Flip over onto your stomach then."

"Gladly."

"I want to squeeze your ass while I fuck you, watch it jiggle while you take me as deep as I go."

"*Yes.*"

She rolled onto her stomach, but I grabbed her waist so she was on her knees. I pinched both of her nipples, causing her to groan, before I smacked *her* ass. I bit into one globe, but not enough to break skin.

"*Dean.*"

"I told you I wanted to mark you everywhere." I laughed as she looked over her shoulder at me, her eyes heated and lips parted. "You're hot as fuck like this, Mack."

"Stop stalling and take me."

"Yes, ma'am."

I guided into her, gripping her hip and being gentle for a few seconds before I fucked her, and holy shit. It was magic. She arched into my every thrust, releasing the most guttural and sexy sounds as I took her rough. I leaned over her back, gripping her throat from behind as I bit her neck. "Hot as fuck."

"My clit," she said, her voice husky from my hand. "Touch me."

I moved the hand from her neck to between her thighs and found the perfect pace of thrusting and swirling her clit. Her throaty sound got louder as she tensed beneath me.

"You're close, baby. What do you need?"

"Harder," she screamed.

I obeyed. It was every fantasy come to life. Her long hair fell all around us, the smell of sex and sweat filling the air as we fucked, rough. She clenched around my cock as she came, and I focused so hard on letting her finish that the second she stopped screaming I let go.

"*Yes, Mack.*" I gripped her ass like I dreamed about as I exploded into her. It had been so long for me that this made my veins hum. My skin tingled, like I plugged into an outlet as the best, most intense pleasure I'd ever had spread through me. "Fuck, fuck," I groaned, the orgasm continuing.

Once it stopped, I could barely breathe, and I rolled onto my back, sneaking my arm over Mack and cradling her against me. "Holy. Shit."

"Ditto," she said, her voice small and cute. She trailed her fingers over my pecs, caressing me. "Sex has never been like that for me."

"Same." I snuggled her closer, not giving a single shit that I never cuddled. I never pulled partners close to me. I never thought about being inside them as soon as possible. Mack had changed the entire game, and I wanted to win the end of it. "How long do you need to recover?"

"What?" she giggled. "You're still panting."

"I know." I rolled her onto me, smiling so hard I couldn't stop. "I want to take you in every position possible. All night. With my mouth and cock and fingers."

"That could be arranged." She combed her fingers through my hair, a soft look on her face. I closed my eyes and leaned into her caress. "You like me touching you today?"

"Every day." I kissed her palm. "How's your pussy? Sore?"

"Eh, it's a good kind of sore. It's been a while for me." She blushed, looking away, like it embarrassed her. Which was ridiculous. If anything, a possessive, jealous inappropriate urge came over me. I wanted to be her only one for a long time.

"Hey," I said softly. I tilted her chin toward me. "It's been almost eight months for me."

"What?" Her eyes bugged out of her head. "Dean, you're *the* playboy—"

"I might've been that for the first two and half years here, but that hasn't been me in a while, and I think you know that." I said it gently but also with a firmness that showed her it was true. "I've done one-night stands, had a lot of hookups—"

Mack winced.

"Sorry, that was crass."

"I don't love thinking about you with others, even though this is just a summer fling we agreed to for the list." She pursed her lips. "Obviously you've slept with quite a few people. It's a fact."

I frowned. "That's true, but no one has come close to this, what happened with us. I need you to know that."

"I do." She smiled, her gaze softening as she sighed in contentment. "So, what happened for you to stop being so much like Callum?"

She ran her finger over my eyebrow, jaw, then shoulder, a thoughtful look on her face. I loved her expressions, how a twitch of her brow or a curve of her lip gave away her thoughts. "I could tell something happened. Lo hinted as much when she worried about you."

"I trusted someone who used me from the start. I'm working on moving on, so I don't want to get into specifics, but she played me, lied to me about becoming pregnant, and really broke my trust with everyone. That's why I'll never date again. I can't risk getting hurt."

"Oh, Dean." She frowned so hard the lines on her face seemed permanent. "I'm so sorry." She leaned up and kissed my heart. "That had to be brutal."

"It was." My voice clogged up, my emotions that I thought I shoved away sneaking out. "The worst part was preparing to be a father. I… I was excited, as fucked up as it is. So then to have it be fake the whole time?" I closed my eyes.

"You mourned the loss." She squeezed me. "No one deserves to go through that. Thank you for telling me. That had to be really difficult."

"It is. I felt like I lost myself and was so damn angry. Then I felt ashamed, like I'd let this happen to me. I'm doing an online therapy session that's helped a little."

"Good. You should keep it up. Look." She pushed up and set her head on her hand, her elbow resting on the bed. Her rainbow hair fell around her face, and there was still a faint redness on her lips. "I hope you realize that you have nothing to be ashamed of. She chose to lie and manipulate, not you. You opened yourself up and trusted her, and she broke that trust. That's all on her. None of it is on you."

I caressed her collarbone, running my thumb over it as I sighed. "This is why this list of yours was so fun to join. You wanted to experience things and go wild before senior year, and I wanted to have fun and stop being angry, without the risk of catching feels."

"You seem less angry." She stared at me a beat before leaning forward and pressing her lips against mine. "I know we'll go our separate ways after this summer, but I promise I'd never lie to you or hurt you. While we're together, I'll take care of you."

The ache in my chest intensified, and the ball of emotion in my throat throbbed to the point of pain. This was *too much.* Way too much.

Distract.

"Come here." I gripped the back of her head and kissed her hard, biting her lip and teasing her until she moaned. I slid off the bed before spreading her thighs and staring up at her. "I'll give you your next orgasm with my mouth so you can recover, then I'm taking you again while you watch in the mirror."

CHAPTER **TWENTY-ONE**

Mack

The soccer clinics had finished, which meant it was one month until the season started and summer ended. Normally, this time of summer meant barbeques and good times, with the anticipation of the next year. I was happier than I'd been in years, smiling more, but the countdown was on and ever present in my mind. Ever since the night at the hotel, I knew I was screwed.

I was in love with Dean Romano. A foolish, break-my-heart-forever kind of love, and it was only going to get worse. I could end it now to save myself the heartbreak later, but doing so would only hurt Dean. He'd been having so much fun with the list, and after hearing what he went through? I couldn't be the one to stop him enjoying life again. That'd be cruel.

Plus, why would I walk away from the best sex of my life? Maybe I was supposed to miss out on so many things in high school to experience them with Dean right now. Because regardless of *why* this playbook happened, I would forever be grateful for this.

I stared at the ends of my hair a few days later, sighing as my phone went off.

Ale: GIRLS. We are in for the lake house trip.

Callum: I love that I'm considered one of the girls.

Ale: And we love you for letting us do the lake house for the Fourth!

Mally: DAMN IT. I can't! Fuck. I'm jealous

Vee: You're always there in spirit.

Callum: Confirmed: Dean, me, Oliver, Ale, Vee, Mack, Lo, and Luca

I tensed. Lo and Luca were going? She hadn't told me. Was that on purpose? We had to talk about it. I felt the wedge every time she walked into the room. We were planning on leaving right away in the morning. My bag was already packed, my Polaroid and list in tow, but my thoughts were dirty and all about Dean. Could we really sneak away and do all the things with Lo there?

Gah.

The front door to our place opened, and I almost jumped out of my chair. I finished doing another video series on healthy fats and proteins to eat if you did a lot of cardio, but I wasn't expecting Lo home.

"Hey, you," she said, smiling. "Guess what I got?"

"Uh, a viral hit?"

"No, but that would be great." She fluffed her hair and set a large paper bag on the table next to my laptop. "All the stuff for s'mores. I convinced Luca to move our trip with his grandma until after the Fourth. I can't miss a night on a lake with my besties."

"You're coming?"

"Hell yeah." She shimmied and pulled out a bottle of Fireball. "This is from me to you, for disappearing on you most of the summer. I hate that this internship and workouts and

Luca are taking my time when we wanted to live together all these years."

"Lo, that's awesome." I smiled, but it didn't reach my eyes. I was the worst friend to feel disappointment instead of excitement. And it was because of Dean.

"You're a shit liar." She plopped down next to me in her cute work blazer and jeans. "You know I love you, right? And that you're a grown ass adult who can make your own choices?"

My throat tightened. "I'm in love with your brother," I blurted, not even trying to ease into this conversation. It boiled over, spilling out like water from of a dam, and I couldn't stop it. "I have been for years, but now it's like, real. This list—him and I hanging out… I'm in love with him, but I know it's a summer thing. We both agreed to that, and we'll end it when our seasons start because we have enough to worry about, and I'm so sorry this happened. I'd never use you to get to him, that was never my plan, and if you want to hate me, I deserve it because I hid this from you."

Lorelei Romano smiled after my meltdown. My best friend could be unpredictable at times, but this wasn't one of them. She chuckled and grabbed my hand. With a serious expression, she said, "I've always known."

"Wait." I shook my head. "Known what?"

"That you had a crush on my brother. It was painfully obvious, but I never once thought our friendship involved him. If that is one of your worries, then you can yeet that right into the sun."

"Oh."

"You are two of my favorite people, so I understand why you'd be into each other. My only concern is one of you getting hurt. That truly is it." She patted my hand and let go. "Thank you for coming clean. I wanted you to tell me on your own, without probing."

"Dean doesn't know how I feel."

She narrowed her eyes. "I won't share that if you're worried."

"Am I crazy? I know it's gonna hurt so badly when we walk away, but this has been the absolute best." I pinched my nose. "I can't stop it. Not when I'm having so much fun, and he's so wonderful, and he's happy too."

"When Luca and I agreed to one night only, it was us fooling ourselves. But he needed to come to terms with changing his life. I'm not sure what you two talked about or agreed on, but you can always renegotiate." She smirked, her cheeks blushing.

"Oh, how did Luca *negotiate* with you?"

"It was hot. I'll say that."

I snickered. "He's made it clear that he's still messed up from that girl and that she fucked with his head and game, so he never wants to go down that path again. I want to respect that decision. He opened up a little about what happened, and I don't want him to feel violated or used in any way."

"He told you?" Her brows rose to her wild hairline. "Holy shit. Dude, he trusts the fuck out of you if he told you about her."

"I don't know her name, but yeah, I got the pieces. It makes me want to take care of him for a little longer." I sighed and melted into the chair. "We were planning on *hanging out* at the lake."

"Ah, that's the flicker of annoyance I saw on your face. Didn't love that."

"I hated lying to you. It wasn't intentional. We are just never alone or have time to talk for more than fun stuff."

"Yeah, that's on me." Lo leaned over and pulled me into a

bear hug. "However this ends, you will always have me. We have matching tattoos, which far outweighs being a twin."

"Not true, but I appreciate you so much. I'm sorry. I wish it was someone other than Dean."

"I don't." She grinned. "Again, you're both some of my favorite people. I think this makes perfect sense as long as you two are on the same page."

Are we? *No.* I wanted more, and he told me it would never happen.

"I don't want this to come between you guys. I'm not sure if you should pretend you don't know or tell him we chatted. I'm torn myself."

"I'm not going to say anything." She stood and tossed her blazer on the chair. "I'm going to pack. Luca is heading over here tonight if that matters to you."

"You know I love Luca. He can be here any time."

"No, I meant… if you wanted to go see Dean. You could." She winked. "I kinda like playing matchmaking super spies."

"That's… okay, enough of that Lo." I laughed. The relief I felt was almost tangible. I never stopped to think that I had the best friend in the world who would support our happiness. She was badass. The best. Her blessing almost made my daydream become more vivid. "You're a dork."

"But I'm *your* dork."

"Yes, forever." I held up my tattoo. "Glad you can join us. This weekend is gonna be epic."

"Sure is."

We agreed that the girls and boys would drive separately. Lo, Ale, Vee, and I hopped into Ale's Jeep with the doors off, and it was glorious. The wind whipped my face on the hour drive to the lake house, and the entire ride was filled with karaoke and dance moves. My heart was so happy since Lo and I talked, and now a drive and lake house trip with my girls? This was the literal dream.

Dean: we're checking three items off the list tonight, Mallinson.

Mack: I'll ask out three dudes we find?

Dean: funny.

Dean: streaking, bonfire, and skinny dipping

Mack: could play strip poker in there too.

Dean: With others? No way.

Mack: It's part of the adventure, you hooligan.

I silenced my phone as we arrived at the house. Callum's family owned this huge ass place with six bedrooms. It was perfect. I wasn't gonna question how or why, but Dean insisted he'd get his own room where I could sneak into it at night. If I roomed with one of the girls, and I snuck off…. They'd know it'd be with Callum, Oliver, or Dean.

"Holy shit." Ale parked the jeep and stared at the massive wooden mansion. "This is amazing, Callum."

"Thank you." Callum walked out the front door, shirtless and wearing aviators. He held a bottle of rum, not a glass, as he took a swig. "Come on in, girlies."

"Give me a swig of that," Vee said, taking it from him. He winked at her, and she grinned. "You horny?"

"Vee, baby, I always am."

I cringed. Vee and Callum? I mean… they were party animals, so it made sense. I shook the thought away as I grabbed my duffel. Lo already went inside, and I took a minute to breathe in the fresh air.

"Hey."

Dean appeared behind me, wrapping his arm around my waist as he lifted me. "You smell good."

"Put me down." I swatted at him, laughing. I spent the night with him last night, and it had been just like the hotel: amazing, hot, sweet, and perfect.

He spun me around and cupped my face, his gaze sweeping across the front as his lips curled up. Then he kissed me. "Mm."

"Had to sneak that in?"

"Yes. Who knows if we'll get alone time ever with this crew."

"Fair point." I grinned at him. I loved how he stared at me, like he took mental notes of every part of my body that he would recreate later. "We'll see how many items I can knock off the list tonight."

"You know my plans." He winked.

"You two, get in here. We're doing shots and then going out on the lake."

"Seems like a smart choice," I said. "Drinking and swimming."

"We're gonna sit on rafts and float, and I'm gonna stare at your ass in a swimming suit." He reached down and squeezed my butt. "Mm, I love this."

"Knock it off, Romano." I walked away from him, swaying my hips more than usual. I went inside, and my mouth dropped. This place was insane. Windows everywhere, beautiful woodwork, a bar top. Callum held a tray of shots as he passed them out, and I stood next to Oliver.

"You know about this secret place?"

"No. I'm kinda pissed it took until senior year to learn." Oliver clinked his glass with mine. "What kind of friend hides this?"

"To our summer before senior year!" Callum yelled, and we all took our shots.

Music played, more shots were poured, and I laughed more than I had in months. Minutes turned to hours, and one drink turned to three. Things were getting silly. *This is what I wanted. This was what I missed.* There was an impromptu dance party where Oliver got way too drunk and danced on the bar.

Vee cheered him on to strip, and he did.

"Holy shit." Lo appeared next to me, her cheeks red from drinking. "This is happening."

"I can't stop watching."

Oliver removed his shirt and tossed it at Vee. She caught it and swung it around her head like a helicopter. "More, more," she shouted.

Oliver then removed his shorts and thrusted in his boxers.

This was wild.

I wore my two-piece bikini that tied in the front and really showcased my ass. It was one splurge I bought a few months ago but never wore it to actually flirt with someone, and I loved how every time I found Dean's gaze, it was on my ass.

Vee pulled Lo into a dance, and the second she was focused on Vee, someone pulled my finger.

"Come with me," Dean said, his voice a whisper.

My stomach swooped as he held my hand, guiding me through the house and into the backyard. It was dusk, so fireworks would start soon. It was light enough to see other houses near them but dark enough to maybe make out? That was what I wanted. "Kiss me, Romano," I said, running my fingers over the waistband of his swimming suit.

"Plan to." He walked us to the dock, and he stopped and crossed his arms. "Take off your suit."

"Wait, what?"

"You heard me. Get naked. Then, you're going to walk down the dock, then back and jump into the water."

"But they could see?"

"They're all plastered. This is the perfect moment." His eyes lit up. "Remember the pact?"

"No!" I shivered. The thought of actually streaking had me nervous. "What is it?"

"We do it together." He smirked as he undid his swimming trunks, letting them drop to the ground as his *hard* cock protruded against his stomach.

"Dean, *your penis!*"

"You better hurry before someone sees how hard I am for you."

"Oh my god." I panicked. I ripped my top off, then my bottoms, and sprinted toward the water. Dean stopped me. "Get in the water!"

"Nope. Streaking requires at least two minutes of exposure. I looked up the rules."

"You're insane!"

"Nah, we're outside our comfort zone. It's the playbook."

"You seem way too comfortable being naked and horny."

He chuckled as he proudly walked toward the end of the dock, then back. I followed, nervous and sweaty, looking over my shoulder every five seconds. No one was in sight.

"Good girl. We get to jump in now." His gaze dropped to my tits, and he licked his lips. "On three?"

"Shit, okay, yeah. One, two, three!" I jumped into the lake, Dean holding my hand, as we were both butt ass naked.

The cool lake water sobered me a bit, and it provided the much-needed protection from being naked as hell. When I came up for air, Dean was right next to me.

"You are beautiful," he said, yanking me against him.

Water droplets clung to his eyelashes, and the urge to tell him my feelings was right there. Enough liquid courage to forget what I should and shouldn't do. I wanted to yell that I loved him, would support him, would be there for him when he felt weird or confused about leadership. We fit together so well, and it would be amazing if he wanted to give this a real try. But I said nothing.

He tweaked my nipple before kissing me.

Top ten moment.

I leaned into the kiss, tasting the saltiness of the water with the sweetness from the rum, and my eyes prickled. How embarrassing. This was about the moment!

"Uh, why are there swimming suits on the dock?"

I yanked from Dean's grasp. *Callum!*

"I think it's Mack's. Yup. She wore red tonight."

"Oh shit! Skinny dipping!" Callum hollered. "Oi, who's getting naked and going into the water?"

Dean narrowed his eyes, our secret moment ruined. "You want me to cover you?"

"There you are, girl." Callum winked before his attention was on Dean. "And Romano? You're naked too? This is crazy. Wow, look at you being wild! I'm joining!"

"Me too!" Vee appeared, her top flying off without a beat as well as her bottoms before she jumped into the water.

Callum followed.

Then Oliver and Ale.

Lo and Luca stood at the edge of the yard, frowning. "This isn't fair. We can't do this because of Dean," Lo shouted.

"You wouldn't do it anyway."

"Yes, I would."

"Do it in the hot tub!" Callum yelled, splashing everyone with water. "We'll be out here for thirty minutes."

"Dude, what the fuck?" Dean shouted.

"What? They can have fun there. We're out here!"

I laughed, hard, absolutely amazed that this was happening. It was a wild, crazy, and perfect moment. I floated, staring up at the sunset as the water flirted with showing my boobs, and I just didn't care. It was utter chaos and joy, the sounds of laughter and motorized boats down the way filling the air. Never in a million years did I think I'd be doing this, leading the charge with a silly list.

"That's quite a smile, Mallinson." Dean swam near me. "I love to see it."

"This list has just been so fun." I treaded water and faced him. "Look at us? All skinny dipping? About to watch fireworks together? This has been a dream. I wish it could last forever."

"I know what you mean." He reached over and pulled a leaf out of my hair, tossing it to the right before gently tugging on my earlobe. "Best summer ever."

"Thank goodness we have four weeks left, huh?" I said, forcing the smile as my stomach weighed me down. It was amazing I didn't sink with how the disappointment grew. All good things came to an end, but damn, I really didn't want us to.

"Thank god we have a month left because I'm going to want to see you every second of it before we gotta end it."

Despite how happy I was, his words twisted my gut. This would end. There was no use dreaming or imagining a different ending because the heartache would be hard enough to survive.

I had to repeat to myself: I wouldn't end up with Dean Romano.

CHAPTER
TWENTY-TWO

Dean

My life flew by faster than it ever had before. Ever since the hotel, things changed. Mack and I almost spent every night we could together, like we knew time was running out between us. She knocked off three more items at the lake house, ones that would remain in my brain forever.

Her dancing on the bar, laughing and being so carefree, and being around her made me want to keep this summer endlessly. Skinny dipping. Streaking. And a bonfire. Callum had a sick-ass pit in the back that we'd fired up after our swimming session, and Lo brought all the stuff for s'mores. Gripping the back of my neck, I stretched before moving onto the next machine. I was at the gym, workouts becoming more intense with August sneaking up, and even though I had the same preseason excitement every single summer, it was partnered with an utter sense of dread.

Football meant no more Mack.

"What *the hell* is she doing?" Callum practically growled,

setting the kettlebell down harder than normal. It slammed against the floor.

"Who?" I wiped moisture off my forehead. Despite it being a leg workout, I was filthy sweaty. "Who are you talking about?"

"Fucking Ivy." He jutted his chin toward one of the trainers, who stood laughing with Xavier and Jayden.

"Ah, the best friend from the past that you clearly have no weird feelings for?"

He glared at me. "I've kept quiet about Mackenzie; you keep your whore mouth shut about this. There are no *feelings* with her. She just isn't into athletes. Never has been. She shouldn't be laughing with them if this is her internship."

Quiet about Mackenzie? What did he even mean? It was temporary. We all knew that. I swallowed down that comment and focused on Callum.

"Because she doesn't deserve joy?"

"You're annoying. I'm going to another machine."

"I'm going to go meet her."

"No, you are not."

I walked with purpose to this mysterious Ivy who had Callum acting out and grinned as she looked at me. "Ivy, right?"

"Hi, yes, that's me." She held out her hand, a sly smile on her lips. "Dean Romano, starting quarterback with three school records and expected to go high in the draft if you play well this season."

"That is me. My favorite color is navy blue too," I said, winking. "Callum shared you two were close growing up."

"Interesting." She pursed her lips, adjusted her thick glasses, and stood straighter as Callum joined my side. "O'Toole."

"Ivy." Callum used a tone I hadn't heard before, almost

like he was angry with her. Callum never got mad. "Your parents must be so proud you're interning with *football* players."

"They are. It's a highly competitive field to get into for sports medicine, and this is a solid program. Despite letting you in, they are by the book and treat their athletes well."

"Sick burn," I said, holding out a fist. She hit it, but her attention was on Callum. Her cheeks turned redder as he stared at her.

"Well, good for you."

"Yeah, good for me." She flicked her hair from one shoulder to the other as she met my gaze again. "It was nice meeting you. Henry is having us visit a few hours before we start full-time with the team. I'll get a formal introduction later, but it was nice meeting the leader."

"See you around, Ivy."

She left us, and as soon as she was out of sight, I nudged Callum. "What happened there?"

"We used to hang out. We kinda grew apart."

"No kinda about it."

"Just don't worry about it, alright?"

"I am because if she messes with your head on the field, then it's gonna make me worry."

"She doesn't have that power anymore." He hit my shoulder. "I need to burn this adrenaline off. I'm running."

Chuckling, I made a note to watch this unfold. In all four years, I'd never seen Callum flustered or hostile toward anyone. Mack invited me to go for a swim at her apartment but only if I spoke with Jayden first. It wasn't that I avoided him, but it was just difficult to accept I wouldn't be the captain visibly on the field.

The sophomore nodded at me as he left the locker room, ready to meet me since I'd asked him to. "Hey, J."

"Romano." He shook my hand, and we did a bro hug. "You look good. Have a fun summer?"

"Yeah, I did." *Two weeks left.* "I wanted to talk to you about something important though. It shouldn't take long."

"No worries. My summer class doesn't start for a few hours. What is it?"

"It's about the captainship." I led us to a bench, where we sat. I leveled my voice, not wanting to sound nervous or insincere. "Coach asked me to pick the next leader on the team, the next person to be the voice of reason or the motivation when everyone is done. The person who calls you on your shit but lifts you up when you need it. It was an easy choice for me, Jayden. You have all the right things to be exceptional on the field, and I want the team in your hands when I leave. This starts now."

"Dude." His eyes widened. "The guys will not like this."

"Why wouldn't they?"

"I'm a sophomore."

"So the fuck what? Years have nothing to do with it. You are a leader, and that's what a captain is. Now, Coach wants to do something official with it. Announce it to the team, but I want you to know if you're in."

"I'm in. Fuck yeah, I'm in, but why wouldn't you be it?"

"Because Coach wants this." I swallowed. "And I'm a position player. My role has me naturally leading. I'm leaving after this season, and you are an outstanding student leader, athlete, and teammate. You've earned this by the choices you make."

"Damn, Romano." Jayden held out a fist, and I bumped it. "Thank you. Don't know how I'm gonna fill your shoes—"

"I'll help you." It was like a lightbulb went off in the back of my brain. This was what Coach wanted. For him to have the captain in name, but I'd be running it behind the scenes and showing him the ropes. No one had done that for me when I was younger. This leadership had just happened, and I wished someone had shown me. "I'll be with you the entire time, talking you through what I've done and what the team needs. You got this, J. I got you."

We parted ways, and any unease or turmoil about Coach's choice disappeared. I couldn't wait to tell Mack. She'd be proud of me and scrunch her nose as she smiled. I fucking loved that smile on her, where her eyes seemed to glow with pride.

I showered, dressed, and drove there within fifteen minutes. Lo was at her internship, Luca still working out, so it was just us. I knocked, my stomach bursting with anticipation. I hadn't seen her in two days. With the guys having a night out together and the girls with their Tuesday meetings, it was a night apart, which sucked. When we had a countdown on our fling, not spending every minute together seemed stupid.

The door twisted, and Mack stood there, all smiles and with tender gaze. "Hi!"

"God, I missed you." I gripped her waist and pulled her toward me, kissing her hard. My heart thudded in my chest, like my body was finally content. She smelled perfect, like summer and sunscreen, and she kissed me back just as hard.

"Wait," she said between kisses. "I have something to ask you."

"Yes, whatever you want," I said, backing us up into her apartment and kicking the door shut. She had to have put on cherry lip balm or something because her lips tasted exceptionally good. Delicious. Addicting. "You taste." I sucked her lip into my mouth. "So good. How?"

"Oh, this lip exfoliating thing I tried." She laughed and put a hand to my chest. "Would you slow it for one goddamn second?"

"Kissing you? No." I lifted her up and set her on the

counter, her legs immediately going around my waist as I rocked into her. "I have stuff to tell you, but my mouth won't stop."

I kissed down her neck, over her collarbone. She wore a black tank top that hugged her body and cutoff jean shorts. Her legs looked ten miles long.

"I have something to say to you to."

"Is it time sensitive?"

"Potentially." She moaned and arched her back as I kissed the center of her chest. "It involves getting naked again."

"Mm, okay." I pulled back, my cock throbbing with wanting to sink into her. Sex with Mack was incredible. I'd been with a lot of people but never when I had this much connection with anyone. I liked her. I liked her a lot. It was so different to fuck someone you liked *and* lusted after instead of just having attraction. I stopped putting my mouth on her, but I kept my hands on her shoulders, wanting to feel her warm skin against mine.

"Thank you for your cooperation." She beamed at me, her hands also resting on my waist. "Now, would you like to accompany me to go camping for one night only? I need to do twenty-four hours without my phone, and I can't think of a better person to spend it with than you."

"Camping?"

"Yes. With me."

"Just you?"

"Yes."

"None of our dumb friends are going to try to tag along?"

"Correct."

Fuck. Yes. "Baby, that sounds amazing."

Her face glowed, and her eyes seemed even bluer. "Yes! Okay, perfect." She wiggled off the counter. "Come look at the list!"

I didn't like that I wasn't touching her anymore. Her shorts showcased her muscles and hugged her ass, so I didn't mind the view as she bent over her table.

"I'm almost done! I have 'get a makeover' and 'lose a cell phone for a day' left! I can't believe this… it went so fast?" Something shifted on her face, her eyes darkening before she masked it into a flirty smile. "I took liberty with the *ask three guys out* and changed it to ask you out three times."

I studied it, an unpleasant heartburn feeling forming deep in my chest and spreading through my limbs. *Two more things left.*

The Summer Playbook

- ~~Buy a guy a shot~~
- ~~Mixologist challenge – ask bartender to let you make a drink~~
- ~~Skinny dipping~~
- Get a makeover
- ~~Tattoo~~
- ~~Take a body shot off someone~~
- ~~Someone takes one off you~~
- ~~Grind with a stranger or someone~~
- ~~Make out with two people in one night~~
- ~~Hook up past first base with a stranger/someone~~
- ~~Be naughty in public~~
- ~~Ask three guys out~~
- ~~Dance on a bar~~
- ~~Streaking~~
- ~~Dance in the rain~~
- ~~Concert~~
- ~~Join a game already going on with strangers~~
- ~~Bonfire (talk to five strangers)~~
- ~~Wear an outfit you normally wouldn't wear~~

- ~~Dye your hair a new color~~
- ~~Crash an event (or wedding for bonus points)~~
- Lose the cell phone for a whole day
- ~~Strip Poker~~

"I'm so proud of myself for these, honestly. They were wild, and my friends can be the worst sometimes, like dancing on a bar? Ugh."

"I believe we got a photo of that here." I pulled out her journal, running my fingers over the printed pictures. She wore her red bikini and held a bottle of beer as her rainbow hair went in every direction. "I wish I could steal this one. You look so hot."

She snorted. "I recall you not getting on the bar even though you were supposed to do all these with me!"

"Mm, the majority are with me. That counts?" I teased. I loved getting her riled up.

"You have selective choices. Anyway, do you want to go camping tonight? I called, and the ground has a spot, I just need to get some gear from Ale's sister. She said I could borrow it! We could leave now and start the twenty-four hours?"

What happens when the list is over?

The pang in my chest doubled in size. I rubbed the back of my neck, trying to come up with an excuse to why we couldn't camp but that I could still spend the night with her. That seemed lame, but if we did this, then she only had one item left. My pulse raced, and I winced the longer she stared at me.

"You sure?"

"Yeah, I don't have anything tomorrow. Wait, I didn't ask if you had morning workouts!"

I don't. But what a way to save the day.

"Ah, I do."

"Shit. Okay." She sighed and spun her phone in a circle on

the table. "When would another night work for you? We could try around your practices. Or the weekend? Damn, my coach wants me running a few day clinics."

"Mallinson," I said, my voice firm.

She glanced up at me, her frown apparent. "Yeah?"

I exhaled and leaned against the wall to her kitchen area, crossing my arms as I chose to be honest. It was terrifying. I hated it. How did people do this all the time? "I can go tonight. I lied about practice tomorrow."

"Great! But wait." She chewed her lip. "Why lie about it?"

"Our seasons start in two weeks, something I'm painfully aware of, and I'm afraid that once this list is done, you won't want to hang out with me." I winced, the little vulnerability leaking through my voice showing weakness. It sucked putting yourself out there like this. Mack could laugh, tell me no shit, or end this now with two weeks left of summer.

"The list has been fun and the reason we started spending time together, Dean." She walked toward me, her eyes sparkling. She ran a hand down my arm, up my chest until she cupped my face. "But even if this thing caught fire, I'd still hang out with you. I know we can't be together, but I love every second I have with you."

"Until the season starts?" I added, without thinking.

Her eyes clouded over, but she nodded. "Yes, exactly. We agreed to a summer fling. Summer ain't done yet, Romano, so you're not getting away from me yet."

Ever.

The thought intruded like a bad case of athlete's foot. EVER. Who the fuck was I? That made no sense. I didn't do relationships. I didn't do feelings. This was a lot for me, experiencing this summer of trust with Mack. Was it even possible to maintain when the season started?

Parties. Practice. Mentoring Jayden. Jayden!

“Hey! I have cool news to share.” I put my hand over hers, our fingers interlocking. “I spoke to Jayden about being the next captain, and it was honestly freeing. I’m going to show him the ropes of how to do it. I think that was what coach wanted me to experience.”

“Yeah? That’s great, Dean. I’m glad you spoke to him about it.” She sighed. “I did say I’d reward you with swimming.”

“I’m sorry I overreacted about finishing the list,” I whispered, staring between her eyes to make sure she heard me. “I love that you spent time researching this and invited me. Let’s do it. Let’s go camping. Let’s knock off the rest of this list together.”

“I’m so glad you wanted to do this with me,” she said, her voice even softer than mine. There was a finality to it, like she was saying goodbye somehow. It caused the ache to worsen, but I’d deal with that later. We still had two weeks left. Plenty of time to stress out.

CHAPTER TWENTY-THREE

Mack

We drove in Dean's car with the windows down, music blasting, and our hands intertwined on the center console. He had this half-smile on his face the whole ride, his dimple teasing me every so often. Seeing him like that had the question on the tip of my tongue: *could we not end this?*

He mentioned the final two weeks so often that it seemed foolish to even suggest going longer. My tongue swelled, and sweat pooled in unsavory places when I even thought about asking him. It wouldn't help us, and it would only cause the final two weeks to be harder. I knew this. It was what we agreed on.

This would be the best summer of a lifetime, where I fell hard for Dean Romano while living life without regret. I had a summer love and went on adventures. When I went through those thoughts, everything seemed *fine,* even though I wanted to break down and cry thinking about not seeing Dean every day or talking to him or kissing him.

Or thinking about him getting with other girls.

"You look thoughtful over there. What's on your mind?" he asked, his voice kind and unhurried.

"You. This summer." I squeezed his hand as he pulled into the campsite. A guard checked our licenses as we gave them our names, but that was it. We had no phones. We agreed to leave them at my apartment to fulfill the twenty-four hours. We told everyone, and they knew where we were. If there was an emergency, they would come here.

The guide handed Dean a map, and he chewed his lip, staring at it.

"We need to go there." I leaned over and showed him the section. "I reserved this one. If you head down the path and go right, it'll lead us to our spot."

He glanced at me with the same happy smile. "Right, yeah."

"Romano is bad at maps. Cute."

"Shut it, you." He flicked my nose playfully as he made the right turn. "Some people are directionally challenged. Like me."

"It's a good thing you're good at real plays then."

He sighed and took my hand again, palm to palm. "You ever think about what you'd do without soccer?"

"No." I laughed. "I want to plan my life around it. Always have. My parents want me to have a fallback plan if I get injured, which I get, but even then, my career would still revolve around the sport. Even if I was a newscaster or announcer or something that supported it. There's just no world where I'm not shouting about women's soccer. It's part of me."

Or maybe even coach and help cultivate healthy athletes, basically be the opposite of Emily.

"I get that. It's how I feel about football. This summer just had me thinking about a different kind of life, even just as a daydream." His voice sounded gruff, thick. "I love the mentoring aspect of the game."

"You could always coach when you get too old."

"True. I just… with what Coach is having me do with Jayden, I think I'm gonna like it. It's weird moving from the headspace of only I matter to the whole team matters."

"Sports are strange, especially when you're a key position player. Our goalie is like that. Games can be won or lost from her actions. So, she worries about her stats more than the team. It doesn't matter if she has thirty or five saves if we only make one goal, you know? She can't worry about our forwards when she has her own shit to deal with."

"This shit with Jessica—well, the girl I told you about, really had me thinking about life beyond the sport. I loved the famous aspect of everything, but this lowkey summer taught me that this makes me happier. The small things."

I'm a small thing? Sadness weighed me down.

"Wait." He shook his head. "That came out weird. I mean… camping and the lake house. Reading an article and drinking coffee with you. Watching you do your social media posts. I've…they meant a lot to me."

"Yeah, me too." I smiled, hiding my mouth from him. I enjoyed all those things too. "Okay, if you could never play football again and couldn't coach, what would you do then?"

"My degree is in economics because I chose it like a dumbass freshman, but any sort of job that requires teaching or mentoring. Not a teacher; that seems hard as fuck. This is hard. You gotta do this question too."

"Outside of soccer? Ugh." I exhaled. "I love watching Lo work with marketing and using PR to spin things in a positive light. I think that's cool, but also running this youth camps is a highlight. I know saying being a social media star is silly, but

I'd love that. Helping explain things to people or highlighting the good. I think I'd do that."

"With your face, yes. You're already killing it now. I love watching your videos. I sometimes watch them at night even if I saw you film them live."

"Wait, really?" I grinned, hard. "You have a crush on me."

"Shut up. Obviously, I do." He rolled his eyes, but the tips of his ears turned red.

"You're blushing. This is so cute." I grabbed the camera and took a picture of him before he could stop me. "I love this. I'm saving this forever. The day Dean Romano blushed."

"I want a picture of you then. That's only fair."

"Okay. Sure." I turned it for a selfie mode and made a kissy face before snapping the shot. It printed it, and I shook it out, rolling my eyes. "I look ridiculous."

"False." Dean snagged it out of my hands and smiled at it. "Perfect. It has your eyes and hair. I love those parts of you. It's gonna be hard to see your rainbow grow out."

"Big fan of the rainbow?"

"Hell yeah." He took my little polaroid photo and put it under his overhead visor. I watched with emotion in my throat. The gesture was so sweet my voice thickened. We pulled into the campsite, then exited the car. I took a deep breath of the fresh summer air.

Cicadas buzzed, and trees rustled in the wind. It smelled like moss and a lake nearby. I pointed toward our post as he neared it and grinned at him. I needed a distraction from these pesky feelings that would never be reciprocated. He liked me, that was clear, but love? Nah.

"Let's make a tent and fuck in it."

"Dream woman."

It took…longer than expected to pitch a tent. Sweat pooled

down my back, my face, between my boobs, but we did it. We made a little tent baby. "I'm so proud of us."

"Why was that so hard? Fuck." He wiped his forehead with the base of his shirt, his white teeth flashing at me. He looked super fucking good with his cutoff workout shirt and jeans. "You're giving me eyes right now."

"I like you sweaty."

"Yeah?" His grin grew as he held up a finger. "Two minutes, then your ass is mine, Mallinson."

"Two minutes? For what?"

He jogged to the car and brought back our duffel and sleeping bags. We had snacks and bug spray, a boom box with batteries for music, and a bottle of rum. The final piece was starting the fire for hot dogs, but my stomach swooped with anticipation over the way Dean looked at me.

Like love.

No. It was the moment. It was magical and perfect but just a moment. I shook off the feeling and covered my laugher as he struggled to open the sleeping bag. "You need help with the zipper?"

"Unless it's your pants, no." He grunted. "It's stuck. Or jammed."

"Or." I walked toward him, carefully. "You're doing it too hard. Sometimes, you need to be gentle."

He narrowed his eyes. "Is this in reference to *me,* Mack?"

I winked.

"God, you're sexy." He laughed and looped his arm around my waist. "I want to feel your sweaty body on me, riding me."

"Well, someone can't open up a zipper, so excuse me for saving the day." I fixed it within a few seconds, and before I could do anything, Dean tossed it into the tent and picked me up.

"Your ass. In there. Strip."

"Wow, you doing okay? You're not using full sentences."

He growled as he shut the tent, struggling to close the zipper again.

"Be delicate, Romano." I giggled at the annoyed look. "I didn't think you'd be more fun to camp with than Zane, but you definitely are."

"Who the fuck is Zane?"

He closed the tent and cornered me, his brown eyes darkening as he ripped his shirt off. "Are you talking about another man in front of me?"

"I mean my church buddy from fifth grade, yeah." I smirked, and he grabbed my ankle and yanked me toward him, making me yelp. "*Dean!*"

He licked up my bare leg, staring at me with a manic face. "I want to lick up your sweat."

"You are… damn." I gulped.

His jaw tensed, and his eyes smoldered. He gripped the edges of my shorts and pulled them down before tossing them to the side of the tent. He kissed right above my pussy before going up my stomach.

"Shirt. Off."

I shivered from the command in his voice. His muscles rippled as he positioned himself over me, holding himself up on his arms as he kissed and teased my stomach. Quickly, I tossed my shirt and bralette to the corner, and his mouth was on my nipple before I could say anything. *"Oh yes."*

"I love how sweaty you are. I want to feel it on me, all of you." He kissed and sucked my pebbled tips before rolling us over so I was on top of him. Cupping my breasts, he looked at me like I mattered, like I was the most important thing. It made me feel cherished, safe.

"Pull out my cock, Mackenzie. I want you riding me with your sexy hips."

I shuddered. He helped me slide his pants and boxers off, so it was just us. Sweat and lust filled the tent, and I groaned as he guided me over his cock. I was already so wet. "God, I want you, Dean."

"*Fuck.*" He groaned, covering his eyes with his arm. "I didn't bring any condoms."

My stomach bottomed out. "No, no, no, really?"

"I forgot! Shit." He closed his eyes, pinching his nose. "I can get you off—"

"Dean, honey." I placed my hand on his chest, taking a deep breath and risking everything. "I'm on birth control. I don't have anything, and I get regular health checks. I would never lie to you about this, so if we wanted to without a condom, I'm game. But there is no pressure, okay? I know this is a lot for you." I bent down and kissed him, wimping out about seeing his reaction. I'd understand if he said no, given what had happened to him.

Except, I was horny as hell.

"I've never…" He breathed hard, deep. He touched my ass, my back, my thighs, as his gaze moved from my chest to between my thighs. He struggled. "Mack."

"Yes?"

"Are you *sure*?"

I nodded, grinding my hips so my wetness coated him. "We can have hot, filthy, unprotected sex all night. You and me."

His entire body trembled as his eyes stared into mine. It took a beat before his gaze softened. "Ride me, baby. Ride me hard."

Love and anticipation coursed through me like a firework. His trust for me had my eyes watering. This was *huge* for him, trusting me to not hurt him, to not betray or lie to him, and I would never take that for granted. I slid onto him, his bare cock filling me and holy shit. This was a first for me, and that made this whole thing more precious.

"*Fucccck,*" he groaned, his gaze never leaving mine. "You are perfect. You are so sexy."

I rocked, taking him deep as I rode him. Sweat pooled even more between our skin, and he used everything he could to touch me. His fingers grazed my nipples, moving up my stomach and up to my neck. I kept going, clenching around him as my heart hurt with love.

I loved him so much. I wanted this, him, us. I didn't want this to end this summer. I'd never find someone who got me so much, who trusted me. The moisture in my eyes spilled over, and Dean caught my tears with his fingers, his eyes understanding.

What started frantic and hot turned slow and sensual, longer touches and slow kisses. It could've been because we both felt it, the love between us, or it could've been a goodbye. I wasn't sure, and I didn't want to think about it. I knew Dean cared for me, but he made it clear he didn't want this to last. Football had to come first for him and soccer for me.

I could fit him in with soccer too. But the question was —could he?

He licked his finger before rubbing my clit, and the pressure grew to a boiling point. With soft kisses and his cock filling me, I grew closer. I tensed, and Dean arched him, sucking a nipple into his mouth as I fell apart.

"You're so fucking gorgeous, Mack." He sat up so our chests were pressed together, his gaze even hotter. "I love watching you come."

He held me tight against him as he thrust into me, his own sexy sounds rumbling from his chest. He dug his fingers into my ass as he sucked on my neck. "Yes, baby, *take me.*"

I clenched around him as he came too, his throaty moans

filling the tent. He clung onto me harder, unless it was my imagination. He also whispered everything he loved about me, which sounded like he *loved* me, but that was my hopeful heart talking.

I made a vow to myself to enjoy every second of this trip. Things were meant to happen a certain way. I'd walk away from my time with Dean with pride and joy because how many people got to experience this with someone?

It was the summer I fell in love.

CHAPTER
TWENTY-FOUR

Dean

I woke up to the sounds of birds, wearing a big-ass cheesy smile. Our legs were intertwined, Mack's sleepy snores right next to my face, and I couldn't recall the last time I was this happy. Years? A decade? She made everything better, and I couldn't explain why or how. My body ached from sleeping at this angle, but it was the best kind of pain.

I slept with her without a condom. This felt huge. Massive growth for me. I mean, fuck, I wasn't even worried about it. A part of me, buried way deep down, wouldn't be that upset if a kid tied me to Mack for the rest of my life either. That was a mindfuck of a thought, so I shoved that aside, content in the moment.

I kissed her forehead, snuggling her closer as I sighed. Two weeks left. There was no way I'd be able to walk away from her and *not* wake up like this. Was I supposed to just pretend this didn't happen and go back to partying? No. That would never happen. That sounded so much less fun that challenges with her and our friends. It wasn't even a competition at this point.

What does this mean though?

Soccer came first for her too. She said it as much, that she never wanted to catch feelings, and here I was planning on asking her to continue this. She'd say no. *But would she?* I was the one who said I'd never do this, not after Jessica. Mack didn't say anything, just respected my words.

I rubbed my hand up and down her arm, enjoying her soft breaths and the way her body heat warmed mine. She was such a mixture of softs and hard. Her toned muscles yet soft hair, her dynamite hard competitive streak with a heart of gold. No wonder Lo claimed her as her best friend.

Lo.

Talk about ruining the moment… I had to talk to her. I had to come clean about this and how it wasn't supposed to happen this way, but it had. She'd understand, but it still felt dirty not sharing this with her.

Okay, game plan. My own *summer playbook.* I had to speak to Lo about this then talk to Mackenzie. I could… hm.

"Morning." She pushed up onto her elbows and smiled up at me. "I like waking up with you, Romano."

My stomach swooped. "You're not so bad, Mallinson."

She snorted and kissed my chest. "You said I was *exceptional* last night, which I'll never let you forget."

"Fair." I hoisted her closer to me. "You sleep okay? Your neck hurt at all from the angle?"

She shook her head. "I feel better than I should, especially with all the rum we drank. It was so worth it though. Best night ever."

"Yeah." I pressed my lips together. After sleeping together without a condom once, we did it three more times, and I wasn't sure I wanted to go back. It felt incredible, *exceptional* as she said. "We still have a few hours without a phone. Did you want to go to the lake or on a hike?"

"A hike would be awesome!" She stretched her arms over her head, completely content being naked. Her rainbow hair spread around her shoulders, and her eyes seemed to match the blue of the sky. Just... beautiful. "I wish we put a hike on the list. I'm so damn competitive I want to keep going."

"You should be proud you only have one item left, right? Your girls' night is in a few days, and you can flaunt it." My fingers itched to keep touching her, so I ran my thumb up and down her bicep.

"True, but Vee has made good progress being less of a party animal and being more focused. That is worth celebrating, even though she definitely got on the counter with Oliver and stripteased."

"They are a fun pair. He is so straitlaced and nerdy for a football player where she is—"

"Wild. I love her and would never want her to change, but her focusing on studies and not messing up her senior year is good. Maybe I can delay the final item until next week, so she can have hers."

Is she trying to delay this as much as me? She admitted it as much yesterday, but with the aggressive urge to continue this, suddenly my feelings felt tense, and my nerves took root. "So, uh, no makeover for a while?"

"I mean, it can wait. I have no fancy plans any time soon. If anything, I should've done it before the wedding we crashed. Which, that was a highlight for sure." She giggled and pulled her hair up into a ponytail. "Seriously, that was a night to remember."

I told her I'd love to take her on a real date that night, not even aware of how hard I was falling for her. Inspiration hit like a helmet to the gut. *I know what to do.*

"Baby, hey, I have an idea."

Her eyes lit up. "Love ideas! Is this a hike and a swim? I

would be so down for that, maybe even another little skinny dip."

"No, well, yes to that." I narrowed my eyes. "For your final item. I want to take you on a date. A nice date, just you and me. You can do the makeover thing to complete the list, but the date is all *us*." My throat was clogged with unnamed emotions, and I had to clear it to get rid of the cobwebs. "If you want."

She stared at me, her lips pressed together as her cheeks pinkened. "So, I get a makeover, and we go on a date."

"If you want," I added, stumbling over my words. God, had I ever asked anyone on a date before? Had it been fucking years? Annoyed at myself, I wish I would've thought this out more instead of blurting it out like a doof. "Can I try this again? I feel like I'm fucking this up, and I don't want to. I need to get this right."

"Well, we are naked in a tent together." She grinned. "Stakes are pretty low."

Snorting, I shook my head as I took her hand. "I'd love to take you on a nice date, thank you for this summer and celebrating you." I swallowed, not saying my ulterior motive of asking her to do this for real with me. "Would you do me the honors?"

Something flashed across her face, but it was so fast I couldn't decipher it. She nodded and gave me a sweet Mack smile. "I'd love it, Dean. It'd be the perfect way to end this summer."

I turned her hand over, running my pointer over her palm. "Do you have plans tonight?"

"Tonight?" she choked. "Uh, I don't know if I can get the makeover done."

"Right." I chewed my lip. I wanted to talk to her as soon as possible so this wasn't hanging over my head. Going after something I wanted was a part of who I was. Waiting around wasn't something I did, and I wanted Mackenzie. The plan formulated easily, without taking into consideration she might not be able to *or want to.*

I mean shit. I could drop her off, talk to Lo, then set up the dinner. Between the afternoon and dinner, I could write out my thoughts and chat with Luca on what to say to her. Him and Lo went through something like this with his obsession with football.

But she didn't seem excited, and that deflated me. "That was a stupid idea—"

"I wish I had my phone so I could make the appointment!" She frowned. "Wait, it's a stupid idea?"

"No! Damn it. I'm being weird about this. I just… want to take you on a date without a list being a reason. I want to take you because I like you and want to spend time with you." My voice dropped low and serious, giving it an even more tense tone.

Any hesitation dancing in her eyes disappeared, and the same warm, glowy look I'd seen recently returned. "I'd love that. Spending time with you is becoming one of my favorite things honestly, so I could even bend the rules and have one of the girls give me a makeover. I mean, it doesn't say it has to be somewhere."

"So yes, tonight?"

"Definitely." She beamed.

"Cool." I ran a hand over my jaw, an absolutely chaotic energy bouncing through my veins. I wanted to kiss her, claim her, and run five miles to burn off this energy. "Want to hike still before we head out? Enjoy this morning?"

"We could even make it a race."

"You're a madwoman. Someone needs to stop you." I pulled her toward me, gently cupping the back of her head. I brought her lips toward mine, gently kissing her before whispering, "Thanks for agreeing to the date."

"Thanks for asking."

All I had to do now was speak to Lo and set it all up.

We arrived back at Mack and Lo's apartment a few hours later after hiking, swimming, and fucking again in the tent before heading home. My feelings only increased, and I doubled down on making this work between us. Even Mack seemed lighter... like the thought of a real date between us made her super happy.

Maybe she wants this to last too.

I walked her to the door, holding her hand as my adrenaline rushed through me. The plan was in place: step one, Lo. "I need to talk to my sister about something real quick. Could you send her out here?"

"Sure." Mackenzie licked the side of her lip, her eyes darting to the door. "She knows about us, if you're worried. She knows that we've been on the same page, so if you feel bad, don't, and I'm sorry if I shared too much with her. I just—"

"Hey, you're okay." I grinned. The ball of worry exploded at her words. "Thank you, for sharing that, but she deserves to at least hear it from me."

"Right, yeah. Even though it's... toward the end?" The lines around her eyes pinched.

"Don't worry about that now. What time should I pick you up?"

"Oh, uh, six?"

"Perfect." I kissed her slowly, my gut tightening with nerves about later. After tonight, I wanted to be with her for real. No list, no summer, just *us.* "I'll see you later?"

"Yes. Yes, you will. Just, thanks for everything Dean." She threw her arms around me, the smell of sweat and lake water and the tent engulfing me. It just reminded me how amazing the entire time was, but her tone made it sound like a goodbye. I wouldn't let that happen.

"Could you have Lo bring my phone out too?"

"Sure thing." She scrunched her nose, lingering at the doorframe. It was like she didn't want to leave this either. *Good sign.* "Okay, well, bye."

I winked.

She shut the door, and it didn't take long for Lo to come out with my phone. Her expression reminded me so much of our mom I laughed. "God, you look stubborn."

"Well, I'm going to either be super right about everything or super pissed, so yeah, I basically am mom trying to raise you." She crossed her arms and arched a brow. "So, which is it? I want to know if I'm going to be mad all night or smug."

I snorted. "Probably smug."

Her brow returned to a normal arch as she smiled. "Okay, great. Love to hear it. Please, tell me whatever it is you want, dear brother."

"I want to be with Mack for real."

"I fucking knew it, you idiot." She punched my arm, three times. "I called it. I knew it. I saw it. I willed it. I win. I fucking win."

"You are insane. Does Luca know this version of you?"

"Shut your mouth!" She pointed at me, hitting my chest this time. "I called it. Goddamn, okay, this is good. No wait. It's bad. No, good. This is great."

"I regret telling you this." I crossed arms, amused as hell.

"Do you need a minute to…I don't know, get yourself together?"

"Oh my god, you're the worst." She shook her head, eyes closed, before she grinned wide. "You two are perfect for each other. She's obviously in love with you, has been for years so this—"

"She's in love with me?"

"Dean. Don't…" She winced. "Yes, but I don't want to ruin this between you. She's always had a thing for you, and I always knew. Never thought anything would happen because she's a relationship, loyal person where you're… not? With friends and family, sure. But not relationships."

"That's changed, Lorelei."

"I know. I *know.* I'm saying this poorly but… I'm happy for you. She's the best and will bring your life so much joy. If you need my permission, you have it, but you can't hurt her. That's the line I'm drawing. You're my twin, my brother, and my longest friend, but I will stab you if you make her cry."

"You'll never have to do that, okay? I lo—" I paused. If I were to say those words, if that was what I felt, Mack deserved to hear them first. "I want this with her. Not just the semester or year, like, long term. I want to travel to watch her play soccer."

"Good. Because soccer is going to come first for her, like football for you."

"We'll figure it out, but I'm going to tell her tonight. I'm going to ask for this to be real, but I had to talk to you first."

She rolled her eyes. "Sure, but let's not pretend I didn't know about this all fucking summer. I appreciate the gesture."

"You are a spitfire pain in the ass."

She wiggled her brows. "I'm aware."

"Thanks, Lo. I love you, and I'm finally getting my head out of my ass." I held a fist, and she hit it.

"Love you too. This makes me happy. Just think! We can

double date with Luca all the time now, oh my god. This is gonna—"

"I'm leaving. Don't push it." I laughed, powering on my phone as I jogged down the stairs. It vibrated consistently until I got to my car, notifications blowing up to the point my stomach soured.

What the fuck?

Texts from Luca, Callum, Oliver. Xavier sent numerous texts. I had four voicemails. *Is the team okay?*

I called Luca immediately. "What's going on?"

"Come to the house *now.*"

"What… what happened?"

"Jessica is here. With a baby."

CHAPTER **TWENTY-FIVE**

Mack

Getting ready for a *goodbye* date had me in a weird headspace. I showered, twice, because I loved camping, but the smell in my hair wasn't the best. Then, I shaved my legs, put myself in my favorite bathrobe, and lay on my bed as sadness overtook me.

A way to celebrate you and the summer.

That was what Dean said. But he asked me on a real date? That had to mean something, right?

A soft knocked tapped on my door, and I got up, unlocking it. Lo grinned at me, brows going crazy, as she clicked her tongue. "Eh? Eh? You and Dean? Maybe we can be sisters-in-law?"

"Okay, crazy." I shoved her as I went to sit on my bed. "Nothing like that. We had a great time this summer, but tonight is it, I think."

Lo tilted her head. "Why would you think that? Dean asked you on a date, right?"

"Yeah, but to celebrate this summer."

"Okay, there are things to unpack here." Lo pulled out the desk chair and sat on it backwards, putting her arms on the back and resting her chin on them. "Dean asked *you* on a date. You. On a date. I'm sorry, has this ever happened before in my entire life? Maybe once in high school? He doesn't date. He doesn't ask people on dates."

My heart skipped a beat, but I didn't dare say a word.

Lo continued, her smile a tad manic. "What do you think that means, Mackenzie? I'll answer for you: he's into you. For real."

"I know he is. We both… we're into each other, but football and soccer will always come first. We spoke about us, and it would be complicated." I chewed my lip, needing to hold onto the reasons why we wouldn't work because if hope slipped into this, I would be done for. "It's easier for us to have this really nice dinner, no list included, and part ways as friends."

"You silly, sweet, naïve friend of mine. That's not what this is."

Glimmers of hope went from my heart to my gut, my stomach swooping dangerously. "You think it's… more?"

"Look, I don't want ruin my brother's game even though he's done that to me so many times, but whatever." She rolled her eyes and flicked her hand in the air, dismissing her own thought. "You love him, right?"

I nodded.

"He has feelings for you and wants this. Let him try to ask you or figure out how to make this work, okay? He's gonna be a mess because Dean Romano has never had to do this before, so make him sweat a bit."

"What if you're wrong?" I blurted out, my voice shaky. "I want this, Lo. I think him and I would be good together if we *both* want to be together, but what if tonight is him saying goodbye? I'm too afraid to hope or want more. It'd be foolish to not prepare for the worst."

"I understand that girl, I do. I know it feels weird to hope or put your heart on the line, but isn't it worth it? Dean might fuck it up. He says the wrong things sometimes, but he wanted to talk to me about you and what it would mean."

I exhaled, my breath shaky. "I need to do a makeover for the dinner tonight."

"Then I mean this with respect, but we're gonna make you look hot as hell for my brother."

"Not too weird for you?"

"Not even a little bit." She pulled out her phone and winked. "I'm calling the girls. It can be a team effort."

My eyes stung, the adrenaline from the glimmer of hope exploding into a full-fledged fantasy. This was the stuff I missed out on all high school. Girls' nights and fun challenges and dating. Falling hard for someone and maybe having them fall back or not. I grinned, finally able to push a bit of the anger at Coach Em away. Maybe things happened for a reason, and I was supposed to go through all this to lead me to Dean…all I knew was that I was *happy.*

"I could be dating your brother for real."

"Yes. That's the right thought."

"Dean and me."

"Yup." Lo grinned again. "I don't know why you'd ever think he wouldn't want this. You're the best. Seriously."

"It's not about putting myself down in any way. It's just football and the lives we lead. It'll be hard."

"You don't think I know that? Hello, have you met my boyfriend? He'd sleep with a football given the chance. People make time for the things that matter to them. Plain and simple. Time is an excuse. If they want to, they will. This applies to friends, relationships, hobbies, all of it. Let him make you a priority. You'll find time if you want it, Mack."

"How the fuck did you get so wise? You're the same age as me."

"I'm like two months older, and I've learned a lot in those sixty days."

I snorted, my emotions regulating more normally. "Okay, well shit. If he's gonna ask me out for real, I definitely want to look good."

"Yes! That's the spirit. Ale, Mally, and Vee will be here in fifteen. Vee has a dress for you too."

"She is way shorter than me."

"Shows more leg then." She wiggled her brows. "Okay, can I just…"

Lo jumped off the chair and threw herself at me, squeezing me in a huge bear hug. "I'm feeling emotional about this. Dean has been so happy, and I love you, and you're happy, and you're happy together." She nuzzled into my robe.

"You're ridiculous," I said, laughing and squeezing her back. "Did you just sniff?"

"Yes. I did. Two of my favorite people finding each other in a weird way? It's beautiful."

"Okay, my robe is falling down."

"Ain't nothing I haven't seen before."

I shoved her off, my mood entirely different than even ten minutes ago. Lo wouldn't say any of this if it weren't true, and maybe that was what Dean needed to talk to her about. Me. Us. This dinner. It was official—I was full of hope and fantasy at this point and oh my god.

Dean Romano was gonna ask me out for real. How did I want to respond? With a cool, *sure,* or *I guess?* Or a jump up and down?

Or be normal and kiss him?

There were so many possibilities.

The girls arrived with outfits and makeup, along with mimosas. I'd done the homecoming and prom thing in high school, and this felt like that but bigger. Ale and Vee did my nails, while Mally started on my hair. Lo had makeup ready, and holy shit, I was pampered.

It was strange but nice. If I was ever famous, I'd get people to do this for me because it was glorious. I had no idea what to do with an eyebrow brush, but damn, my brows looked good. So did my lashes. They had to be fake?

"You're like my own Barbie. This is so much fun." Vee stood in front of me, doing something with my hair so her tits were right in my face. "I love these rainbow tips. They are perfect for you. You're so serious, but you have these colors that show the real you."

"Deep, Vee."

"It's kinda like Oliver. He's so serious and quiet, but he has this longish hair with a half-bun thing and those glasses? Oof. You know he's a freak inside."

"Man, you and him dance on a bar together and you're into him?"

"Oh, god, no. He's… he's just a hot, complicated dude. That's all. I'm on a hiatus from dating or sleeping around for this semester. I need to graduate, and I'm short a few credits which… that's a conversation for another time. Now, if this was Xavier we were talking about, different story." She grinned, but her smile didn't reach her eyes.

If I wasn't such a weird mess about Dean, I'd be digging harder.

"I'm adding some color around your eyes. They are gorgeous." Vee bent down, and her brows came together as she grabbed a different brush. "I love that this summer playbook brought you and Dean together. You've been happier, lighter somehow. You weren't unhappy before, but you have more… joy to you. I hate the shit that says your partner should make you happy, we gotta make our own selves happy, but he's brought more light to your life. I love this for you."

"Why do you all feel like my moms, and you're preparing me for my first date?"

"Because we are."

We both laughed, and she finished the makeup with Lo, them talking about Callum and the latest gossip with the guys and our team. Mally had flirted with someone who happened to be the cousin of her ex, so that was fun.

Callum had been acting weirder the last week, and no one knew why.

More drama and silly rumors that made us laugh as we finished up my look. They hadn't let me see my outfit until now, where they brought out the floor-length mirror from Lo's room.

"Okay, are you ready?" Lo said, excitement pouring out of her voice. "You look *so good.*"

"Yes, I'm ready!"

They counted down, and on three, I opened my eyes and gasped. Holy shit balls. I looked insane. My makeup only enhanced my features: my large blue eyes, my high cheekbones, my lips. It was still me, but the makeup was on point. Then the hair. It was soft and curled and reminded me of the influencers I saw all the time. Then the dress. Damn! It was black with a deep vee in the front and a slit on the side. It covered everything tastefully but flirted with my skin. "Whoa."

"You are always beautiful, Mack. You know this. But it was fun playing dress-up with you." Mally looped her arm through mine as Ale snapped a few pictures. She also grabbed the Polaroid and took a photo, the sound of printing filling the room. "Dean is gonna fall over. What time is he coming anyway?"

"In five minutes." Lo clapped her hands. "Six, right?"

I nodded.

Everyone slipped out, except Lo, saying goodbye and giving me all sorts of hugs and good lucks.

Five minutes. Oof. Nerves overtook me, my insides an absolute mess. I wanted to tease him, just to hear from him before everything changed.

Mack: wait until you see this dress

Nothing. He was the quickest texter I knew, but if he was driving, then that made sense. One, two, three, four minutes went by. Then it was more than five minutes. Still nothing.

I walked to the front door, anxiously glancing through the hole to see if he was here. He was always on time too. I blamed it as an athlete thing, but for it to be 6:01 and nothing was weird.

Mack: there is a huge slit in the front that you'll like.

Mack: hey we're still on for six, right? You've never been late before

Nothing, again.

6:10.

"This is weird." Lo ran a hand over her forehead, smoothing down her worry lines. "He's never late. Has he texted you at all?"

I shook my head, my heart sinking. He changed his mind. He backed out. He chickened out. He realized he didn't want this and didn't want a messy goodbye. "He hasn't responded to my texts too."

"That's unlike him. He doesn't bail, and he's never late." She frowned, hard. "Shit, what if something happened to him?"

"Or what if he backed out?" I asked, my heart in my throat. "That could be it."

"Eh, if that was the case, he would tell you. He doesn't play games; you know this about him. Try not… okay, I understand this is hard, but I don't think this is intentional, Mack. Does standing you up seem like something he would do?"

I thought about it. Ignoring the hurt and shame of being dressed up and waiting for him when he wasn't there, I focused on the Dean I spent all summer with. He wouldn't do this. He would know this would hurt me. He would call. Or text. "This doesn't seem like him, no."

"Can I call Luca? I don't want to get in the way, and I won't if you say no, but I feel like something happened. Maybe it's my twin thing or the fact he didn't show up. I saw how he spoke about you earlier. He was so excited to do this for real. He wouldn't change within eight hours."

"Sure, yeah. I want him to be okay." I wrung my fingers together, my eyes prickling with unshed tears. It would ruin the mascara, that was for sure, but worry wedged its way into my gut. *Was* Dean okay?

"Okay cool, yeah." She had the phone to her ear, biting down on her lip with worry. "Hey, babe, is Dean with you?"

She listened, her eyes widening. "What? No fucking way. Are you… at the house? Jesus. Okay. We'll head there."

Every part of my body felt wrong from her tone. My skin was too tight, my shoes were too small, pressing against my toes like my feet were going to explode out of them. My tongue was too big, my mouth uncomfortable as I gripped the sides of my dress. Lo's tone was curt, angry, and worried.

Is he okay? Please be okay.

She hung up, her mouth hanging open as she stared at me like she saw a ghost. "We need to go to the house."

"Okay."

"The girl who fucked him up?"

"Jessica?"

Lo swallowed. "She showed up with a kid today to *speak* with him. No one knows what she said, but he's been a mess since and won't talk to them."

My heart fell into my stomach, aching so much I wanted to throw up. "We have to go help him. He's been doing so well—is the baby his? God, he has to be freaking out."

"Don't know. Come on. Let's… fuck." Lo's hand shook. "I'm so angry I can't even drive."

"I can." I took her hand. "Let me take care of the Romanos tonight. It's something I'm getting pretty good at."

This was *not* the night I imagined, but it was reality, and if I knew anything right now, my feelings didn't matter. Dean had to be freaking out after he'd made so much progress. He might not love me back, but I loved him enough to help him right now. Because that's what love was—sacrifice.

CHAPTER **TWENTY-SIX**

Dean

I regretted the shots.

Taking four of them seemed like the right thing to do when the woman who fucked you up showed up with a baby that wasn't yours. She wanted to *apologize* and *make amends* now that she was a mother. She wanted to live as an example for her son, and that meant going on a forgiveness tour of everyone she screwed with.

It had the opposite effect on me.

Hence the shots.

It might've been more than four.

"S-what time is it?" I asked Callum, staring up into the summer sky. It was dusk now, the sun setting and turning into night. There were stars, and I bet Mack would've found this romantic. Ugh, Mack. It was a punch to the gut, a smack to the sternum. A tackle to the chest. That woman was incredible, but we'd never work. Not… now. Maybe that morning, but Jessica reminded me feelings weren't worth it.

"It's seven." Callum handed me a water bottle. "You should drink this."

"Nah, I'm not trying to sober up. I want to feel this."

"Drunk? Bro, you're gonna feel like shit tomorrow. I don't want that for you even though it seems like that chick messed you up."

I burped. "Yeah. She told me I was going to be a dad, lied about losing the baby, then told me she cheated on me and was pregnant with someone else's." I hiccupped and took another swig of the vodka Sprite, which was really more vodka. "How fucked is that? I thought I was going to be a father, then thought I lost a kid, then none of it was real."

"Holy shit." Callum's mouth fell open, and he sat in silence. That never happened. *That's right, Cally Boy.*

"You look stupid with that face, but I like how quiet you are," I said, pointing at him and laughing. "Yeah, now you see why I'm drunk? It's the right choice. Even though Mack and I were gonna be together for real. Not now. I'd be foolish to do that now. You saw Jessica and the baby. And me."

"You are not making a bit of sense, but I see why Luca took your phone." Callum ran a hand over his face, groaning loudly before hitting my knee.

"Ow." I covered it, wincing. "Don't injure your QB. Football is the only thing I have going for me. Fuck, where is the bottle?"

"I love you, man, I do, but you're a fucking mess, and I don't like it. Yeah, seeing Jessica fucked you up after what she did. I don't condone violence against women, but I kind have the urge to punch her. I'm sure Lo could handle that for us. But you are acting like you deserved this or some weird shit. You didn't. No one does."

"I don't deserve it. I know that," I said softly, the blip of reality crashing down from the alcohol. "My online counselor and I are working on that." I coughed and stared at my friend, who moved side to side. Or maybe I moved side to side? Unclear. One of us was moving.

"You wanna know what my plan was tonight? Mack and I." I groaned as my stomach bottomed out. "I never canceled on her. Oh fuck. She thought I was coming at six to take her to a real date. I was gonna ask her out for real, then this shit happened and—"

"Worry about that later. Focus on yourself first." Callum cracked his knuckles and winced, looking at the back porch. "I was going to say you need to sober up and sleep it off, then worry about making up with Mack because dude, she's perfect for you. You know this. We *all* fucking know this. But the girls are here, and they look fucking pissed as hell."

My damn heart hadn't gotten the memo that Mack and I were done yet. It sped up, excitement coursing through my blood at seeing Mack. I wanted to curl into her, smell her familiar scent, and lose myself in her body. It was a fucking joke that I woke up that morning ready to do this with her, be with her, give her my heart to take care of but then Jessica reminded me it was too painful. I'd never survive something like this again, and I'd liked Jessica. My feelings for her were nothing compared to what I felt for Mack, so this pain would be a million times worse. Un-survivable. It was a word, I swear.

No thank you. My best friend, vodka, agreed with me.

"The girls?" I slurred, thinking about making a run for it. My body wasn't really firing on all cylinders though. Even the idea of running had me falling over in my chair. I didn't want to see them. right?

Did I? No? Yes? I needed water. Or another drink.

"Where the fuck is she?"

My sister's voice carried over the night air, the anger and bite slashing through the night and hitting me. She was furious at me. I deserved it. I told her I was gonna step up for her best friend and then abandoned them. Lo was a word wizard and always said the right thing at the right time, so she'd murder me with her insults. And I would take it.

"S'right here, Lolo. Let me have it." I raised my hand in the air, my free one, and took another long swig. The alcohol burned my throat. "Come over here."

"You? I'm not here to deal with *you.* Where. The fuck. Is. *Jessica?*"

I shrugged, still not facing her or Mackenzie. *Uhh.* My chest ached so badly, I had to scratch it to try and ease it. It was like the worst combination of heartburn and indigestion. "Don't know. I told her to get the hell out of here."

"Lo, you're not going after her." Luca joined the conversation. He could handle my sister.

I'd just keep drinking.

Callum stood and said something to someone, but I tuned them out. The baby didn't look like me, but the timing, man… fuck. It could've been mine. That was the wild part about it. We did the paternity test last fall, when shit hit the fan, but seeing the kid's little face… I groaned into my hands.

"Romano," Mackenzie said, her voice calm and strong. Her familiar perfume welcomed me, and I breathed it in, still not looking at her. Disgust and shame engulfed me.

"Why are you here?" I asked into my hands.

"Because I hate to see someone I care about upset. Because I know you're beating yourself up over this. And—" She paused, crouched in front of me and spread my knees apart so she could wiggle between them. She placed a hand on either thigh before nudging my face out of my hands. She waited until I opened my eyes, and she knocked the breath out of me.

Her face… was different, but the same. Her hair looked so soft and perfect. "Fuck, you're beautiful."

She smiled, a soft, tender look in her eyes. "Thank you. Dean, listen to me, you get to be upset and mad tonight but not tomorrow."

"Not that simple."

"It is that simple. You've worked so hard to move on from this, and *fuck her* for coming back." She cupped my face. "You did nothing wrong. This is all her choices and her apology tour or whatever was to make herself feel better, not you."

"The kid was so cute. It could've… it could've been mine."

A wrinkle formed between her brows. "Any chance it is? Did you ever take a test to be certain because I wouldn't trust her."

I shook my head. "It's not mine, for sure."

"Hey." She tilted my chin up. "Even it was, it wouldn't change a thing about how I feel about you. I need you to know that."

She ran her thumb over my chin, caressing it with sweet touches that I leaned into.

The amount I'd drunk bubbled up, and I felt a wave of sick, but it could've been from guilt. "I stood you up."

"Luca explained he took your phone, so it's not entirely your fault that you forgot to cancel."

"I got drunk instead of telling you. I'm so sorry." I hung my head, refusing to look at her. "Look---"

"If you're about to break up with me, I don't accept it. Plain and simple." She puffed out her chest.

"I'm a mess."

"No, you went through a mess. *You* are not a mess."

"I hurt you." God, my stomach was bubbling. Sweat covered my body. My vision blurred. She looked so serious though. I had to hang on. Just another minute.

"I mean, I was angry you didn't show up, but that wasn't like you. You're kind and sweet and communicative. You care about your friends so deeply it's amazing. You don't ghost us. This isn't the norm. You helped me dye my hair. You helped me pee outside yesterday. You are nice and protective, and honestly Dean? I love you. I'm just gonna say it. You're drunk and probably not gonna remember this, but I love you." She licked her lips before smiling, her blue eyes crinkling on the sides as she stared at me *hard.* "I love *you,* Dean, not the footballer, not the popular guy on billboards or the guy who won some awards. I love your heart and playfulness and the way you see the world. I love your scars and how you laugh. You might not want to do this for real, but what we have is rare."

My eyes flickered, and the last thing I remembered was feeling an insane amount of joy and luck that she'd said those things. Then, night took over.

A construction company formed home base in my skull. That was the only explanation to the bangs and crashes going around me. It was so bad I wondered if this was a slow death. But I wouldn't feel the sheets against my skin if that was the case. If I moved either to the left or the right, a throbbing pain reminded me of last night.

Jessica. The baby. *Mackenzie.*

"Fuckkkk." I hit the pillow, but then someone stirred next to me. Who the fuck…I bolted up, terrified beyond anything about not remembering the night before when a familiar scent hit me. *Sunscreen, flowers, grass.*

My girl was here, next to me.

"Hi." She yawned and slowly pushed herself up to sitting. She gave me a sleepy grin, her face having lines from the pillow all over it. The shirt hung off her shoulder, showcasing her collarbone and a little freckle she had there. "I have sports drinks, medicine, and cold bacon for you, since I know that's your favorite hangover cure."

How did she… why was she… my brain wouldn't compute the equation. The playbook was unclear.

"What?" I asked, dumbfounded that I was staring at her in my bed, with me, when she should've punched me in the face and ran. "Wait, why are you *here?*"

She blinked a few times, and a blush crept up her cheeks. I loved that red color on her skin.

She cleared her throat, her voice hoarse and lacking her normal confidence. "Uh, I wanted to make sure you were okay. You passed out and were a bit of a mess."

"But you're in my bed." My slow-ass brain was still drunk or hungover because why the hell would she want to be with me? After I ghosted her for a date? With my literal baby mama drama. "I don't understand."

"I'm sorry, I can… I might've misread this; I think. I just…" She jumped from my bed, clearly flustered. She hopped from one foot to the other, grabbing her stuff.

She wore one of my shirts, and that was it. Her long, toned legs and bare feet were gorgeous, and I had to take a deep breath before I connected the dots. "Wait, I'm not mad you're here."

"Are… are you sure?"

"Mack, oh my god." I shook my head, then winced. "Don't leave. Please. Give me a second."

The pounding subsided enough to slide out of bed. "My mouth tastes like a bowling alley dumpster, my head feels like a band is playing in it, but I'm trying to explain and doing a shit job."

"Explain what?" She held onto her things tighter and moved farther from me.

"I figured you were pissed at me. I want you here, fuck, I do. But I stood you up. Hell, I don't even know where my phone is." I shrugged and regretted it instantly. "I messed up my shot with you, a real shot."

"Your phone is charging on your desk over there. Luca helped me find your stuff. He also helped me get you to bed after you passed out."

"That's… embarrassing." I ran a hand over my face. "I've never passed out before."

"You had a lot on your mind."

"Would you stop backing up to the door and sit with me for a second?" I asked, my voice scratchy. "I'm worried you're about to run for it, and while you probably should, I want to talk to you if you'll let me."

She set her clothes down on the chair and glided toward the bed. She sat upright and faced me with an expectant look, like she thought I had the answers to everything.

I knew jack shit.

I raised my hand, hoping inspiration would hit, but nothing profound entered my dumbass mind. Just a plain old apology. "I'm so sorry. I'm fucking sorry about all of this. This wasn't my plan at all."

"I'm not angry with you. I'm hurting *with you,* for you, wishing I could do something to help you. Same with Lo and Luca and the guys. No one is mad at you. We all lo—care—want the best for you. No one is upset with you if that's on your mind."

"Even though I missed my chance with you?"

"Why would you think that?"

"I asked you on the date last night for a reason." I fell back onto the pillow, choosing to be a coward and stare at the ceiling instead of her. *No. Be better.* It'd be simpler to take the easy route with this, but Mack deserved more. Facing her, I took one of her hands in mine. "I said I wanted to celebrate the summer, but my dumbass thought it'd be better to surprise you with the truth. I wanted to talk to Lo about it first before confessing how I felt about you, to you. I should've just told you when I woke up in that tent happier than I ever have been. It would've been more romantic than this shitstorm. Jessica showing up sent me spiraling."

Mack nodded, understanding written all over her face. "Do you recall what I said to you before passing out last night?"

I frowned. I recalled feeling overjoyed, but I blamed the vodka. "No. And I'm sorry if that upsets you."

She laughed and kissed the back of my hand. "I told you I loved you."

My jaw clenched, and my lungs seized. Loved. Loved. "As in, you don't anymore?"

"Oh my God, are you always so literal hungover? Not past tense. Current. Hopelessly. I love you. In love with you. I don't give a shit about football, to be honest, I just love you as the person you are. Even the messy parts."

"You love me." I repeated it, my heart thudding so hard it was a little worrying. My limbs tingled. My throat closed up. Everything felt too much all of a sudden. Was it hot, or was that the sweats? "Mackenzie." I gulped. "Mackenzie. You *love* me."

She giggled, a sweet, glorious sound that I wanted to keep for the rest of my life and nodded. "Yes. I think I always have a little, but after this summer? You are incredible." She traced her pointer finger over the back of my hand, the gesture sending bolts of electricity through me.

"I came over here to make sure you were okay. Because that's what you do if someone you love is hurting. If you're worried about blowing it or missing your shot, you didn't. I want to be with you if you want this too. Even if you don't love me but care for me, I'm not someone who demands it back. I'm telling you because it matters to me that you know. Even if we end this, I don't regret a single thing with you. I never will either. This summer has meant more to me than you'll ever know."

I swallowed down the ball of emotion, and it felt like swallowing a rolled-up sock. She stared at me with so much fucking love it was overwhelming. She'd made me *cold bacon* —my favorite hungover snack. She stayed with me all night, even after I'd ghosted her. No one had done anything like this in my life. She took care of me. I was so used to ensuring everyone else was okay: my sister, my teammates, my housemates. But no one went out of their way for me.

I pinched the bridge of my nose, overcome with feeling everything. How could I be with this woman when I'd never done the boyfriend thing? I'd mess up. I could come up with all the reasons, but she deserved the truth and nothing else. Staring at her eyes, I took a final breath.

"I've never been in love before, Mack. I mean, I love my team and my family, but with someone else? It's a new thing for me. Is love thinking about someone all the damn time? Because I do. I see you in the sun and the way the fresh-cut grass reminds me of you or rainbows. Hell, every time I see a color, I think of your hair and the way you smiled at me in the mirror when it was done. Is love feeling your actual heart beat faster around someone? Because feel my chest, Mack."

I took her hand and put in over my heart. "It's beating so fucking hard because of hearing you tell me you *love* me? Its… its maddening in the best way. Is love wanting to be with you all the time? Because I do. Is love putting yourself so far outside of your comfort zone it scares the shit out of you? Because I'm there. I want to try this with you. I want to date you, and even though my heart is fucked because of Jessica, I want to try this with you. I want your smiles, your laughs, your lists, and to celebrate your wins and help you through loses." I gulped down the feelings and exhaled. "Does that sound okay?"

She nodded, her eyes watery as she blinked back a few tears. "Sounds a little like love, Romano."

"Then I guess I'm a little in love with you, Mallinson." I said the words, then shook my head. "No, I'm definitely in love with you. Nothing little about it." I grinned, ignoring the searing pain in my head, and laughed. "Holy shit. Yeah, I love you. I've never said that in this way before, and I thought it'd be scarier."

"I'm scared." She chewed her lip, scooting closer to me. "I'm terrified, Dean, but that won't keep me from wanting this with you." She traced a finger over my eyebrow, a small smile teasing her lips. "I want to wear your jersey at your games. I want everyone to know you belong to me."

"Deal. Done. Yes." I pulled her into my lap, nuzzling my favorite spot by her neck and collarbone. "We can figure out a schedule that works for us. We'll compromise. I don't want this adventure to end." I kissed her temple, her cheek, then her mouth softly. "I'd kiss you more, but my breath is probably brutal."

"Oh, it's horrible, but I don't care." She kissed me again, laughing into my mouth. "If we're shifting from the summer playbook to the dating playbook, I have a few rules."

"Yeah?" I tilted her chin, unable to keep my smile off my face. "Name 'em."

"The first—you *never* ghost me again. I'm forgiving this time, but next time I'll kick your ass."

"I'm sorry I hurt you, but that will never fucking happen again." I kissed her forehead, still hating that I hurt her at all. "What's your next rule?"

"If you're sad and want to get drunk, call me. I'll join you. We'll either do it together or find a challenge to complete."

"I can dig it. Anything else?"

She pursed her lips. "Nope, that's it for me."

"Okay, good." I flipped her over onto her back, and I crawled up her body. The hangover was still there, but it dulled in comparison to how happy I was right now. "My rules, are you ready?"

She nodded.

"First, you wear my jersey on game days. Maybe even *just* that."

"That can be arranged."

"You're *never* getting a tattoo at that place without me. I can't have my girl getting hit on like that."

She rolled her eyes. "Jesus, Romano. Are you some possessive boyfriend? I wouldn't have guessed that."

"With you, apparently. Never really been a *boyfriend* before." I grinned. "I like the sound of it coming from you though."

"Okay fine. No tattoos without letting you know."

"Mm, not what I said, but I'll let it go. Thirdly, you tell me what you need or if I mess up or hurt you. I want this to work, Mackenzie. I want to be with you and talk about your social media posts and how you want to scale the game and hear about your game plans, and I want us to make our own lists. I'm going to mess up and say the wrong thing, so please be patient with me. I'll always make you a priority. Promise me you'll always tell me?"

"I promise. But love is a conversation, and we'll always do it together." She pulled me down, kissing me softly. "I love you, but—"

"I love you too," I said, loving the fact I could say it back.

Her eyes lit up. "Dork. What I wanted to say, was that I love you, but you need a shower and mouthwash."

I snorted. "Fair. Any chance you want to join me in the

shower, girlfriend?"

She smirked. "Only because you asked nicely." She slid from the bed and tossed her shirt to the ground, revealing the fact she was completely naked underneath.

I sucked in a breath. "Damn, my drunk ass didn't even take advantage of this." I ran a hand over her back, her ass, enjoying the feel of her skin. "God, you're sexy."

"You should see the photos I left on your desk that I took." She winked. "I'll get the shower started. You brush your teeth first."

She blew me a kiss before strutting toward my bathroom, and I scanned my desk for photos. Two Polaroids sat there, one from the two of us at the wedding we crashed. She looked so fucking perfect it was amazing. The second one though.

Hot damn.

She posed naked for me, and holy shit. I'd be keeping this one with me close. I stared, admiring the curve of her ass when she cleared her throat.

"You could look at the real thing, you know."

"Yeah, but this feels naughty." I grinned, tapping the desk twice before joining her in the shower.

I wasn't one to question how we got to this point because things happened for a reason, but I couldn't believe my luck. This was the best summer of my life, and instead of it ending, we were going to continue. I was giving this a real shot with her. Jessica had messed me up for sure, but my girl understood and was patient. It was unreal to me that she wanted this, but I would never take her for granted. Ever. I knew what pain felt like, and I knew what being the happiest I had ever been felt like.

Mackenzie Mallinson wasn't in my playbook to start, but she still made me feel like I won the game.

And I'd make damn sure to never stop trying to win her.

EPILOGUE

Spring break...

Mack

The seagulls made a shit ton of noise. It wasn't like I hadn't been to a beach before, but it had been so long since I visited that I'd forgotten the smells, sounds, and the feeling of sand in my toes. I shifted from my stomach to my back, groaning a little.

"You need more sunscreen, soccer star?"

I rolled my eyes. "Offering to put it on me *again,* Dean?"

"Anything to touch this ass." He nudged his body with mine before he smacked my ass. He grinned and kissed my shoulder with a sparkle to his eyes. "No big deal, just smacking my girlfriend's fantastic ass. Why is she awesome? Oh, she just got drafted to Chicago. You hear that, people? My girlfriend will play for *Chicago!*"

"Jesus, stop it," I said, laughing and shoving him away. He had been doing it nonstop since the NWSL draft back in January.

Did I go first round? Yes.

Was it to my top three teams? Yes.

Was I beyond excited? Also, yes.

Was I also terrified? Yes.

Terrified because this was the next step? Sure, but it was about Dean. My stomach flipped, half excited, half worried about what the future would mean. I would live in the city, but he could end up anywhere in the country.

Could we survive distance?

I swallowed, shaking off the nerves. I hated being this person, worrying before something happened, but it was hard when the NFL draft was in a few weeks, and our future would be determined. Even if we did somehow end up in Chicago together, we could be traded at any time, doing distance, always trying to see each other…

"You're doing it again, aren't you?" Dean tensed his jaw, his gaze darkening. "Thinking about all the situations and stressing." He ran a finger over the strap of my swimsuit, gently caressing my skin around my neck with a soft sigh. "What has you stressed, baby? Us living in different cities?"

I nodded, my eyes prickling. My throat tightened, and I focused on the couple ahead of us. They were an older couple with young kids and smiling. I wanted that. "I just—"

"I want a fucking life *with you.* That means, accepting all parts of you, which includes soccer. I can't wait to see you play in Chicago and wear your jersey. I'm so proud to be with you, and we can get through anything."

"I know, I feel the same." I pinched the bridge of my nose. "What if you end up in California? That's a long flight. One we—"

"So, we take turns visiting each other. We rack up all the points we can and take a bad ass trip to Australia in a few years. Always wanted to go there." He rolled over and caged my face in his hands as he stared at me hard. "It honestly doesn't matter where we live. You own me completely. There is no world with you and me in it where we aren't together. We get each other's good parts and bad and push each other to be better. I almost wish I could propose right now and see Romano on the back of *your* jersey, just so everyone knew you were mine. Might be dramatic, but I'm a Romano, and that's all we know."

My eyes stung more, and a tear slid down my cheek. He swiped it with his thumb as a soft look crossed his face. I loved that tender look, the face only I got to see because he was the quarterback to everyone else. "You sound so confident."

"Because I am. Do we need to make another list of all the reasons this will work? I can. It can be our professional athlete playbook."

"You're a dork." I sniffed, laughing at how excited he seemed. "I know this spring break trip was supposed to be a way to relax and have fun, but every time I'm not doing something, I think about the draft for you and how hard the next year of our lives will be."

"So, we work at it." He narrowed his eyes for just a beat. "You're not backing out on me, Mack, are you? My girl doesn't back down from a challenge. She embraces it at every angle."

"No, I'm not…I just…I've loved this year more than I ever thought, and I know I have amazing friends and a teammate, and I was drafted, but I love *you* so much it scares me. Life outside Central State will be different. We won't see our friends all the time, we'll grow apart, and—"

"And yeah, we do new things. It's gonna be awesome as hell." He frowned, his gaze bouncing between my lips and eyes. "You keep biting your lip, and it's cute, and I want to kiss you, but this is serious, so I'll be right back."

He rubbed the upper part of my back before jogging away from me. We were early risers, so we were at the beach before our friends. We'd rented a house with the girls and guys, hoping to party it up as our senior year spring break. It was our last day there, and it had me feeling melancholic.

Which wasn't me.

I embraced life. I took it and enjoyed every second. *So why was I freaking out?*

Because I loved Dean so much and was worried about our futures changing. Luca and Lo were moving in together after our lease was done. Wherever he got drafted, she would follow. No questions asked. Her career could follow his. Callum and his girl had a plan, one that wasn't tainted with distance, and Oliver, well, him and his new girl were both townies, so they'd always wanted to stay in central Illinois.

I pushed up and took a long sip of water, the Florida sun warming me up. If I focused on the pinpoint of stress—it was the fear Dean wouldn't want to stay with me after a few months. I could do it, succeed in my career and endorse his. Because one thing wasn't going to change with this: me giving up soccer. That would never happen. Coach Em started me on this path and honestly, with some distance, I was thankful. She might've done it in terrible ways, but she prepared me to get to this point. I'd never hug her or thank her for the emotional damage she did, but my dream was happening. I'd play professional soccer *while* keeping my friends and being with the love of my life.

Even if that meant we did distance for ten years, the only other option was to break up, and that… no.

No.

Not fucking happening.

I could only control what I could control (Wise, I know), but we both would never give up our sport or ask the other to, so that meant accepting the things we could change. Like being together long-distance or traveling or sharing a place in our off-seasons. Hell, we had three months of no season at all. Maybe we could afford two places? One in each city? Yeah. We could do that.

"Okay, Mack, I have it."

Dean jogged back to me, his muscles rippling with the movement. He tanned well and fast, and mama likey. Even after all these months together, I still thought he was so hot. It made me giggle sometimes that I got to kiss him anytime I wanted.

I smiled, and he noticed, his brows furrowing. "What's with the grin?"

"You're sexy and all mine. Just appreciating that fact before your face is nationwide."

"Mackenzie Violet, *you* have been hit on in front of me more than I have. Don't start with that. You have a million followers." He sat next to me, a small notepad hanging from his hands. "Of all the doubts you have going on in your brilliant mind, none of them should be about what I want. I want *you.*"

"I know, I do. I'm sorry I made the moment a downer."

"Never apologize for feeling the way you do. For us to do this for real, we have to be honest. So, this starts now. Here is our list until I get a ring on that finger."

"Sounds serious," I said, ignoring the flip of my stomach. Dean had mentioned marriage on and off since January, and every time, it didn't seem real. Marriage... at twenty-two...it wasn't unheard of, but damn. Was I ready?

"Baby, I know you're not ready." He laughed and tilted my chin and kissed me softly. "I also know you love me. You brought me back to life, so I'm willing to wait as long as you need."

"You're being so fucking cute right now I don't know if I want to cry or jump you."

"Both. Do both." He chuckled and nuzzled against me in a hug, the smell of seat salt and sunscreen filling my nose. He was home. He was strength and vulnerability, tough and soft, kind and hardworking. "Okay, here is our new list."

Attend the other's game in their jersey

Attend the other's game in every type of weather (four seasons, x2)

Take a free trip together after earning flight miles

Buy jersey of the other person

Wear jersey and snap selfies

Wear just jersey while we fuck

I snickered and elbowed him. "You would put that."

"Can't change me. You're too sexy, and it makes me wild thinking about you in an NFL jersey with my name. Keep going though."

Sharing copies of keys

Buying a place together in between our cities

Yearly trips to see our friends

Create our own pregame traditions

Take a trip to the lake with our friends

Spend holidays together, in any city

Get engaged

Get married

I sucked in a breath. "Wow, this is sure a list."

"Yeah, and next year, before your season starts, we're coming back to Central State and making sure every single one of those items is crossed." He pulled me against him, resting his chin on my head. "I love you, Mackenzie. I know I should be more excited about the draft, but I'm honestly ready for this next chapter of life *with you.*"

"I love you too, and I'm sorry I was scared. I feel the same, you know. I'm so ready for this next level, but I'm selfish. I want to keep spending every second together."

"Well, that's what we're gonna do until we know what happens for sure." He kissed the side of my neck. "Because no matter where I end up, it doesn't change a thing for me, and if I have to prove it for a few months, then I will."

I smiled, the tension easing in my body. He was right. The location didn't matter. We would figure our relationship out and make our own lists. We'd work through any distance life through at us. Because he was my endgame, the long game, the prize at the end of day. Relaxing, I snuggled closer and made a promise to not let fear prevent me from being happy.

Dean and I had fallen into each other's lives at the same time, and we'd stay in them, even if it got hard because just like being on the field, winning games wasn't easy. It was a challenge, but goddamn it, it was worth the effort. Life had a funny way of rewarding you for the time you put in. Dean and I had chosen each other every day the last eight months, and that wouldn't change even if we lived an ocean apart. Because when you wanted something, you sacrificed everything to get there.

We sacrificed our bodies, time, and energy to make it in a sport we loved. We knew how to put everything on the line and tune everything out. We'd do that for each other every single day until… well, until forever.

I'd never stop playing for Dean or stop trying to win for us. We'd get to do life together, our own way, and wasn't that the best prize of all?

ACKNOWLEDGMENTS

Rachel R—don't make it weird, but this story wouldn't have happened without you. From you sending me photo inspirations for the ridiculous t-shirt scene, to reading these two and telling Dean to get his shit together, from proof reading and being such a good friend. I love the fact reading romance books brought us together and now you're an integral part of writing books for me. Thank you so much. I'm not saying we need to hug or anything, but please know I love our friendship and will always cherish it.

Star Child Designs—thank you a million times for putting up with me during the cover process. You are so talented and amazing. I'm so grateful we're able to work together and I am always ITCHING to get covers for book 3 and 4 done!

Kat M—when people talk about their editors and how they can't live without them? Yeah, that tracks. I hope we can continue to work together for years because you're stuck with me at this point. I appreciate how you help me take every story to the next level.

Also—to all my coaches. I had amazing coaches (I will not name them because they should never under any circumstance read this book!) The coaches I had pushed me to be the best version of myself on and off the field. I'm a lucky one. Most life lessons were learned from playing sports and that's why so much of what I write focuses on it.

Lastly—all of you who have haters or who say you can't do something. Do it anyway. Succeeding is the best revenge.

ALSO BY JAQUELINE SNOWE

CENTRAL STATE FOOTBALL SERIES

First Meet Foul

The Summer Playbook

Third Down Deception (Spring 2024)

Snowed in for Christmas

CENTRAL STATE SERIES

The Puck Drop

From the Top

Take the Lead

Off the Ice

CLEAT CHASERS SERIES

Challenge Accepted

The Game Changer

Best Player

No Easy Catch

OUT OF THE PARK SERIES

Evening the Score

Sliding Home

Rounding the Bases

SHUT UP AND KISS ME SERIES

Internship with the Devil

Teaching with the Enemy

Nightmare Next Door

STANDALONES

Holdout

Take a Chance on Me

The Weekend Deal

ABOUT THE AUTHOR

Jaqueline Snowe lives in Arizona where the "dry heat" really isn't that bad. She prefers drinking coffee all hours of the day and snacking on anything that has peanut butter or chocolate. She is the mother to two fur-babies who don't realize they aren't humans and two amazing kiddos. She is an avid reader and writer of romances and tends to write about athletes. Her husband works for an MLB team (not a player, lol) so she knows more about baseball than any human ever should.

To sign up for her review team, or blogger list, please visit her website www.jaquelinesnowe.com for more information.

Printed in Great Britain
by Amazon